DEAD BEFORE DINNER

A Shadow Valley Manor Novel

KERRY SCHAFER

DEAD BEFORE DINNER

A Shadow Valley Mystery
By Kerry Schafer

CHAPTER ONE

Matt lies flat on his standard-issue mattress and stares at the ceiling. He's taken to creating recognizable shapes out of the stains, the way people look for pictures in the clouds. Over the course of two long weeks, he's discovered an arachnid that's missing three legs, a genetically altered amoeba, and a sadly misshapen ghost. And that's it. The game is much more limited than finding shapes in clouds, because the stains aren't going anywhere.

Neither is he.

There are worse places to be than jail, but there are also better places. Much better. Hell, for instance. Right now, he'd be grateful for flames and a little pitchfork-poking. At least that would give him something to do, something else to think about, some way to atone for his sins. Two weeks, and the only human contact he's had is with stone-faced deputies, and then only when they bring him meals.

They're calling it protective custody, but he knows better.

"Can't take any chances on a wayward incident happening to you," he was told, when he was locked in here away from the general population. It was implied that this means from the other inmates. He knows the real danger is law enforcement and jail staff.

Matt is a cop killer. Judged, convicted, and sentenced. Doesn't matter that the sheriff isn't dead—yet. Or that, technically, Matt didn't pull the trigger. Given the lack of witnesses, the multiple sets of fingerprints on the gun, and the identities of the three people claiming responsibility for the shooting, he's the one who has to have done it.

Say you're law enforcement and you have three possible suspects. Are you going with the eighty-year-old stroke survivor who can only speak in snatches of verse, the sixty-year-old, frail-looking woman with the obvious limp, or the twenty-six-year-old sharpshooter with special forces training?

Slam dunk. Which was exactly what he'd intended when he claimed the shooting in the first place. At the moment, it seemed like the right thing to do. He owes Maureen, big-time. But now that he's deep into what amounts to solitary confinement, with nothing to do but think about the lives he's taken and the mistakes he's made and the devil's bargain he's right square in the middle of, he's reconsidering every life decision he's ever made.

He sits up at the sound of approaching footsteps, alert and ready to go down fighting. He relaxes when he sees it's Deputy Ito—the guy might hate Matt's guts, but he's morally upright. Matt likes him. Under other circumstances, they'd call each other Hank and Matt and probably get a drink together. As it is, Ito exhibits only professional tolerance, and Matt's surprised by how much that stings.

"You have a visitor, Pennington."

Ito unlocks the cell and holds out not only handcuffs but ankle chains as well.

"Is that really necessary?"

"For you, yes."

"Who's here?" Matt asks, hungry for human interaction. "My attorney, finally?"

Ito indicates with sign language that Matt should shift his right leg. The truth is, Matt doesn't have an attorney. He'd hoped the Unit would pull some strings. They could have had him out of here in a matter of hours. The lack of contact makes it likely they've decided he's more liability than asset and will take advantage of this opportunity to fortify the case against him and keep him locked up for the rest of his life.

That, or have someone kill him.

"Come on, Ito," Matt cajoles. "It wouldn't hurt you to tell me who I'm seeing."

"Not my job." Ito locks the chains around Matt's waist and then follows him out of the cell and down the hall to the conference room. It's a small jail and there's none of that phones-and-glass setup. Just a table, bolted to the floor, and two plastic chairs.

A man sits in one of the chairs, relaxed, casual, harmless. He's short, no more than five foot five, and chubby, with the sort of baby fat that should have left him when he hit puberty. Male-pattern baldness has set in, leaving him tonsured like a monk. He wears unfashionable glasses with thick lenses. A button-up shirt strains across his middle, gaping between buttons.

Matt pauses in the doorway, his heart skipping a single beat before he gets himself in hand and his vitals settle into a regular, steady rhythm. Ito gives him a nudge, and he jangles and clanks across the room and settles into the chair. Neither he nor his visitor says a single word until the door clangs shut and a key scrapes in the lock.

"Charlie," Matt says. "How you been, man? Thought maybe you'd gone off on vacation."

The little man, about as innocuous as an Ebola virus despite his benign appearance, shoves his glasses up on his nose and leans forward in his chair. "I'm curious. How does one interpret an order for 'surveillance only' as "shoot the county sheriff in a church in front of a crowd of innocent bystanders'?"

"Things got. . .complicated."

"Really," Charlie drawls. "Do tell. Inquiring minds and all that."

"First off, there were only two innocent bystanders." Even that is an exaggeration. Sophronia is far from either innocent or a bystander. In truth, the accurate count of innocent bystanders is precisely zero. Meanwhile, there is a lot of intel Matt desperately needs and a lot of secrets he needs to keep. He decides to go on the offensive.

"Are you here to spring me or kill me? Either way, let's cut to the chase and get it over with."

Charlie sighs, shoving his glasses up the bridge of his nose and then raking one hand through his hair, pausing at the bald spot in surprise, as if he is just now discovering something missing. "I've told you, I have no interest in eliminating you or anybody else."

"Good to know," Matt says, as if he believes the line of propaganda. But he's well aware that any number of unfortunate accidents could occur while he's locked up. He could accidentally strangle himself. Choke on his dinner. Right here, right now, during this visit, he could have an unfortunate heart attack or seizure. So unexpected. So tragic for a man so young, although really for the best, you know, given his psychopathic tendencies.

Charlie sighs. "I do have some. . .concerns. Can we trust you, Matthew?"

"To investigate and deal with dangerous paranormal anomalies? Absolutely."

Charlie pulls out a recording device, lays it on the table, and clicks it on. "Official debriefing of agent Matthew Pennington. December fourth, 2017. Please summarize in your own words the events that led up to your arrest."

Matt begins, selecting his words carefully. "As per my assignment, I've been observing Maureen Keslyn and have gained her trust. She's apparently done the same with the sheriff, and he brought her in on the investigation into the death of Dason Williams. Maureen also discovered some intel about the suspicious death of a teenager, which she figured had something to do with both the Unit and the Medusa. Keslyn got pretty obsessive about that. Don't ask me how, but she figured out that the Medusa would show up at the church, and she went there to confront the thing. Why and how the sheriff or the old woman came to be there with her, I can't tell you. The girl, Sophronia, had run away a few days previously, and I also can't surmise why she showed up."

"And why were you not observing Keslyn during this time?"

Matt snorts. "She sent me on a wild-goose chase to the cemetery."

"Why do you think that is? Does she suspect you?"

"Do you *know* Maureen? She suspects everybody! She's the most paranoid old bird I have ever met."

Charlie taps his lips with an index finger, and Matt hopes the man is buying the spin. Impossible to tell. He has a poker face that could make him a millionaire.

"What happened next?"

"I waited in the graveyard. My primary directive was to earn her trust, so I did what she told me. Did I not interpret my directive accurately?"

"Go on, Matthew."

"I heard shots fired in the direction of the church. So, I scampered over there like any good citizen and found things out of control. The shot was necessary to mitigate risk to bystanders. Called the ambulance, provided first aid, and that's the end of it."

"Oh, Matthew." Charlie shakes his head, sadly. "You are no good to us here."

"Then get me out. You can totally do that, right?"

"If we break you out, we blow your cover and you're off the Shadow Valley case. I'm not sure we're ready to do that. The best thing will be if the sheriff wakes up and tells the truth that you didn't shoot him. Please tell me that is the truth."

"How *is* the sheriff?" Matt evades.

"Hanging in. They've got him on a ventilator and are keeping him sedated. Doc says he expects the man will live. Whether he'll have his memories or not is another thing altogether."

"And if he doesn't?"

"We could help him to some new ones. Or come up with another plan. For now, you stay here."

"Come on, Charlie. Get me out of here."

"Bored, are you? Learn a foreign language. Get a degree. Catch up on the soaps."

"You're hilarious. What's happening with Maureen?"

"Back at the Manor, going about her business." Charlie gets up without another word and buzzes for the guard.

Matt feels a sting of hurt and resentment. Maureen out and about, free, while he rots away here. No message. No attempt to bail him out.

Not that I know of, he reminds himself. Who knows what she is up to?

Other than this piece of intel, he has learned exactly nothing other than that the Unit has no grand plan to get him out anytime soon. Ito escorts him back to his cell and he flops onto his mattress, heavy with something dangerously close to despair.

Movement flickers in his peripheral vision, where a shiny metal plate bolted to the wall serves as a mirror. He tries to ignore it. Whatever is reflected there isn't real, just the shadow of some future thing that might or might not happen. His mother had the sight, and his grandmother before her, and it didn't serve either of them well. As a teenager, when his first vision ambushed him in the school restroom—

"No," he says, both to that memory and to the current vision, and lies back, eyes closed, hoping to fall into a very long nap.

But of course he can't sleep, and it seems like hours that he lies there, steadfastly resisting a compulsion to look at what he doesn't want to see. Finally, he can't bear the tension and gives in, as he always does, sooner or later. At first, all he sees in the mirror is his own face, and he's about to turn away when the images begin to flash across his vision. Crawling things. A flurry of black wings. A series of dead bodies. The images flash by too fast for him to latch on to them, except for the last one: Maureen, lying on a metal table, her face as white and still as death, a raven perched on her breast.

CHAPTER TWO

Renny shuffles the deck, her motions fluid, smooth, and faster than my eyes can follow. I watch her hands, trying and failing to catch her in the lie as she deals. The stakes we're gambling for—a half-smoked cigarette and a solitary match—are pitiful by real-world standards, but two weeks of jail-enforced nicotine abstinence has induced a powerful craving that makes it worth the effort.

Not that anybody but Renny will be winning this game, at least not so long as she's the dealer. I'd suggest a change, but getting on the wrong side of Renny would be a mistake, so I don't call her out on the cheating. The other players exchange glances and also say nothing. They are short-timers and it's not worth their while.

Me and Renny are the hard cases, both of us in for murder. Never mind that there hasn't been a trial yet; we are guilty until proven innocent. Unlike me, Renny isn't, and doesn't want to be, innocent.

"I killed him once and I'd kill him again if that son of a bitch would just come back and give me another opportunity," she told me about five minutes after she found out I was in on a charge of attempted murder against an officer of the law. I could have told her that just because I shot the sheriff, it doesn't mean I meant to kill him, but I kept my mouth shut about that, too. Having a reputation as a cop killer, even when said cop is still hopefully alive and one of the few people on the planet I care deeply about, creates a wide circle of respect around me that I don't have to work for.

The population of women in lockup changes frequently, most of them out on bail within a day or two. Shadow Valley jail is small, and today there are ten of us on the women's side, including me. Six of us are playing cards. Two are in bed, sweating and shaking and puking through obvious opiate withdrawals. Last night's arrival is hung over and keeping to her cell, flat on her face with a pillow over her head.

Number ten shouldn't be in here at all. She's got to be over eighty, shriveled up, wizened, and frail. Her orange jumpsuit bags on her, the pants and sleeves too long. Wispy gray hair floats around her wrinkled face. But her age isn't the only reason she doesn't belong. The woman is clearly in late-stage dementia. We don't know her name or why she's here, and she can't put a coherent sentence together to fill us in. While we play, she ghosts around the room, skirting the perimeter, patting the walls with her hands, searching, ever searching, for something we can't see.

"Here or here or here or here. Over. Under. Above. Below." She trips over a too-long pantleg and steadies herself, looking down, puzzled, as if it's the floor that tripped her up.

"Bloody hell," Renny explodes, throwing down her cards. "They need to get her out of here before she hurts herself. Whole system is totally fucked up." She gets to her feet and approaches the old woman, slowly, hands outstretched, softening her voice. "Easy, Granny. Just take it easy. Let me fix you."

The old woman's eyes are wide, nostrils flaring, as if she's a wild thing facing danger, but she stays where she is while Renny kneels and rolls up the legs of her jumpsuit so they can't get caught under her wandering feet.

"Pain in the ass if she falls and breaks a hip," Renny says when she returns to the table, deflecting the idea that she might just have engaged in an act of kindness. "Now, are we playing cards or what?"

"What do you think she did?" one of the new girls asks, eyes still on the old woman, who has resumed her circuit of the room.

"Gotta be pretty bad for them to put her in here in that condition," another one says. "God, Renny. Can I get a redeal? These cards aren't worth shit."

Granny starts pounding her blue-veined fists against the wall, shouting, "Open this door at once!"

I get up and hold back her hands, already bloodied, to keep her from damaging herself further, but her outrage, or fear, or whatever it is that's driving her, makes her strong.

Renny hollers for a guard.

Deputy Smith materializes like a genie. She's a solidly built woman as no-nonsense as her name, and of all the deputies running the jail, she's my favorite. Fair, forthright, and not without compassion.

"Ellen," she says, putting herself between the old woman and the wall. "Hey, now. That's not a door. Come sit down. Take a break." The old woman goes suddenly limp and docile, allowing herself to be led to a chair.

"She's not safe in here," I say. "Somebody needs to do something about that."

"Yeah, yeah," Smith says. "Tell that to the powers that be. You think we haven't tried?" I can hear the frustration in her voice and can only guess that they've worked all the angles without any luck. "Anyway." She shifts gears. "Somebody here to see you, Keslyn. Come with me."

She unlocks the door and motions me out into the hallway.

"After you," she says, not even bothering to put me in handcuffs. I rankle at the inference that I'm a zero threat but keep my mouth shut. Her carelessness means that I've been successful at portraying myself as feeble. I've whined about my bad leg until I want to shoot myself to put us all out of my misery, and I make a point of hobbling whenever I walk, as if it's all I can do to power myself under my own steam.

When she opens the door to the visiting room, I pause before entering, assessing the situation.

A small man sits at the table, peering at me through thick lenses that make his eyes look gigantic and alien. I've never seen him before. My first thought is that he is something else masquerading as human. My second is that the phone call to my almost-ex-husband asking him to find me a lawyer has hit pay dirt. Come to think of it, that means he still probably qualifies in the not-quite-human department.

"Take a seat, Keslyn," Smith says.

I limp across the room and ease into a plastic chair that is definitely not designed for comfort. The little man smiles blandly. No briefcase. No paper. No pen. I almost revert to guess number one—and then it hits me. I know exactly who this is, though not why he is here.

"Thought you might have had me strangled in my sleep by now." I lean back in the chair, feigning casual, all of my reflexes sharpened by a rush of adrenaline.

"Pardon me?" he asks, looking bewildered and affronted. "Have we met?"

"No, and that's why I know who you are."

He continues to give me the innocent act.

"Fine. I'll spell it out. It's not Sunday, which is the only open day for visitors, so you're not some do-gooder volunteer. You're not a minister or a priest. You're not my lawyer. I don't think you're actually an alien. So, I know who you are, more or less. What I can't work out is why you're here."

My visitor smiles then, guileless and open, confirming my

impression that he's a lying snake-in-the-grass bastard. I've got
not a single weapon on me, not that it would do me any good if I
had. He says nothing. I say nothing. Both of us are playing the
game of making the other speak first. Unlike him, I've got
nothing but time.

Finally, he tugs his shirt down over his paunch and adjusts
himself a little in the uncomfortable chair. "You can call me
Charlie."

"Or you can go away and I'll call you nothing." I stifle a yawn
and inspect the fingernails on my left hand as if they are the
most important thing in this room, giving myself time to cover
up a fit of murderous rage. Charlie works for the Unit—the real-
life equivalent of *Men in Black* but with less charitable intentions.
Officially, they are responsible for responding to and containing
paranormal activity. Unofficially, they have a history of commit-
ting monstrous moral atrocities, including human/paranormal
experimentation. I worked for them for thirty years before they
discarded me for the sins of being female, aging, and injured, and
followed that up with an attempt to kill me because I know too
much.

"Perhaps you should listen to why I'm here." Charlie's voice
sharpens.

I pick at a hangnail, not even looking up, and keep my voice
lazy and bored. "Fly away, Charlie. Your angels are waiting. I
have no interest in anything you have to say."

He leans forward and lays his hands on the table, palms up
and open, a calculated gesture meant to inspire my confidence.
He's gotten himself back under control, his voice now soft and
even. "Let me begin by conveying my sincere regret for the policies that led to the unfortunate deaths of people you cared for. I
was not responsible for that, and I have instituted changes in
policy to ensure that such things do not happen again."

Now I do meet his eyes. "And I should believe you why?"

"You're still alive," he says, mildly.

"Which could indicate a policy change, or merely that you still need something from me."

"Or both." He folds his hands together now, ready to launch into his pitch.

I sigh. I've got nowhere to go. Not a weapon within reach. And I have to admit that curiosity and self-preservation are both clamoring to hear what he's got up his sleeve.

"Spill it, Charlie. I've got little tolerance for games."

He laughs. "Now, that, Maureen Keslyn, is a lie. Admit it. You love games."

"Point for you. But I prefer to select the players. And to choose the game."

"Don't we all? Let me start by laying out the stakes we are playing for. Maybe you get out of jail today and go back to your Manor. All charges dropped. In plenty of time to spend Christmas with your loved ones."

"Bah, humbug. I have no loved ones. What would I do in exchange for this pulling of strings?"

"We are releasing an inmate to the Manor. One of your cellmates, actually. You will watch her with your usual efficient paranoia and ensure that she stays there and causes no harm."

He sits perfectly still. No fidgeting. Apparently relaxed. His round, innocent eyes gaze earnestly through those ridiculous oversized glasses into mine. All of which tells me he needs this. Which means whoever this inmate is, she's dangerous. I run through the women in lockup with me and can't imagine who it might be.

Curiosity and elation brush aside my common sense.

On an ordinary day, running Shadow Valley Manor is just as mind-numbingly boring as rotting away in jail. Fortunately, the boring spells tend to be interspersed with excitement and danger. I inherited the place thanks to my old friend and partner, Phil Evers, one of the people whose deaths rests at the Unit's door.

"I'm listening," I say, making it a point to remain nonchalant.

Charlie's lips tuck into an almost smile and I know he thinks he's hooked me.

"She's an elderly woman, so she'll fit right in. Her name is Ellen Ellis—"

"Granny? You want Granny at the Manor?"

He carries on as if there's been no interruption. "She's eighty-two, suffers from dementia, and is here on charges of attempting to murder her husband. It's been determined that she's not fit to stand trial, but we can't find a placement for her."

"Oh, come on! The woman needs a psych hospital, or at least a skilled-care placement. The Manor is for high-functioning seniors. With money."

"Eastern State Hospital no longer accepts dementia patients, and there's no psych unit or nursing home in the state that will touch her."

"All very sad, Charlie, but since when does the Unit care about the difficulty of placing combative dementia patients?"

He folds his hands on the table and tries to look compassionate while he evades everything I've said and heaps on some flattery. "If anybody can manage her, Maureen, it's you. I've heard about your resourcefulness. You're legendary."

"Resourcefulness has nothing to do with this. The woman needs proper care and I can't offer that. What do you want?"

"In order for me to tell you that, you need to come back into the fold. As an official consultant, you'll be filled in on everything you need to know."

"Not interested."

"Maureen—"

"You killed people who mattered to me. I'm done." I bite my tongue to keep from mentioning the other things the Unit is guilty of. Paranormal-human research, for example, some of it done without consent on a batch of pregnant teenagers, back in the days when the Manor was a home for unwed mothers.

"I've already told you, we regret those deaths," Charlie says. "We're restructuring."

"Good for you." I push back my chair. Cross the room. Push the button for the guard. "You didn't want me after I got injured. But now I do have something you want, so you're trying to reel me back in. Fuck you, Charlie. I'm so out, I'm in another galaxy."

"You haven't asked about Matthew Pennington," Charlie says, conversationally. I turn around to see a completely different man. The glasses are gone. His posture is alert, centered, the expression on his face focused and lethal.

"Didn't know my facility cook was your concern."

"Oh, come now. I know better than that. I doubt you worked with him for more than a day before you'd figured out he was one of our agents."

I say nothing, embarrassed to admit that it took a week and a murder before I'd figured that out.

Charlie presses his advantage. "If you walk away from my offer, Matthew will get a death sentence for the murder of Sheriff Jake Callahan."

The words run me through and through with a spike of fear and loss. I'd hoped and almost prayed that Jake would pull through. But I am not going to feed Charlie with my grief and say only, "Matt didn't shoot him. I did."

Charlie shrugs. "Yet he's been in solitary confinement since the shooting happened. You'll both be convicted, of course, but your charges will leave you locked up for the rest of your life. Matt will get a lethal injection."

"Jake is really dead, then?" I spit out the question, needing the answer.

Charlie smiles, holding out his hands in a what can I do about it gesture. "I understand he's balanced between life and death. It would be a shame if he took a turn for the worse."

I resist the urge to draw in a breath of relief, school my face to remain calm. "I'm disappointed, Charlie. What happened to the kinder, gentler Unit and the change in policies?"

"Ah," he says, removing the glasses from his pocket and wiping the lenses as a key grates in the lock. "But the sheriff is not one of ours, you see."

Smith opens the door and glances from me to Charlie, who is wearing the glasses and looking harmless and inept once again.

"Take me back to my cell," I say. "And I'm going on record that I don't ever want to talk to this asshole again."

"You'll get a message to me by seven o'clock tonight," Charlie says, holding out a business card. "Just let one of the deputies know. Yes, to agree. No, to refuse. Remember the people who are counting on you when you make your decision."

I stay where I am, my brain sifting and sorting and scrambling for a third option. But Smith crosses the room and takes the card from Charlie. She examines it as if it might be contraband, then holds it out to me. Years of conditioning, in which I went along on the surface and never, ever exposed Unit secrets, take over. I accept the card, glance at it casually, and allow Smith to lead me back to lockup.

The others are where I left them, except for Ellen.

"You want in?" Renny asks, shuffling the deck.

"Where's Granny?"

"No idea. They came and took her away while you were gone. Told us to say goodbye."

I drop into a chair and pick up my cards, pretending to study my hand while my brain races to a bunch of dead-end options. My pride utterly rebels at the idea of being dragged back into the fold after the Unit hung me out to twist in the wind, killed people I cared about, and ordered a hit on me.

On the other hand, I have no doubt that Charlie will make good on his veiled threats of helping Jake over the edge into death and seeing that Matt gets a lethal injection. This is what comes from letting myself get attached to people. Now I'm vulnerable to leverage.

By the time seven o'clock rolls around, I've utterly failed at finding an alternative.

Smith comes to find me. "Your lawyer called, the one from this afternoon. Pushy bastard. Wants to know what you've decided about the defense strategy."

I sigh. "Tell him yes. I agree to his plan."

CHAPTER THREE

Long after lights out, I'm lying awake regretting my deal with the devil when I hear booted feet headed in my direction, and then a jingle of keys.

"Get up, Keslyn. Let's go."

Deputy Whiteacre. I'm sure she was Queen Bee Mean Girl in high school. The inmates call her Wiseacre, and any opportunity she gets to make life harder for us, she'll take it.

"Another visitor? At this hour? It's like living in a frat house." I pretend to be too comfortable on the lumpy cot to be interested in getting up.

"You've been sprung. Come on; let's go."

I stay where I am, eyes half closed. "Nice joke, Wiseacre. Nobody's paying my bail."

"Charges dropped."

"Right. And the Easter Bunny drives a sleigh and delivers Valentine cards in August."

Whiteacre's voice sharpens. "Let's go, already, before I slam this door and let you cool your heels until morning."

Rolling off the cot, I follow her out of the cell and out to booking, where I'm given back my clothes and belongings and allowed to change. It feels good to be back in jeans, but the bastards have taken my revolver and my knives—and not even Charlie could shake loose a weapon involved in a cop shooting.

I walk out the door a free woman—at night, in a small town, with no transportation. Charlie's not about to make it obvious that I'm back with the Unit, so I don't expect he's orchestrated a ride. It's a seven-mile walk up the mountainside to get back to the Manor, and taxis, buses, and Ubers do not exist in this part of the world. My bad leg amps up its aching at the very thought of the ordeal.

But a panel van sits idling in the parking lot. It's white, or would be if it weren't mud-spattered. The legend FRANK'S FULL SERVICE CREMATORIUM AND BURIAL SERVICE adorns the side, accompanied by a garish illustration of a funereal urn and flowers. I happen to know that there is no Frank. The undertaker's name is Lysander and the van is usually driven by his daughter, Sophronia.

Before I can expend too many brain cells wondering if Charlie has somehow gotten to Sophie, the passenger door opens. A man eases himself out and turns toward me. His face is pale and thinner than when I saw it last, the cheekbones too sharp, the skin around his eyes pinched and tight with pain. He stands with his legs braced wide, holding on to the door, as though he might crumple into a heap if the van weren't there to hold him up.

All things considered, he looks pretty good. Definitely a whole lot better than Charlie implied. The floodlights are too bright, all at once, and I blink repeatedly to clear my vision.

"Shouldn't you be home in bed, Sheriff?" In addition to the problem with my eyes, there's an unaccountable hoarseness in my throat.

Jake smiles, slightly. "Always knew you'd shoot me one day," he says.

I take a step toward him, my eyes locked with his. "You're

welcome. Just let me know next time you need killing, and I'll be sure to be ready."

He starts to laugh. Stops abruptly with a hand on his chest.

Sophie leans toward the open door from the driver's seat and calls, "Are you two getting in or what?"

I see that Jake has a dilemma, and one that I recognize. The simple act of getting back into the van is going to hurt. A lot. He won't want me to see it, and he won't want my help, so I brush past him and clamber up to sit in the middle.

Jake climbs back in, a sharp hiss of breath escaping him as he does so, and then he sits perfectly still, not reaching for his seat-belt, not even breathing, as Sophie shifts the van into gear. He hisses again as we lurch into motion. His arm, where my shoulder presses against it, is damp with sweat even though it's chilly outside.

"When did they let you out?" I ask, silently planning to murder Charlie in his sleep for implying that Jake was still hovering between life and death.

"This afternoon." His voice is tight.

"And you're not taking pain meds and you're out running around—"

"Since when did you learn to hover?" There's a dangerous edge to his voice, and I smile. That's better. He's okay, more or less.

I turn to Sophronia, who is frowning ever so slightly but otherwise looks as normal as it's possible to look when your hair is night black, your eyes are vividly green and heavily lined with kohl and you look more like an ancient Egyptian priestess than an eighteen-year-old girl from small town USA. So, that, too, is good.

"Well, give me the rundown." I adjust my position to something resembling comfortable while trying not to jar Jake or jab him in the ribs with my elbow. His presence beside me is distracting, and I have a completely uncharacteristic desire to lay my head on his shoulder and dissolve into tears.

"They haven't released Matt yet," Sophie replies. "Jake spent the afternoon talking to the DA and explaining the accidental shooting—"

"Better fill me in on that," I interrupt. "So I know what I actually did if anybody asks."

Jake answers, his voice almost normal now. "There was a perp with a gun threatening innocent civilians. You took a righteous shot at the guy but I wasn't paying attention and stepped right into the path of the bullet. The suspect then ran off, and here we are."

The story sounds thin, even to me, particularly since both Matt and Val, a fragile Manor resident, both also claimed to have pulled the trigger. Still, the story is more plausible than the truth.

"Description of this suspect?" I ask.

"Middle-aged white male, medium height, wearing a ski mask, jeans, and a T-shirt. Fled on foot."

Good. The description is so vague, no innocent guy is going to get picked up on suspicion of a crime that never even happened.

"As of this afternoon, the DA was planning to drop charges against both you and Matt," Jake goes on. "But just now, the jail said they couldn't release Matt on some sort of technicality. I reminded them I'm the Sheriff and last I heard had some sort of authority, and was reminded that I'm out sick and my interim still has final say. Subtext—something's going on and she wouldn't tell me what."

"Huh," I say, staring hard at the windshield in front of me.

"Maureen?" Jake knows me all too well. "What do you know?"

"Not a thing," I say, primly. "I've been locked up for two weeks. Soph, if you could slow your roll a little, I might not bounce around like a bullet in a brain pan. I've got nothing to hold on to. Besides, these roads are slick and you're going to put us in the ditch."

"I'm driving like I always do. Just tell us what you know." She steps on the accelerator and I'm forced to grab Jake's thigh to keep myself in place. Before I can recover my balance, he covers my hand with his and keeps it there.

"If there was a body in the back, it would be rolling around on the floor by now," I grumble.

"If there was a *person in transition* in the back, I would obviously drive with more respect," Sophronia counters. "I'm trying to get you to the Manor before ten-o'clock lockdown."

"I have a key."

"Huh," Jake says.

I glance at his profile, and then at Sophronia's. "What are you two not telling me? What's going on with the Manor?"

"Jill is going on with the Manor," Sophie says, grimly. "Running things."

"What? I thought Jake arrested her." My memory definitely confirms that the last time I saw Jill, she was in handcuffs.

"Didn't really have valid charges," Jake says glumly. "Plus, you shot me before I could actually take her in and get her booked. Nobody else had a clue as to what was up."

"Meanwhile, back at the Manor," Sophie says, "she's got an attorney looking at her father's will to see if him leaving the place to you can be contested. I've been banned from the premises, by the way, so if you have any people in transition, I'll have to send Craig out to fetch them. Lysander is basically useless."

Her voice leaves no doubt that she is royally pissed about this situation, and I can't imagine Craig is happy about it, either, since he prefers to keep his badly-scarred face out of public sight. The residents also won't be happy. Last time Jill made a power grab it only lasted a day but caused an uprising none-theless.

All of this makes me feel better. A little battle of wills and wits with Jill will clear the cobwebs from my brain nicely.

"Let me out." I jab Sophie with an elbow, and she opens her door and hops down to the ground with the careless ease of the young. I slide under the steering wheel and very nearly take a spill when my feet land on a patch of ice. Sophie steadies me, which is hard on my pride, so when she says, "There's something else you might want to know," I snarl, "Later," and stalk toward the front doors without looking back.

CHAPTER FOUR

Even in the dark, illuminated only by a couple of security spot-lights, Shadow Valley Manor looks as ordinary and boring as any run-of-the-mill retirement home, maybe even more so. The building was originally part of a Cold War government installation and later was converted into a home for unwed mothers, known to the locals as HUM. When that organization dissolved, the place was remodeled and put to use as an upscale residence for well-to-do seniors. In keeping with its military origins, there is nothing either beautiful or interesting about the building's exterior.

Fortunately, appearances can be deceptive. I keep my senses on hyper alert as I walk up to the front door. The sidewalk is well lit, but there are plenty of shadows and shrubs that offer hiding places. Anything might be lurking: creatures that make the monsters hiding under children's beds look as harmless as the ones in a Disney movie. Unit assassins. Old enemies.

I reach the front door unscathed, only to be confronted by an oversized evergreen wreath decked out in shiny balls and pinecones. I wasn't kidding when I bah-humbugged Christmas; I hate fake glitz and extravagant sparkle. Muttering under my breath at Jill, who has got to be responsible, I tug at the door. It's locked, which is normal. My key doesn't fit in the lock, which is not. In addition to hanging this obnoxious wreath, that infuriating woman must have changed the locks.

No way in hell am I going to ring the buzzer at the door of my own Manor and then stand here like a supplicant while Jill makes her leisurely way down to gloat over my predicament. But when I reach into my pocket for my lockpick set, it's missing. Naturally. Another precious item confiscated by the jail when they booked me.

My next thought is to hunt down a nice rock to throw through the glass, but the Manor belongs to me, not Jill, and if I break something, I'm the one who will have to pay to fix it. So, I step away from the front doors and follow the sidewalk around the side of the building, stopping at the dining hall. As expected, given the time of year, the French doors are locked.

Next, I try the kitchen. It gets hot in there, even in the winter. Matt, trained by the military and then further conditioned by the Unit, opens the windows while he works but is meticulous about closing and locking them at the end of the day. Hopefully, whoever is filling in for him is laxer. The first window I try is latched, and I start thinking about rocks again, but the other window—smaller, a little higher, and inconveniently located over the scullery sink—is wide open.

Six months ago, before the paranormal slug feasted on my innards, and the bullet that killed it shattered my femur, the window would have been easy. As it is, the only gymnastics competition I'm likely to win is the debilitated-senior division. But at least I'm still wiry and thin, so after two awkward runs, I manage to leap high enough to get my head and chest lodged in the opening and wriggle the rest of my body through, coming down into a sort of handstand in the sink while my feet are still in the window.

I lack the abdominal strength to maintain the pose without

support, so when my feet come free, I collapse onto the drainboard with a clang of pots and lids. I scramble to right myself, not wanting to be found in an embarrassing tangle of limbs and cookware, but nobody comes to investigate the noise.

This is not surprising. Most of the residents wear hearing aids, which of course are out at night, and Jill's suite is on the third floor. I straighten my shirt, adjust my jeans, and make sure to close and lock the window behind me before venturing farther into the Manor.

The kitchen is dark and empty. The dining room is dimly lit by strings of brightly colored lights and, of all things, a Christmas tree. Cursing Jill to hell and back, I make my way down the hallway—strung with tinsel garlands—to my office, just down the hall from the front doors. When I flip on the lights, I see an organizer on my desk, filled with gel pens containing pink and purple ink. A day planner, not mine, lies open next to a pair of glitter-coated ceramic snowmen capering with a red-hatted penguin. An annoying haze of perfume lingers in the air.

Passing the office, I carry on down the hallway to the front door, noting that the alarm system is armed and ready to go. "Sleep through this, Jill," I say, as I unlock and open the door. A piercing siren blares out of a speaker right above my head. Another speaker is located in my suite, which is right across from Jill's. If she doesn't hear that, she's either deaf or dead.

As well as I can, given that my leg is not happy with either the inactivity in jail or the adventures of this night, I stomp back down the hall to the office. I pull out the chair from behind the desk—my chair, though the height and tilt have been adjusted—and sit down to wait. With an effort, I manage to get both feet up on the desk, tilt the chair back, and light up the first smoke I've had in two weeks, thanks to the pack that, fortunately, was hidden under random papers in the bottom drawer, where Jill didn't see them.

When she appears five minutes and thirty-three seconds later —an abysmal response time, and one that I can beat by two minutes, even from dead asleep—I'm near the end of my smoke and flipping through her planner, which is full of saccharine motivational quotes and notations in pink ink.

"What the hell, Maureen?" Jill shouts, completely forgetting her usual faked French accent. Her hair is sticking up on one side of her head and flattened on the other. Free of makeup, her skin looks dull and sallow. Her bathrobe is silk and aims at elegance, but her fuzzy slippers and disordered hair make her look exactly like the middle-aged woman she is instead of the Parisian fashion plate she aspires to be.

I blow smoke at her. "Seems like I should be asking you that question. You wanna turn that thing off?" I shout, partly because shouting feels good but mostly to be heard over the racket made by the alarm.

I can see that Jill would like nothing better than to shoot me, right here and now. I smile, cheerfully and provokingly, and blow more smoke in her direction. Her face turns an unbecoming shade that is closer to purple than rosy pink, but she scurries off down the hall. The alarm stops, dropping us into a beautiful silence, broken only by the shuffling thump of an angry woman trying to stomp in slippers.

"You can't smoke in here" is her opening salvo when she reappears in the doorway.

I take another long drag, then slide my feet to the floor and turn to face her more directly. "Care to tell me why I'm locked out of my own Manor?"

"It needed better security. The locks were inadequate." She tries to look dignified, but again: Robe. Fuzzy slippers. Wonky hair. "I was worried about the poor old people. They might be murdered or robbed in their beds—"

"Most likely by you." I drop my butt into an empty water

glass she's left on my desk and light another. Normally, I'm not a chain smoker, but it's been so long and it's an easy way to annoy Jill. "Clearly, we do need better security, since it only took me about thirty seconds to break in. I will get on that first thing in the morning."

Her lips tighten as she takes two steps toward me, waving a finger. "Not so fast. You somehow manipulated my father into willing this Manor to you. But you shot the sheriff. I have no idea how you got out of lockup, but you have no business whatsoever being in charge of a bunch of helpless people—"

"Whereas, the last time I saw you, I believe you were in handcuffs, waiting for your ride to jail."

"There was no crime to charge me with."

I lean forward and fix her with my best glare. "We both know there were plenty of crimes you could have been charged with had I not, as you pointed out, shot Jake. But now that he's out of the hospital, perhaps we can remedy that situation."

Jill straightens her shoulders and tightens her bathrobe belt, which is trying to come undone. She glances hopefully down the hallway toward the door.

I laugh. "Security isn't going to save you, *ma belle*. I'm sure you're hoping I escaped from jail and can be sent back, but I was released. All charges dropped. They are not going to arrest me for breaking into a building that legally belongs to me. You can either call now and let them know this was a mistake, or apologize when they get here. Whichever you like. I'm going to bed."

She smiles. It's not a pleasant look on her. "Good luck with that," she says. "Sleep well."

I show her both of my middle fingers before making my way down the silent hallway, past the elevator, and to the stairs. I avoid elevators whenever possible. They are essentially moving prisons where you can be trapped with somebody or something that wants to kill you. On stairs, at least you have some freedom of movement.

Thoughts of my suite give me the burst of energy I need to make the ascent. I think about my tiny kitchen and my personal coffeemaker. The private bathroom with a shower that actually has a curtain. My favorite comfy old armchair. A secondary stash of weapons. Most of all, my bed. The luxury of my sheets, my comforter, a mattress that is both cushy and firm. After two weeks sleeping on a lumpy jail mattress, it holds the allure of the holy grail.

But when I reach the door to my suite, it's unlocked. This means trouble. I have five locks on my door. Sophie is the only person who has keys, and if she's found reason to enter my space, she knows to lock things up behind her. I've always suspected Jill's father taught her more than she'll let on, lock-picking included. Maybe this is part of her power play. If I were properly armed, I'd be up to confront any danger, but I am not reckless enough to barge in without a gun or a knife or any weapon at all.

A step behind me spins me around, my hand reaching yet again for my missing revolver.

"Is there a problem?" Jill asks, smooth as silk, her accent back in place.

"No problem at all." I ease the door open and switch on the overhead lights.

An open suitcase sits on my couch. Clothing that I wouldn't be caught dead in hangs over the back of a chair. An empty cup and plate sit on the counter by the sink, in need of washing. And in my bed—my precious, so much longed-for bed, there's a person-shaped lump under the covers. Anubis, the huge orange cat I inherited with the Manor, is curled up beside the pillow. He blinks at me but doesn't offer to come and say hello. I don't like cats and only tolerate him for Phil's sake, but the betrayal still smarts.

"Care to explain?" I ask Jill.

"Hush," she whispers. "Don't wake her."

At this point, I don't care if I wake the dead, even though zombies are damnably inconvenient and annoying.

"You put somebody in my suite. In my bed."

"Well, you were in jail. And we had no other rooms available."

"There's this simple little word you say in those situations. No. N. O. As in *We have no rooms; we cannot accept a new resident at this time.*"

"He was very. . .persuasive."

"He who?"

She opens her mouth, then stops, eyes widening as she realizes she wasn't supposed to tell me this. I don't need her answer. A terrible suspicion is rising in me. Striding across the room— my room—I peel back the quilt, exposing a wizened, wrinkled, bony woman. Her face is half-hidden by the pillow and a tousle of gray hair, but I know who she is.

"Wake up!" I shake the thin shoulder. Anubis, disturbed from his comfortable position, swears at me in feline. Ellen rolls onto her back and stares at me out of wide, uncomprehending eyes, then sits up, scooting backward against the headboard, whimpering in fear.

"What the hell were you thinking, Jill?" I demand. "We don't have care available for somebody with this level of dementia. A *violent* person with dementia." This is all Charlie's doing, of course, but he's not here to shout at.

"She's violent?" Jill gasps.

I give her a withering glare. "Why do you think they'd put an old woman with dementia in the jail? Embezzlement, maybe? Fraud? She brained her husband with a sock full of rocks."

Jill shuffles her feet and glances away. "The very kind man who called said only that the poor old dear was in jail and it was no place for her, and they had no other placement options at all. What could I do?"

I know damned well Jill is no more inclined to act out of mercy or kindness than Charlie is, and I wonder what kind of deal *she* made with that particular devil. I add that question to a rapidly growing mental list, then assume a patronizing and exaggeratedly patient tone.

"Running the Manor isn't fun and games. It means making hard decisions and asking good questions before admitting residents. Who do you think is going to take care of her? Give her meds, help her get dressed?"

An evil smile spreads over Jill's face. "Well, it's your Manor. So, I guess she's your problem. I'll just go to bed and turn the responsibility all back over to you where it belongs. Good night, Maureen. Sleep well."

And with that, she slams out the door, leaving me with an unwanted and potentially dangerous guest and the promise of a long and sleepless night.

Ellen sits there staring at me, wide-eyed and frightened, covers drawn up to her chin. Anubis, belatedly remembering that I'm the one who feeds him, is winding around my ankles and purring. He wants me to believe he's happy to see me. He's not. Ignoring him, I turn my attention to soothing Ellen. But soothing is not my strong suit, and even though I try to speak gently, my words come out more like military commands. "Lie down. Go back to sleep."

"Where's Richard?" she whimpers. "Isn't he coming to bed?"

"Not tonight."

Her face crumples as if she's maybe going to cry, and I add, "Maybe we'll find him in the morning." I have no idea who Richard is, but I hope he's alive, because while I might welcome a good altercation with a vampire or a werewolf, I am not in the mood to be joined by ghosts or revenants.

Tears track pathways down Ellen's wrinkled cheeks. For possibly the first time in my life, I don't know what to do. She's the picture of a frightened and confused old woman, harmless and in need of shelter and protection. But she *did* try to kill her husband. And I've been fooled by seemingly harmless and confused old women before. Since Charlie is involved, I have to assume that Ellen is really a highly dangerous paranormal that he hopes will kill me in my sleep.

"How about I make us some tea?" I ask, buying time. "And then you can go back to sleep. Everything will look better in the morning."

She sniffles and wipes her eyes and nose on the sheet. *My* sheet. The one I should be snuggled under this very minute. Shoving that thought aside, I put the kettle on, thinking that what I really need is a stiff shot of whiskey. Make that three shots. But I need to keep sharp until I figure out who or what Ellen is and why she is here. I do, however, pour a shot in her cup, hoping it will either send her back to sleep or activate her true nature if she isn't human. Paranormals tend to have unusual reactions to alcohol.

She sniffs at the brew suspiciously, refusing to drink until I sip from my own mug. Even after she finishes the tea, she doesn't want to go back to sleep. She needs to use the bathroom. She wants to go outside on the balcony. I coax her back into bed three times and finally get her to lie down.

"Tuck me in," she says.

No way in hell am I tucking her in. Somewhere behind those hazy gray-blue eyes, she's probably laughing at me, picturing the day when she gets to tell Charlie and other operatives about how she manipulated me into falling for her act.

But her wrinkled face crumples and tears track down her cheeks once more. Soft sobs increase in volume, becoming wails.

Hellfire and damnation. I pull the sheets and blanket up to her chin. "There, happy?"

"Kiss me goodnight."

"Look, I'm not Richard, whoever Richard is, and I'm not your mother—"

She begins to wail again.

"Fine," I tell her. "Just stop crying." She stops with a little hiccup, gazing up at me expectantly. Somebody is going pay for this.

I lean down and drop a dry kiss on her forehead. Her eyelids lower, then rise again. "Sing me a song."

"Just go to sleep."

"Sing." Her thin lips push out into a pout.

I can't carry a tune, and I don't know a single lullaby, but I'll do just about anything to hush her at this point. So, I give her a badly butchered rendition of "Yellow Submarine," the first thing that comes to mind, and by the time I'm done, she's snoring.

Checking repeatedly to make sure she's not feigning sleep, I locate my backup knife and the little .22 I confiscated from Jill when she first showed up at the Manor. I'm still not properly armed, but it's better than nothing. Ellen's eyes are closed and she's still snoring, so I step into the walk-in closet and check the door at the back. It's closed and invisible to anybody who doesn't know it's there. I want to go down the secret staircase and check on the lab, but I don't dare leave Ellen unattended.

Wearily, I sit down in the armchair to keep watch. Something rubs against my legs, and I jerk and startle, but it's only the cat. He meows, then launches himself into my lap. I grab him and cuddle him—only to save myself from the claws he will employ for traction if I don't. And then I stroke his fur, but only because if I don't, the claws will come out again; certainly not because his purr is a comforting sound and the weight of his body is pleasant.

I need to stay awake. Essentially, I'm on stakeout, or stake-in, to be more accurate. But my head keeps nodding, my eyes keep closing, and I keep jerking awake while the clock stubbornly refuses to move. After a while, I get up and open the sliding door to my balcony, hoping the cold air will do the trick, but even shivering does little to keep me alert.

When I sit down in the chair again, I tell myself I'll rest my eyes for just a moment.

And it feels no more than a moment before I startle awake in the midst of a full adrenaline surge. My eyes fly open. My head snaps up. Somewhere in the Manor, a woman is screaming.

CHAPTER FIVE

I'm wide awake in a heartbeat. Years of conditioning kick in and I roll up onto my feet and assess the situation. My immediate surroundings are secure. The door to the hallway is closed and locked. The Ellen-sized lump in my bed stirs, murmurs something incomprehensible, and resettles. The screaming comes from the direction of the balcony. When I step out and look down, I see and hear nothing moving in the dark. The sound is too muffled to be coming from outside anyway, and I estimate its source to be on the main floor, in the dining room, two stories below me.

I slide the .22 into the back of my jeans, lock the sliding door to the balcony, set all five locks on my room door, and activate the personal alarm system that will vibrate in my pocket if the door is opened. If the screaming is a distraction meant to remove me from my room, it won't be easy for any entity, human or other, to sneak in—or out—while my back is turned.

By the time I descend two flights of stairs and follow the racket to the dining room, a clump of wheelchairs, walkers, and slow-moving oldsters in pajamas and robes already blocks the hallway. I forge a path through the middle of them and stop at the dining room doorway for a quick assessment of the situation.

Sylvia stands in the center of the room, shrieking at the top of a pair of very capacious lungs. "Dead. Oh my God. She's dead!"

Chuck stands next to her, hyperventilating and making gibbering noises. Ginny, managing to look elegant even in her bathrobe and minus her diamonds and makeup, is pale but composed, attempting to calm the screamer.

The cause of the commotion is Ida Mae Franklin, lying spread-eagled on dining table five. She's respectably clad in a flannel nightgown and crocheted slippers. A seasonal placemat— bright red, printed with green wreaths and pinecones—has been laid out on her torso and topped with a dinner plate and a vase holding a single white daisy. Her face is peaceful, eyes closed as if she's asleep. There's no sign of violence.

"Oh, *mon dieu*," Jill wails from behind me. "Why are you just standing here? Call 911. Does she need CPR?" She attempts to sweep dramatically into the room, but my arm comes out and catches her hard in the midsection. She doubles over with a whooping sound.

"Stay there," I command. "Do not move or I will shoot you."

I double-check to make sure Ida Mae is actually dead. There's no pulse, no breath, and her skin is already cooling, which tells me there's no point in CPR. Her eyes don't fly open when I surreptitiously touch a silver ring to her skin, which is a pretty good indicator that she's also not *undead*, a deceptive condition I learned about the hard way.

My next move is to preserve and document the crime scene. I snap pictures with my phone camera, issuing other directives to the residents, which are totally unheard over Sylvia's earsplitting screams. Ginny continues to pat the hysterical woman on the shoulder and chant, "Hush now, you're safe, you have nothing to worry about." This approach is clearly not working, so I walk over and administer a slap to one side of the well-tended face and then the other. Sylvia freezes, mouth open, eyes wide. A blissful silence descends, broken only by Jill's attempts to get in a good breath and Chuck's hyperventilating.

Picking out one of the most sensible residents from the crowd at the doorway, I call out, "Dan. Call 911. Tell them we have a murder, would you?"

Gasps. Clamoring voices. As if I've said something startling. As if they think Ida Mae chose to voluntarily expire on a table with a place setting on her belly.

"Nobody is to enter this room; is that clear?" I raise my voice to be heard above the chatter and they all fall silent again. "Nobody is to leave the Manor until the police have come and gone and given their okay. Who found the body?" I snap some pictures of the shuffling throng, just to aid my memory of who is here.

"Sylvia, it would appear," Ginny answers. "At least, she was the one in here screaming when I came down. Chuck followed me in."

"You didn't see anybody else leaving the room?"

Ginny shakes her head.

My attention focuses on Sylvia, who continues to stare at me, her mouth still open. "You hit me," she says, shock giving away to resentment and anger. "I'll report you to—"

"Don't be ridiculous. You couldn't stop screaming, and now you have and can tell me what you saw."

Her chin comes up. She's an imperious old bird, born to money and used to people giving her what she wants. "I don't have to tell you anything."

"Fine. You can wait right here for law enforcement."

"Of course," she says, attempting to smooth her carefully colored hair into some sort of order. "I'm the one who found her."

"You'll also be their prime suspect."

Her jaw drops open again, her face goes pale, and she sways a little on her feet. Damn. Maybe I've overdone the tough routine. I catch myself looking around for Matt before remembering that he's still moldering away in jail. Damn it. I'm used to him being here to back me up, and now I have to do all of this myself.

"I couldn't sleep," Sylvia says, employing the sort of diction movie stars used during the time of my youth. But then she shudders and her face contorts, as if holding back either a fit of weeping or maybe more screaming.

"She said she came down to get some milk; isn't that right, Sylvia?" Ginny prompts.

Sylvia sucks in a breath and pulls herself together. "Right. Yes. I wanted some warm milk to help me sleep, and came down to get some from the cooler. And then I saw. . .*that thing.*" She shudders, dramatically.

Before she can lapse back into hysterics, I ask, "Did you see anybody else out and about between here and your room? Or was there anybody in the dining room?"

She shakes her head. "No. I was thinking the whole time I was glad everybody was sleeping so as not to be seen. . ." She gestures at her thin silk robe. I'd had my suspicions about Chuck's apparent panic, but they evaporate when he doesn't so much as leer at her or make one of his usual piggish comments. He just keeps sucking in great gasping breaths, wiping his hand across his mouth and onto his pants, over and over in a repetitive gesture.

"Ginny?"

"I heard the screaming and came to tell the screamer to desist, as my sleep is precious and was being ruined. Chuck was already here. I saw nobody else."

"Chuck. What did you see?"

He gasps, his eyes bugging out of his head. "Dizzy. Hands. . .numb."

"You're fine. Slow down your breathing."

Which of course he doesn't do. No paper bag handy to get him to breathe into, so he'll just have to either figure it out himself or pass out. Which would take care of the problem just fine, only he's a big man with a huge belly, and the crash might make him another casualty if he falls hard enough, not to mention corrupting the crime scene.

I herd all three of them across the dining room and sit them in chairs as far from the body as possible. "The three of you stay here until a deputy can take your statements."

Turning back toward the group in the hallway, I ask, "Anybody else see anything? Hear anything?"

"Just Sylvia screaming," somebody says, and a murmur of agreement follows this.

"Jill, did you reset the alarm after I came in?"

"*Bien sûr*. Of course." She smooths her hair, trying to look dignified and offended at the question.

If she's telling the truth and the alarm was set, then nobody came in through the door after I went upstairs. Which means one of four things. One, the murderer used a window. Two, he or she knows how to access the subterranean passages. Three, the murderer is a resident or employee of the Manor. Four, we're got a dangerous paranormal on the loose. In any case, my residents are at risk.

"Okay, everybody, listen up!" I wave both arms above my head and shout, to get their attention. "You are all going to go directly back to your rooms and stay there. Lock the door. Don't let anybody in unless it's me or law enforcement."

"Why can't we wait together somewhere?" Julia objects. She's a spoiled trust-fund baby, despite her years, and objects to being told what to do. If I'd told her to wait with the group, she'd want to go back to her room. She's not the only one. Fortunately, I have some pretty good ammunition, in the forms of logic and intimidation.

"In case it's escaped your attention, Ida Mae has not died of natural causes. We don't know who killed her or where that killer might be."

I let that sink in before I go on. "This is for your own safety."

That does it, and they disperse, Julia in her wheelchair very nearly running over a frail old man with a walker. Jill, of course, takes the opportunity to edge toward the body, and I call her off with assignments and responsibility. "I need you to wait by the front door and let in the deputies and the coroner and anybody else official who shows up. No residents leave the building and nobody else comes in, understood?"

"Do I have time to get dressed, first, perhaps?"

I stare her down. She shuffles her feet and says, "Of course, yes. This is important. I'm going."

"Maybe call Cathy while you're at it. Ask her to come in early."

"Um, about that. . ."

"Oh my God, Jill. Did you let her go?"

"She quit. The woman is completely incapable of following orders. But don't worry; I am looking for another—"

"Just go, will you? We'll talk about this later."

It's not the first time Jill has managed to get rid of Cathy. The last time, I was only gone for a couple of days, and it still took me some sweet-talking and a serious pay raise to get the woman back. But Cathy is a problem for later. My first priority right now is to preserve the crime scene and keep an eye on my witnesses.

With a shock of surprise, I realize how much I miss my team. Matt, competent and potentially lethal, knowing exactly what needs to be done without being told. Sophie, outraged on behalf of Ida Mae's spirit. And Jake. . .a warm feeling in my chest at the thought of Jake goes well beyond my confidence in him as a lawman. But the team is temporarily disrupted, even Cathy is gone, and I'm stuck with Jill, who I trust about as much as a rattlesnake hyped up on methamphetamine.

As if to emphasize this point, the official troops roll in. Or, more literally, the troop. Singular. One lone deputy who looks like he should still be in high school, wide-eyed, apple-cheeked, and already perspiring.

"Deputy Garrity," he squeaks, his eyes darting from me to Chuck, who is still loudly hyperventilating, to the two old women in nightclothes, and finally to the disturbing tableau of Ida Mae. His face pales dramatically. He swallows, repeatedly, his throat making an ominous clicking noise. He opens his mouth to say something, but all that comes out is a gargle, and he runs into the hall, where I can hear him retching. At least he had the sense to clear the crime scene first.

I hear footsteps in the hall, and Jake appears in the doorway. He's pale and unshaven, but his eyes are clear and intense as he takes in every detail of the scene.

"Shouldn't you be in bed?" I ask.

"I can do without the hovering," he growls. "Fill me in."

More footsteps, and a commotion in the hallway.

"That is thoroughly disgusting," a bass voice booms. It's Mac, the county coroner. "Whatever you do, do not let that creature anywhere near the crime scene or I will personally flay the skin off both of you."

"Morpheus, stop it," Sophronia's voice says, then adds, "Oh, whatever. Saves cleanup."

Mac stomps into the room. He's a large man, with a stern face and long black hair tied back out of the way. "Must be an ugly one," he says. "You've got a deputy puking in the hallway. Hope there haven't been a horde of senior citizens contaminating my crime scene."

"Ewww, don't lick me," Sophie's voice says, still in the hallway. "Not where that mouth has been. Sit. Stay. Oh, fine, lie down then, just don't come in here."

I suppress an inappropriate grin of exhilaration. Of course,

I'm sorry for Ida Mae, but I'll admit there is nothing like a beautifully freakish murder to make life feel worth living.

"Dispatch is getting mighty efficient if one call to 911 brings you all in at once," I say.

"Scanner," Mac rumbles.

"Me too," Sophronia says. "Sit, Morpheus."

Morpheus, the mutt we rescued after his mistress turned out to be an insane, out-of-control soul stealer, doesn't sit, of course. Instead, he bounds across the room to me, demanding to be petted.

"Do none of you sleep?" I question, bending down to pat him so that he'll settle and not disturb evidence.

"Well, that's not at all disturbing." Mac sweeps his gaze over the bizarrely posed victim. He dons a pair of gloves and checks for a pulse. "Definitely dead," he says. "I can't assess further without disturbing evidence."

I grab the dog's collar and hold him as Sophronia approaches the body and stands there, head bent, eyes closed, a remote, listening expression on her face.

"Let's be clear." Mac glares at her, and then at me. "This body will be going to the medical examiner. We don't need an undertaker or any civilians contaminating evidence." I suspect that by *civilians* he also means me, but he ought to know me well enough by now that I'm not going anywhere.

"Anything, Soph?" I ask.

Her eyes meet mine. Troubled. "Weirdness. Creepy, incomprehensible weirdness." She withdraws her hand and wipes it on her black jeans.

"Hold up," Mac says. "Are you saying you can talk to the dead?" He's encountered Sophie before but isn't up to speed on all of her abilities.

She sighs dramatically. "Anybody can talk to the dead, Mac. It's easy. Stop talking *about* her and talk *to* her." Demonstrating, she leans closer to the body and croons, "We'll get you out of here soon, Ida Mae. Hold tight. We'll figure this shit out." Her hand lifts to touch the woman's forehead. Mac intercepts.

"Do *not* touch the body."

Sophronia rolls her eyes, teenage-fashion.

I watch Mac and Jake take in the scene, and run my own eyes over it again, looking for anything that I missed. Ida Mae lies on her back at the center of table five. Her arms and legs are spread out from her body as if she's been doing jumping jacks or making snow angels. There's no sign of a struggle or disturbance. No chairs knocked over. No footprints on the floor. The other tables are wiped down, the chairs all neatly in place. Nothing smells wrong. Nothing feels wrong. There's not even so much as a hint of a chill in the room that would indicate some super-powered spirit wreaking an unlikely vengeance.

"Could we please remove all of the civilians, Jake?" Mac growls. "And *pets*, for God's sake."

"On it," Jake says. "Where did Garrity get to?"

"Here, sir," The young man's voice sounds green and fragile.

"Go watch the entrance," Jake orders, having mercy. "Nobody in or out without checking with me, understood? And call for backup."

"Everybody's sleeping," Garrity protests. "I'm the only. . ."

Jake glares at him and he takes a step backward, nearly tripping over his own feet. "Yes, sir. I'll have dispatch wake them, sir."

"You reset the alarm last night after you broke in?" Jake asks, turning to me.

"How did you know. . ." Realization dawns. "You knew Jill changed the locks and you didn't warn me."

"You seemed in need of a challenge."

"Did you also know Ellen was moved from the jail to here?"

I watch his face closely, wondering if Charlie has gotten to him, too, but don't see so much as a twitch as he responds, "Who is Ellen? And can we focus on the crime scene?"

"Ellen was in jail with me and is my new roommate. Jill admitted her while I was gone and she is currently asleep in my bed. As for the alarm, I believe Jill set it, but you'll have to ask her and hope she tells the truth."

"We should talk to this Ellen person," Jake muses.

I shift, uneasily. This would be the time to tell him about my new entanglement with Charlie and the Unit, but years of secret keeping win out and I say only, "Good luck with that."

"Meaning?"

"Meaning she can't string two words together that make sense."

"And what's up with these people?" Jake jerks his chin at Chuck and Sylvia and Ginny.

"Witnesses. Sylvia found the body. The other two came to investigate when she started screaming and were first on the scene."

"Can you take them to wait in the library? And then I guess we'll need to talk to every one of the residents. Where are they?"

"I sent them to their rooms. Hopefully, they went."

"Thoughts on Jill?"

Our eyes meet and hold. "We have no reason to believe she's actually ever killed anybody," I say, slowly. "Not directly, anyway."

"Unusual to hear you defending her."

"For the record, I am confident that she is capable of killing any number of people, but I'd see her as more of a knife or gun type than something so. . .extravagant."

Jake rubs his jaw, thinking. "Well, we'll watch her."

I can see the lines of pain etched into his face, the way every movement is hesitant and stiff. He won't appreciate me coddling him, so I take another tack. "Are you supposed to be here? We don't want to mess up chain of custody or create inadmissible evidence or whatever."

"I'm touched by your concern for my health," he says. Then adds, "And your sudden and uncharacteristic attention to the rules. None of my deputies know how to work a murder, Maureen. I need to be here."

"But all of these other people do not," Mac says. "Maureen, you are not a part of this investigation. In fact, you'll also need to give a statement. And Sophronia will need to have a conversation with the deceased later—"

"It's not a conversation," she protests. "It's not like I can hear her talking."

"My mistake." Mac infuses supercharged irony into his words. "Please forgive my lack of understanding of. . .whatever it is you are and do. Now, would you take those witnesses and get. Out. Of. My. Crime. Scene."

CHAPTER SIX

I'm not scared of Mac, even though he's a large man who can appear intimidating and downright threatening, but he has a point. Somebody's got to wrangle the witnesses, and I guess that somebody is me. Besides, this gives me the opportunity to be the first to question them. Unofficially.

"Come on, people, you heard the coroner. Let's move. Soph, I guess you're with us." Normally, they would argue, if only for the sake of being contrary, but our witnesses head for the door like horses to the stable. Slow horses, mind, with a hitch in their giddy-up, but definitely happy to get far away from Ida Mae. Even Sophie stalks along beside me without arguing. Morpheus barks and bounces around, hoping for pats, but even he settles down and trails behind us, toenails clacking on the linoleum.

Halfway to the elevator, Chuck recovers himself enough to put his arms around Ginny and Sylvia's waists.

"Don't touch me," Ginny warns, venom in her voice.

"Just trying to be supportive."

"That's not what supportive feels like." She whispers something else that I can't hear, and he immediately drops both arms and keeps his hands to himself.

The library is on the second floor, just down the hall from the elevator. It's furnished with cushy armchairs and two reading tables. Shelves full of books line all four walls. Christmas has invaded in the form of paper snowflakes dangling from the ceiling. As a decorating choice, that makes sense. It's always cold in here, thanks to the library ghost that I assume is floating somewhere near the ceiling, since Sophie nods and waves in that direction.

I don't waste time on the invisible, being much more concerned with the feet and pajama-clad legs sticking out from behind one of the armchairs. Last I saw those pajamas, they were tucked into my bed, and there's no good reason for them to be here.

"Oh, damn it. Everybody stay where you are."

I pick my way forward, one slow step at a time, making sure I'm not stepping on any evidence. With the .22 in hand, I edge around the chair. Ellen lies on her side. One slipper is half off. A stretch of blue-veined leg is visible between her foot and the hem of her pajama pants. Her right hand pillows her cheek. Just like Ida Mae's, her face is peaceful.

Unlike Ida Mae's, her chest rises and falls with regular, easy breath.

Alive, then. And from the looks of things, sleeping. I know damn well I left her locked in my room and that I set the alarm, which is still in my pocket but has certainly never gone off.

"Ellen?" I call softly, and then louder. "Ellen! Wake up!"

Morpheus escapes Sophie's grip on his collar and bounds over, licking the wrinkled face with great enthusiasm. Ellen's eyes fly open and she scuttles back toward the wall like a frightened animal, drawing her knees up to her chest. She doesn't make a sound, doesn't move again, as if by staying perfectly still she is invisible.

"Hey." I hold my hand out to her, speaking softly, while internally cursing Charlie and the Unit extensively and fluently. "Soph, call off this infernal creature, would you?"

But Ellen now has her arms around the dog's neck and he flops down onto the floor with his head in her lap. Spinning around to the rest of the group clustered behind me, I snap, "What are you all staring at? Sit down already."

"What is that woman doing here?" Ginny asks, her aristocratic nose tilted upward in distaste. "This facility is for functional people. And could we possibly be permitted to change into appropriate attire before being interviewed by the police?"

Chuck scratches his belly and yawns. "Don't see why I can't wait in bed." He's not fooling anybody with this pretense. His hands are still shaking, his face is unnaturally pale, and he keeps repetitively wiping his mouth and scrubbing his hand on his jeans. "If we do have to be up, you'd think we could at least have some coffee."

Sylvia perches on the edge of an armchair, managing to convey that it is hard and uncomfortable and possibly dirty and flea-infested as well. "I'll be expecting a discount on my payment this month, to compensate for tonight's distress." Behind those words, I hear the unspoken plan to contact an attorney at once and see if there might be a case for a lawsuit on the grounds of mental suffering.

"Go get coffee for us, would you, Soph? And while you're at it, since we both know you have keys to my suite, would you fetch my walkie and check that I remembered to lock the door?"

She flops down into a chair. "I'm not your errand girl, Maureen."

"No, but you are in possession of two good legs and the aforementioned keys. Plus, I ran off in a hurry and may have left the closet door open. If you could just close that, please. I hate it when the cat sheds on my clothes." Sophie's green eyes widen just enough to let me know she's received the message that I want her to check the secret passage.

Her rebellion dissipates in a flare of curiosity and she stalks off, leaving me with a lot of questions and three captive witnesses. The pressure of silence will be good for all of them, and I sit quietly, contemplating the ceiling and planning an interrogation strategy. A spider dangles above Chuck's head on a length of silk, slowly but steadily lowering itself until it dangles right in front of his eyes.

He screams, rearing backward in his chair and windmilling his arms. "Get it away from me. Get it away from me!"

Sylvia emits an undignified little squeal of fear. The dog begins yapping an alarm.

I get up and clap both hands together, sharply, then wipe the resulting spider smear on my jeans. All three witnesses gape at me, even Ginny, their faces shocked and white.

"You killed it," Chuck whispers, as if I've just run a sword through a human being right in front of their eyes.

"Oh, for heaven's sake, people," I remonstrate. "You've just discovered a murdered body and a spider gets you all spun up? Now. Let's go over what happened one more time."

Before I can formulate my first question, Ellen starts to warble in a quavering voice, "The itsy-bitsy spider went up the water spout. . ."

"An unusual form of interrogation," Jake says, appearing in the library doorway. Morpheus runs to greet him.

Ellen's voice rises in volume. "Down came the rain—"

"Meet Ellen. You still want to interview her?"

"And washed the spider out—"

Jake approaches Ellen. She hisses, snapping her teeth together sharply, her eyes fixed on his face. At least she's not singing anymore.

"Maybe mental health?" he suggests. "Or an ambulance? Surely, the medical system is more equipped to manage her than we are."

At this moment, Sophie saunters in with a carafe of coffee

and a stack of paper cups, along with the radio I use for staff communications. "All doors were locked," she says. "And the cat was on your bed."

"Took you long enough," I grumble, pouring myself a cup while my mind works away at the question of Ellen and how on earth she got from my room to here without triggering my alarm.

"You're welcome." Sophie injects a great deal of sarcasm into those two words.

Jake speaks into his radio. "We need mental health out at the Manor."

"Cancel that," I tell him.

"What? Why? I thought you—"

"We need her here."

Our eyes meet and hold, and then he sighs. "Dispatch, cancel that. Hold off on mental health." And then, to me: "Care to explain?"

"Long story. Just believe me that we need to keep her for now."

He sighs again. "Can you get her out of here, do you think?"

"I can try. Ellen. Shall we get you some tea?" I coax. "Like last night."

Ellen's head tilts to one side and she smiles, almost childlike, but there's something cunning and sharp about her expression as she says, "Sing to me."

Unaccustomed heat rises to my cheeks. Jake's eyebrows go up. His lips twitch. "Didn't know you were a singer, Maureen."

I give him a murderous glare. If I find out that Ellen is really aware and cognitively together, she will pay for this in many inventive ways. For now, I'll go along and do whatever it takes.

"Out came the sun. . ." I sing, picking up where she left off. "And dried up all the rain. . ."

She lets me take her hand. Her fingers are cold and tremulous. Sophie reaches for her other hand, and I watch the girl's eyes for any flare of reaction, but there's nothing. Ellen peers up at her and says, "You too. Sing."

"You have got to be kidding," Sophie protests, but then she joins in. Together, we get the old woman up onto her feet, and the three of us head down the hall, singing like a trio of drunks, the dog at our heels.

MATT

"Wake up."

The command breaks into Matt's dream, sending it skittering off like a cockroach fleeing the light. Speaking of light, a very bright one is shining in his eyes. He can just make out the silhouette of a deputy standing in the open door of his cell, flashlight in hand.

"Midnight visit? That can't be good," he says, rolling off the cot and onto his feet in one fluid motion, half-blind but fully alert and adrenaline-charged. The odds are stacked against him, but he won't go down without a fight.

"It's not midnight," the guard says. "Three a.m., give or take."

"Nice of you to visit, but can't it wait? I was dreaming."

"If you don't want to be released, go back to sleep. By all means."

"What's this about release?" Matt suppresses the rush of hope, suspicious that this visit is part of a game of cat and mouse, designed for his torment and the deputy's amusement.

"Sheriff is out of hospital. Says you weren't the shooter. You're out of here."

"Well, in that case, I guess I can forgive you for waking me," Matt says, still not believing.

But fifteen minutes later, he stands shivering on the street outside the jail beneath a sky bright with stars, breathing in the freezing December air. He's been offered no apology and no ride home, even though the Manor is seven miles up the side of a mountain. He could probably call Sophronia to come and get him, but there are several very good reasons not to do that. Besides, after two weeks of inactivity, he's actually looking forward to stretching his muscles and reveling in the freedom.

The pleasure of free movement fades three miles into his trek. By mile five, he's cold and tired and laser-focused on a cup of coffee and a hot breakfast in his beloved kitchen. But as soon as he rounds the final curve that brings the Manor into view, he sees that trouble is brewing.

Two black-and-whites are parked outside the door. Despite the early-morning hour, Sophronia's van is in the lot, as is Jake's pickup. Matt breaks into a run, weariness forgotten in an adrenaline rush that is half-dread, half-curiosity.

A deputy meets him at the front door, barring his entrance.

"Sorry. Nobody in, nobody out."

"I live here," Matt protests. "And I just walked all the way from town."

"So sad. I've got orders."

Matt takes a step forward and makes an obvious production of reading the man's name tag. "Garrity, is it? I'm coming in, Garrity. Get out of my way."

The deputy backs up a step before suddenly remembering he is armed. He reaches for his service weapon and aims at Matt's chest, his hands trembling visibly.

"Oh, for God's sake," Matt says. "Radio Jake, would you, and tell him Matt is here, before that thing goes off accidentally and you put somebody's eye out."

A moment of hesitation, and then Garrity does as he's been asked, still pointing the gun more or less at Matt.

"Clarifying orders, sir," he says, into his radio. "Man at the door requesting entrance."

"Nobody in or out," Jake's voice comes back.

"Yes, sir. I told him, sir, but—"

"Jake. It's me," Matt interrupts. "Can you tell this guy to let me in?"

"Well, that's a different story," Jake's voice crackles over the radio. "He's clear, Garrity."

Matt doesn't wait for more. He grabs the deputy's wrist and shoves his arm down, aiming the gun toward the ground, then crowds past him, not asking or answering any more questions.

He slows his pace when he reaches the office. Jill is sitting at Maureen's desk, disheveled and makeup-free and wearing a bathrobe. She leaps to her feet. "Oh, *mon Dieu*. You are safe. You are back." Her face crumples dramatically, and she sobs, though she fails to summon tears to her bloodshot eyes. "It's so horrible."

She's as good a source of information as any, so he enters the office, whereupon she predictably catapults herself toward him. He puts his arms around her and pats her back while she sobs and sighs with her face against his chest.

"What's happened?" he asks.

"A murder. Shocking. Terrible."

"Dear God. Who?"

Jill's only answer is to cling to him, her weeping escalating into wails.

Matt's vision—Maureen dead—flickers behind his eyes. He grabs Jill's shoulders and pushes her away from him so he can see her face. "Who, Jill? Who's been murdered?"

"It 'appened in the dining room."

He shakes her, raising his voice. "Tell me who is dead!"

"One of the residents," she gasps. "Where are you going? Don't leave me alone. The murderer might be anywhere."

The murderer might be you, he thinks but doesn't say, already striding down the hallway toward the dining room. He's unarmed and doesn't like it. He's got knives in his room, but the kitchen is closer. He'll swing by and grab the sweet little paring knife that even has a case. Not as effective as his usual, but discreet and portable.

But when he reaches the kitchen, he finds it already occupied.

A woman stands at the cutting board, chopping up a chunk of bloody meat. She's nearly as tall as he is and packs more muscle. Those biceps would be the envy of any bodybuilder, male or female. Her yellow hair—definitely yellow, nothing so ephemeral as blond or golden, is braided and wound around her head. She looks like she stepped out of central casting after a call for Viking shieldmaidens—except for the bloodstained apron she's wearing and the cleaver in her hands, which make her look more like she just landed the starring role in a horror flick.

"Hey," he says, suppressing his irritation at the sight of somebody else occupying his space. "I'm Matt. Regular cook around these parts."

She whirls around and glares at him, cleaver raised. "This is my kitchen now. I am the cook."

There's bitterness in that final word, if he's not mistaken. He offers his best smile, the one most women find irresistible. He slides his hands into his pockets, keeping his posture casual and easy but infusing his tone with insolence. "Interim cook, maybe. Temporary? Thank you for taking care of things, but I'm back."

"Nobody said anything about *interim*." Her hand, larger than his, tightens on the handle of the cleaver.

His cleaver. If there's anything he's more possessive about than his kitchen, it's his knives.

Even so, a sliver of doubt pricks at him. Maureen has never

trusted him fully. Would she take the opportunity to replace him while he was in jail? Crowd him out of the Manor? What if this woman isn't a temp but a permanent hire?

"What's your name?" he asks, edging through the doorway and placing the island between them. "Do you live in Shadow Valley?"

"I am Karin," she says, eyeing him suspiciously, not answering the second question. "I was hired for this job and I am busy. Go away."

Before he can formulate an answer, he's distracted by the sound of voices in the hallway, singing loudly and off key. What the hell? Somebody drunk at this hour, with a murder investigation underway?

The singing stops. Uneven footsteps fill the silence, and moments later, Maureen and Sophronia appear, arm in arm with a frail old woman he doesn't recognize. The mutt dog, Morpheus, is right on their heels.

"Matt!" Maureen exclaims. "You're back. Perfect timing. Care to make me a cup of coffee? And some tea, for Ellen here."

Typical Maureen. No "Welcome back," or "Thanks for trying to protect me," or even "When did you get out?"

At least her greeting is an indication that he still has a job.

Sophie says nothing, but her eyes meet his, level and clear, and her lips curve in a smile. She looks okay, normal even. There have been long hours, locked away in his cell, where all he could do was replay the sight of her— undeniably *other*, those green eyes glowing as her hair blew in an invisible wind—and worry about whether she'd crossed that line so far that she wasn't coming back.

"Coffee is brewing already," Karin says.

"Great, I'll just come in and grab a cup." Maureen takes a step into the kitchen.

Karin bars her entrance, cleaver in hand. "You can't come in here."

Matt has no doubt that Maureen's got a gun and knows she's a quick draw, but if Karin attacks and gets herself shot, his beloved kitchen will become a crime scene. He braces himself, ready to intervene as Maureen steps forward again, her nose nearly touching Karin's prominent and somewhat alarming breasts.

"Given that the Manor belongs to me, I believe I can go anywhere I like."

"My kitchen. My rules. You are not the manager." Karin's knuckles whiten on the handle of the cleaver.

Matt grabs her wrist in a lightning-swift gesture, applying pressure to just the right spot. Her eyes widen, her fingers go limp, and the cleaver bites into the floor at their feet with a *thunk*.

Maureen bends down and tugs it free it from the flooring. "How about we all get acquainted." She straightens. "I'm Maureen. I own this place. Karin, I'm guessing you were hired by Jill in my *temporary* absence."

Interesting, Matt thinks. Charlie told him that Maureen has been out for some time already. The old bastard was obviously lying, so what angle was he trying to work?

Karin scowls. "I do not have time to get acquainted. I was preparing breakfast before this man's rude interruptions. I must deliver coffee to every room now, I've been told. And then a breakfast which is to be served to all of the residents, also in their rooms. As if I am a delivery girl. This will require more time and make me late with lunch."

The coffeemaker gargles and glugs into the community-sized carafe. Maureen hands Matt the cleaver, crosses to the cupboards, grabs a mug, and fills it. She takes a long swallow and chokes. "What did you do to it?" she gasps, red-faced, one hand going to her throat.

Matt surges forward and grabs the mug out of her hands.

"Are you okay? Is it poisoned?" He sniffs it, immediately wishing he hadn't.

Karin growls, a guttural animal sound that raises the warning hairs on the back of his neck. "I resent that. It is good, strong coffee. No fancy nonsense."

"Bracing," Maureen says, breathlessly, one hand still clutching her throat. "Here's what we're going to do. Matt is going to make some less. . .medicinal. . .coffee. And then the two of you are going to figure out how to work together."

"You did not hire me; you are not the boss of me." The woman's chin thrusts forward belligerently. "I do not answer to you." Clearly, she doesn't know who she's dealing with. Maureen returns her arctic glare with interest.

"Jill brought you in, but trust me, I can take you out. Jill works for me. Matt is supreme ruler in this kitchen and you will assist him. End of story."

Matt tries a conciliatory tactic. "I am sure you already have everything well under control. Maybe for today I can act as sous-chef? I'll get coffee out to the residents and then help you out. It's not easy shifting gears. Trust me, I know. Maureen made me switch up from Thanksgiving turkey to pizza once."

To his surprise, the tactic actually works. "Waste of good bird," Karin says, glaring at Maureen.

He seals the deal by handing back the cleaver, even though he still resents seeing it in hands other than his own and he's not quite sure she won't use it to take off somebody's head. Karin accepts it as if he's gifted her with a sword fished from the depths of a magical lake. A flush rises to her cheeks and her head dips in what is very nearly a small bow.

"I'll make that new batch of coffee," he says. "Not everybody can handle a bold, robust cup." He pours himself a cup of what Karin has made, prays for strength, and takes a long swallow. Pure battery acid, but he manages to make an appreciative noise. His heroism doesn't go to waste. Karin smiles. She carries the cleaver to the sink and scours it with hot soapy water before returning to the cutting board and getting back to work. The cleaver *thud*s rapidly, jarring the counter and rattling the glassware in the cupboards.

"We'll still have the beef hash I had already planned, but we will stuff it in a bun," she says. "I do not have time to fill all of the cups with coffee and juice to go to every room. And I will need somebody to deliver trays."

"I'm your delivery boy," Matt says.

"Tea?" Ellen queries.

"Got it." Matt fishes a teabag out of the cupboard and puts it in a mug, filling the cup with steaming water from the attachment at the sink. "Milk? Sugar?"

"Both," Maureen answers. Her eyes are full of the questions he is asking himself. Normally, she would slide onto a stool by the counter for a chat. Today, with Karin present, there's nothing to talk about other than inquiring after the health of Odin and Thor and asking whether Ragnarök is coming anytime soon.

Matt moves to the fridge to get the milk and stops, frozen, at what he sees reflected in the stainless steel door. Another vision. Maureen again.

"Matt?" Maureen's voice says, behind him. "You okay?"

"Right. Yes." He opens the door and retrieves the milk. When he hands Maureen the mug, her eyes meet his, and he nods, slightly, assurance that he understands his mission to watch Karin, even though his curiosity about who has been murdered and how is now at a fever pitch.

"Walkie me when there's good coffee, would you?" she says, a signal for him to check in, and also her way of saying she's glad he's back, and that maybe she even missed him.

He's missed her, too. Cares about her more than is healthy. "Be careful," he calls after her. But he knows Maureen. She'll run headlong into any possible danger, and nothing and nobody, certainly not him, will be able to stop her.

CHAPTER EIGHT

Jill is still in the office where I sent her earlier. Sitting in my chair. At my desk. Typing on my computer. When I direct Ellen to a chair, she complies willingly, sitting down with her mug in both hands and sipping, her eyes peering over the rim, curious as a child.

I glare pointedly at Jill. She keeps her eyes on the computer screen, as if she's unaware of my presence, but her fingers move faster and faster until I'm sure she's just pressing keys and not making words at all. Finally, she stops and looks up at me. "Can I help you?"

"You most certainly can. Get out of my chair and clear all of your shit off my desk. Especially that Christmas claptrap."

"Are you so sure the desk is yours?"

"Move, before I move you."

Before I can enforce my threat, Deputy Garrity ghosts into the room, looking apologetic and abashed. If he had a cap, it would be in hand, but he doesn't, so it isn't. He clears his throat and murmurs, "The sheriff wants to take your statement."

"Well, go on, Jill," I say. "You heard the man."

Garrity clears his throat again. "Ma'am, it's you he wishes to speak to, if you would come with me?"

I don't appreciate being summoned like a suspect, and I hate being ma'amed, but I'm more than happy to have a conversation with Jake, so I'm willing enough to go. First, I need to figure out what to do with Ellen. Jill is right here and might as well make herself useful. Yes, she's capable of murder, but apparently so is Ellen. Maybe the two of them deserve each other.

Jill notices me staring at her and narrows her eyes in suspicion. "What? He said it is you who must go."

"Right. Of course. I was just wondering. . .but it's beneath you. I couldn't even ask."

"Tell me."

"Well, it's just . . . I need somebody to do Cathy's job until we can hire a replacement. For a minute I thought . . . but you're not trained."

Jill rises to the bait. "But of course I can do it. How hard can it be?"

"Really? You think you could handle it?" I radiate as much skepticism as possible.

"I will begin at once. There is a list, I believe, of every resident and what they need to have done?"

"Well, I guess maybe . . ." I say, doubtfully.

"I will begin at once!"

"Excellent. That's such a relief. For starters, you'll need to keep an eye on Ellen. She can't be left alone; do you understand?"

"I am not a babysitter," Jill protests.

"Cathy would have watched her. But the job is very difficult, and you are not—"

"I will do it. Ellen will stay with me. And later we will check on all of the residents together. Right, Ellen?"

Ellen stares at her blankly.

"Okay, take me to Jake." I follow Garrity to the door, then turn back to Jill. "If she gets restless, sing to her. She likes that."

Before we make it to the end of the hall, I hear a surprisingly melodic voice singing some mournful tune I'm not familiar with.

"Thought you might bring me coffee," Jake says, as I enter the library. "Also, why is it so damned cold in here?"

"It's cold because of the ghost. And trust me, the coffee brewed this morning would likely kill you in your weakened condition."

"There's poison in the coffee?"

He's come a long way since we first met, I think, as I sink into a chair. His only reaction to mention of the ghost was a quick glance around the room and a tiny shiver.

"Nothing as straightforward as poison," I explain. "The interim cook prepared a beverage that could melt a spoon; whether by intention or accident is still up for debate. Matt is making some good stuff now."

"Damn. I really need a cup."

He looks like he needs a whole lot more than coffee. A couple of weeks in bed, for starters. His cheeks are hollow, and his skin is two shades too pale. We're alone for the first time since the shooting, and what my crusty old heart wants me to do is put my arms around this man and hold him. Tell him how relieved I am that he is still alive. Maybe even distract him from his pain by revisiting an interesting episode that was rudely interrupted by my former lover's ghost.

But weary and battle-scarred as he is, Jake has his professional face on. He needs to take my statement, and he needs to do it without distractions. I shift my weight in the chair, seeking a more comfortable position for my own aching bones, and dive in.

"Beginning with the beginning," I say, "you should know that I came in through the kitchen window last night and that it was already open."

"Are you *sure* the coffee wasn't poisoned?"

"You think Karin killed her?"

"Please, Maureen. I don't know who Karin is." He holds up a hand. "Don't tell me yet. Just answer my question."

"Fine. I drank one swallow of coffee. Matt downed a fair bit of the stuff and was still standing. He's helping her with breakfast."

"So, by *her* you mean Karin, and by *Karin* you mean Matt's temp replacement," he says, somewhat plaintively.

I open my mouth to explain but he asks another question. "Do you think that's wise?"

"Which part? Matt being left alone with Karin? Or Karin being in the kitchen at all?"

I'm trying to entice him into giving up some information, but he's still in professional mode and just gives me a look. I sigh.

"As you already know, the door was locked when you dropped me off. I came in through the kitchen window, which was already open. By the way, Karin would never have fit through that window. She's rather sturdily built."

Jake rubs his head as if it aches. "Your statement."

I'm wounded by his tone and deliberately act like the usual scattered witness. "My goodness. I'm so distraught over seeing that ghastly body, I just can't think straight. Who could do such a thing? So shocking and distressing. I arrived at the Manor last night but I wasn't wearing a watch and I really don't know what time it was. You could ask Sheriff Jake Callahan—he gave me a ride, so he would know, maybe? The front door was locked, which can also probably be confirmed by the same person, who was very likely watching from the van and laughing at my predicament."

"Maureen—"

"Right. Okay." I revert to my normal voice and give him the details he's looking for. "I walked around the side of the building and saw nothing moving. The dining-room patio doors were locked. The first kitchen window was also locked. However, the small window over the sink was not only unlocked but open. I climbed in through it and closed and locked it behind me.

"There was nobody in the kitchen. The lights were out, all except for a nightlight, but it was bright enough that I can be sure that the room was empty. Nothing was out of place or in disarray. The dining room also looked as expected and was visible because somebody, not to mention names or anything but probably Jill, has strung up Christmas lights. There was certainly no dead body lying on, or under, a table."

"Are you sure?" Jake asks, pausing in jotting down notes. "It was late. You might not have noticed if there was a body in the corner."

"I would have noticed a body, Jake."

"All right. That helps to establish time of death."

I make a noncommittal sound and he glares at me. "Speak up, if you have an opinion."

"I'm only a humble civilian. I couldn't possibly have an opinion."

"Just tell me."

"Fine. My timeline doesn't help to establish time of death, only the time that Ida Mae was put on the table. She could have died anywhere, and at any time, as far as we know."

"Right." Jake makes a little note on another piece of paper. "What happened next?"

"I walked down the hallway to the front door and opened it."

"Of course you did."

"Aren't you going to ask me why?"

"I know why. You did it to set off the alarm so Jill would have to come down and you could tangle with her."

I smile. "You know me so well. It warms my heart."

"Just forget about your heart," he growls. "Dammit, Maureen, this complicates everything. Did she lock the door and set the alarm again after your little prank?"

"I told her to. She walked down the hall in that direction and I heard the buttons beeping on the control panel."

"All right," he says. "Let's assume she locked the door and set the alarm. And you had closed and locked the window. There would have been no access to the Manor after that time. What happened next?"

I have a point of disagreement about possible entry, but I decide to table it for later. "I went to my room and discovered that Ellen was sleeping in my bed, thanks to Jill."

"Tell me about Ellen. Why is she here, again? Damn it, Maureen, getting a statement out of you is like pulling teeth without a pair of pliers."

He is not going to want to hear the rest of this, I know. The poor man is hoping for a nice, normal murder, or at least as normal as a murder can be when the victim is posed like an invitation to dinner.

"Maureen?"

I sigh. "Ellen is the favor that Charlie wanted from me."

Jake looks injured, as if I've said this on purpose to hurt him. "You're sure there's no coffee?"

I text Matt. *Coffee ready?*

It is. Not sure I should leave.

Good point. Send Sophie. Tell her to bring some for Jake.

A short pause, and then a text comes in from Sophie. *Really? I am not an errand girl.*

"Sophie's bringing coffee," I say.

"While we're waiting, suppose you skip over the part about who Ellen is and why the Unit is interested in her and tell me how the crime first came to your attention."

"Ellen was sleeping in my bed—sorry, I can't skip over all reference to her. I was awake in my chair so as to watch her, but I must have fallen asleep. I woke to the sound of screaming."

"Where was the screaming coming from?"

"The dining room."

"Surely, you couldn't hear screams from the dining room all the way up in your suite."

"They wafted up via the balcony. I had the door open. In fact, at first I thought they were coming from outside. I immediately checked that Ellen was still sleeping and locked her into the room."

Jake frowns. There's a pesky law about locking people in rooms, but for now I gloss over it and keep on talking.

"I took the stairs. When I arrived in the dining room, Ida Mae was as you saw her. Chuck and Ginny and Sylvia were all present. Sylvia was screaming. Chuck was hyperventilating. Ginny was surprisingly calm. Residents were gathered. I took pics of them as a roll call. Here, I'll transfer them to your phone."

He looks at the pics I airdrop to him. Consults his notes. Shoves them aside, which means now he's done with my official statement and I get to tell him what I think.

"In summary," he says, trying to stretch, and wincing as his body reminds him that he's recently had his chest cracked open and put back together, "Ida Mae was killed somewhere in the Manor, possibly by some form of poison. She was lifted up onto the table by somebody strong enough to do so, and this happened between the hours of ten and four. Unless somebody came in that window, or was overlooked and locked into the Manor for the night, it would have to be one of the residents."

He already looks unhappy with this summary, and I haven't even started yet.

"I'm not going to like your take on this, am I?" he says.

"You'll definitely need coffee first. Maybe a month of vacation."

"Well, I don't seem to have either, do I?" he barks. "Sorry. Not your fault. Although, Maureen, I have to say that town was quieter before you moved into the Manor."

At this moment, Sophie stalks in with an oversized go cup for Jake. And for me, a tiny Styrofoam thimble.

"You don't deserve coffee," she says.

"What did I do?"

"It's what you didn't do."

Jake takes a long, appreciative swallow and smiles at her. "Thanks, Soph. You can go now."

"Aren't we having a team meeting about this?" She sinks into a chair in the boneless way of young people who don't yet know about joint pain and stiffness and smiles at him.

"This is not a team project," he growls. "This is an official murder investigation. No civilians."

"About that," I murmur.

Jake glares at me. I smile back.

"We'll have a team meeting as soon as Jake is done here and has had a chance to go home and rest," I say, calmly. "Maybe at your house, Jake? Gathered around your bedside, so you—"

"Sophronia," Jake rudely interrupts. "Go. If Maureen calls a meeting, *in the lab*, I'm sure she'll let you know."

"Whatever." She gets up and tosses her hair. "Just so you know, something is weird about Ida Mae's soul."

"So you said." Jake levels a gaze at me. "You are about to give me some rigmarole about how this is not a human killing and why the Unit is involved. Let's get it over with."

"Wouldn't dream of it," I say, getting to my feet. "My opinions have nothing to do with your official investigation. I'll tell you during the team meeting. In the lab."

"Maureen." Jake closes his notebook. Presses both hands over his eyes.

I take the opportunity to pick up his mug and refill my own tiny cup with its contents. "Welcome back to the Manor." I grin at him. "Come on, Jake. Cheer up. This is going to be fun. Team meeting tonight at eight."

CHAPTER NINE

A sharp, businesslike knock on my door at seven fifty-five signals Jake's arrival. Sophie would just unlock the door and come in. Matt has a rap once, wait two seconds, rap twice pattern. Jill taps.

His reaction when I open the door is entirely predictable. He looks over my shoulder and demands, "What is she doing here?"

Since he already knows Ellen is my new roommate, I'm pretty sure the *she* he's asking about is the twelve-year-old girl sitting cross-legged on the floor with Anubis purring in her lap.

"Hey, Jake," she says. "You're out of the hospital!"

"That's Sheriff Callahan to you," I correct, but Jake is less interested in respect than in the question of what a child is doing at the Manor when there's a murder investigation underway.

"Seriously," he says. "You need to go home, Guinevere."

"It's Gee, and I can't. My parents are gone."

He looks at me, and I shrug. "I told your deputy to let her in. Her parents are not answering their phones. Apparently, she planned on staying the night with Val."

Val, sitting in my armchair, waves at him and smiles. Ellen, occupying the sofa, hunkers into the corner as if trying to make herself invisible.

"And they are here, in your suite, why?" he asks, turning his attention back to me.

"They are going to hang out with Ellen while we have our meeting." I try to dazzle him with a smile, but it doesn't work. I'm not exactly comfortable with the arrangement myself.

I've spent my day obtaining a new revolver, getting a bed brought in for Ellen, and figuring out what to do with her during the meeting. Of these tasks, the revolver was the easiest and finding a babysitter the hardest.

Even in a small town like Shadow Valley, obtaining a weapon is surprisingly easy, especially when you're in possession of an FBI badge. My new gun, nestled in the holster at the small of my back, is unregistered and unlicensed, but I don't have a problem with that.

As for the bed, the owner of Shadow Valley's one and only furniture store knows full well that his is the only business in town and doesn't give a damn about my creds. I ended up paying way more than the bed is worth, especially since Ellen likely will not be with us long, but I have no intention of spending another night in my chair.

Jill has informed me in no uncertain terms that doing Cathy's job is a daytime-only shift and she will not be performing Ellen duty in the evening. I can't leave Ellen alone in my suite, and I don't believe in her dementia quite enough to let her join our meeting. The only person outside of our team that I can trust is Val, who is sharper than 95% of the population, but she can only access speech through fragments of songs and stories and well-worn clichés. So, if Ellen vanishes or turns violent, Val can't communicate the situation easily. Which makes Gee both a problem and a solution.

The child is a troublemaking stray whose parents are missing in action most of the time. She has bonded with Val and spends more time with the old woman than she does at home. She also knows most of the Manor secrets, has blackmailed us by threatening to expose them, and very probably has some paranormal gifts of her own. Given that we've had a murder in the Manor and there might be danger, she shouldn't be here, but since getting rid of her isn't easy, she might as well make herself useful.

"Really, Maureen?" Jake demands. "Come here, Gee. I'll drive you home."

On cue, her face screws up and tears begin pouring down her cheeks. She gulps back a pitiful sob as she puts the cat aside and gets obediently to her feet.

"Okay." She walks over to stand in front of Jake and tips her head back to look up into his face. She does something with her posture that makes her looks smaller, and younger, and very pitiful. "Only, the house is dark, and there's nothing but cereal in the cupboards, and not even any milk."

Another well-timed and very convincing sob follows this announcement.

I've heard it all earlier in the day, and wait for Jake's reaction.

"Surely, there's a friend you could stay with," he protests, trying to hold his ground.

Gee breaks down into full-fledged sobbing, her words now nearly incomprehensible. "I don't have any friends."

I suspect this statement is actually the truth.

Jake is recognizing the inevitable but hasn't quite conceded full defeat. "If she must stay here, she and Val should go back to their room and lock the door—"

"But we're watching Ellen," Gee objects, her tears vanishing as suddenly as they came on. "I mean, Val is watching her, and I'm here to do the talking."

Jake glares at me. I shrug. "I can't leave Ellen alone. She can't come with us. And I think she's basically harmless."

"Basically?"

"I'll explain at the meeting."

Footsteps sound in the hallway, and Sophie's voice calls out, "Traffic jam?"

Jake, still barring the doorway, steps into the suite. Sophie and Matt follow him, just as Jill's door opens and she asks, "Is there a difficulty?" Her eyes light on Matt, and her accent becomes so thick, she is nearly incomprehensible.

"What is 'appening? Is it a *soirée*? I may be invited, *n'est-ce pas?*" She crosses the hallway. When she catches sight of Sophie, she shrieks dramatically, clutching Matt's sleeve with one hand and making the sign of the cross with the other. "Keep that. . .creature. . .away from me. *S'il vous plaît*, don't let her kill me."

"Oh, for God's sake, Jill, stop it," I say. "Sophie is not going to hurt you and Matt is half your age. Go away."

I shove her backward, then close and lock the door with her on the other side.

"Sophie!" Gee crows. "When can you teach me more stuff? Where's Morpheus? Did you leave him at home?"

"Maureen?" Jake growls. "I won't be party to a child involving herself—"

"She's not involving herself in anything. Are you, Gee? She's just helping Val keep an eye on Ellen. They are going to keep all of the doors closed and not open them for any reason. They will not let Jill in. They will message me at the first sign of any strange behavior or agitation from Ellen. Isn't that right, Gee?"

"The lady doth protest too much," Val says, laughing.

All of us stare at her. It's the first time she's laughed since she entered the Manor, at least to my knowledge. She crosses the room and opens the closet door, then makes a sweeping gesture with her hand to indicate we should enter.

Sophie and Matt go first, neither of them seemingly bothered by the fact that I'm leaving Gee and Val and Ellen to watch each other, but then, neither of them cares much for the usual rules and both are considerably more versed in the moral flexibility required for dealing with paranormal situations than Jake is. I know the poor man is still hoping his murder will be quickly solved and there will be no paranormal elements attached to it. I also suspect he's wrong.

He does not look happy, but he passes through the secret door. I follow, closing it behind me. He'll be even less happy in a few minutes.

As it turns out, none of us are happy. Things in the lab are definitely not the way we left them.

In my opinion, a clandestine lab should look like a clandestine lab. We'd scrubbed the bloodstains off the concrete floor, removed the metal gurneys, and brought in a table and chairs and a coffeepot. Otherwise, it was still a dark and creepy place with cobwebs in the corners and a few storage cabinets. I liked it that way.

Now our battered table and gloriously mismatched but comfortable chairs have been replaced by a gleaming conference table and wooden chairs designed to be looked at, not relaxed in. Running along the walls is an array of sleek, shiny lab equipment. I walk over and examine the unwelcome additions. A centrifuge for blood samples. A high-powered microscope. A few machines I can't begin to guess the purpose of. This will be Jill's doing, and she's probably installed at least one snooping device while she was at it. We all look at each other for a long moment and then I whisper, "Stay put. Don't say another word. I'll be right back."

By the time I reach the stairs, I'm cursing my bad leg with what is left of my breath. Before I was wounded, I could have run this distance without breaking a sweat. My inactivity in jail did not help with either my mobility or my stamina, and now the stairs look like a military obstacle course. Nothing for it; I don't want to tell anybody else where to look for what I need. So, I drag myself up the stairs and into my suite.

"About time you showed up," Mac says, from a comfortable position on the couch right next to Ellen.

"Goddamn it, Gee," I curse. "What were the rules, again?"

"Don't open the door. Call you if anything is out of order."

"And Mac walked through the walls, I presume?"

Mac sips at a cup of what appears to be tea and takes a bite of the cookie in his other hand. "Easy," he remonstrates. "She was just—"

"She was just completely disobeying my directions."

"She's a child."

"I'm twelve!" Gee protests. "Besides, I didn't let him in; Val did." Her face is flushed, eyes bright with outrage.

Val shrugs and turns both hands palm up. "Words cannot express," she says.

"Please don't send me home," Gee pleads. "Next time something happens, anything, no matter how tiny, I will call you immediately. Cross my heart and hope to die."

"Nobody is dying," I say. "And, as you said, Val let Mac in, and he is, after all, the coroner. Come on, Mac. You might as well crash the team meeting. Oh, damn it, wait a sec. I almost forgot." I open the safe that holds some of my high-tech equipment, carefully screening the combination from Gee's curious eyes, and draw out my portable bug detector. The child literally has her bottom lip caught between her teeth, her big eyes fixed on my hands, her body vibrating with curiosity, but she doesn't want to risk getting sent away and keeps her mouth shut.

"Take good care of Ellen and Val," I tell her. "Call me if anything or anybody wants to come into the room or if any little thing is off, and later I will show you what this is and how to use it. Deal?" Maybe bribery will work better than threats.

She holds her hand out to me and we solemnly shake.

Mac is in on some of our secrets, but he has never been down to the lab and sucks in a breath of surprise when he sees the secret passageway, but otherwise follows me in silence. When we reach the lab, I put a finger over my lips and everybody waits while I run the bug snooper. I locate one listening device on the underside of the conference table. Another attached to the new lab equipment. I remove that one and smash it under my heel.

Then I lean down to the one under the table and say, "Jill. We are not stupid." And then I smash that one as well. Then I look up at the others, who are all looking at me. "Well, what are we waiting for? I thought we were having a meeting." I lower myself into one of the wooden chairs, which seems designed to deliberately make the sitter as uncomfortable as possible. "Mac knows enough that he might as well know everything. Let's do this."

There's a little flurry of activity as people pull out chairs and get settled. Matt brings over the coffeepot, which he has thoughtfully run while I was upstairs, and starts filling mugs.

I open a notebook. "All right, then, what do we know? Mac? I assume you've got something or you wouldn't have stopped by."

"I've got a whole lot of nothing," he answers in his big, soft voice. "The body is with the ME and she won't get around to the autopsy for a couple of days. I've asked to be present but I'm not holding my breath. She's not exactly happy with me since that stunt we pulled last time."

"Hmmm. Yes. I don't suppose she loved being on our suspect list for Dason's murder. If you don't know anything, why come see me?"

Mac grins. "I figured you were up to something, Red. A murder so bizarre? I was driven by curiosity. Also, I do know one thing. I took a blood sample before I sent the body to the medical examiner."

"Not a body," Sophie snarls. "Ida Mae."

"And?" Jake asks.

"It came back negative for any commonly known poisons and has been sent off for more extensive testing. There were no marks of trauma on the body. I'm thinking this murder has a hint of the otherworld about it."

"Hellfire and damnation!" Jake shoves his chair back from the table, then freezes, one hand splinting his ribs. When he can breathe again, he proceeds. "Every murder doesn't have to have a paranormal component."

"Of course it doesn't." Mac shrugs. "Want to tell me why are you hanging out down here in secret, involving civilians, if you don't think there's something a little unusual going on?"

Jake sighs. "Because this is the Manor and nothing can ever be normal here. But before we dive into wild and fantastic theories, let me share what the *evidence*"—he exaggerates the word—"has revealed so far. There were no fingerprints left on the plate or the flower vase. Nor are there fingerprints on the tables or chairs, which were apparently all thoroughly wiped down after dinner, according to Karin, because that is the protocol. Maureen came in through the kitchen window at a little after ten, and the body was discovered at four."

"Time of death probably between ten and four. That fits with the body temp and state of rigor," Mac agrees.

"Footprints consistent with Maureen's are in the snow outside the window," Jake continues. "No obvious trace evidence was found on Ida Mae's clothing or skin, or anywhere in the dining room, which was remarkably clean. There is no sign of a struggle in Ida Mae's room or anywhere in the Manor. Her bed had not been slept in. We've dusted for fingerprints, and those are running through AFIS now. As Mac says, it will be a couple of days before anything comes back on the tox screen, which is also being run for obscure poisons."

"Any suspects?" Matt asks.

"She has no known enemies and family hasn't visited in several weeks. No life insurance policy. Only a few thousand dollars in the bank. Her kids were paying her costs at the Manor. I can't see any obvious motive.

"So," I venture, "no suspects, no evidence, no leads."

"Yet," Jake says, frowning.

"Could it be one of the residents?" Matt asks.

"Well, it wouldn't be the first time we've been blindsided by somebody pretending to be infirm. But given that any one of them can barely get themselves into a chair at the table, let alone haul a dead weight body up onto a table—"

"Someone might have induced her to get up there herself," Jake suggests.

"I suppose she could have crawled up there," I concede, "although she did have bilateral hip replacements, which would have rendered that somewhat difficult."

Jake slams his cup down on the table harder than is necessary. "All right, Maureen. Let's hear your theory. You've been waiting all day."

"Oh, I don't have a theory." I smile at him in the way that tends to make people want to kill me. "But I have a lot of questions. And an early suspect list."

Jake sighs again. "Let's hear it."

"Well, obviously the three witnesses."

"Obviously," he says, with great sarcasm. "Any particular reason, other than that they were found at the scene of the crime?"

"That's enough for starters, isn't it? But here are my reasons. I don't like Chuck. Sylvia was way too hysterical and Ginny was too calm."

Jake jots them down. "Noted. But I hope you've got something better than that."

"I do. Let's talk about Karin, the temporary cook."

"Reasonable suspicion, given that our victim was killed in the dining room," Mac approves.

"Found in the dining room," I correct.

"Plus, she's new and the killing happened after she was hired. How long has she been working here, Sophie?"

"Like I would know," Sophronia says, bitterly. "Jill banned me, remember? I was here for a bit the night you shot. . .the night that Jake got shot. Haven't been back since, until this morning."

"And Maureen was released when?" Matt asks.

I can immediately see what he might be thinking. "A few hours before you were."

"If I might?" Jake interrupts. "According to Jill, Karin started work here the day after I was shot. She needed somebody to feed the residents immediately, and she chose Karin. What's your take on her, Matt?"

"She's territorial and has a temper, but I've seen worse tyrants in the kitchen. The only thing she was interested in talking about is food. She graduated from the Culinary Institute of America, but for some reason she did not wish to divulge, has been compelled to take what she considers demeaning jobs in less-than-five-star restaurants and now is employed here. If I were to guess, I'd say she lost her previous jobs due to complete inability to accommodate or adapt. Where she was born, whether she has family or friends or a lover, or why she's in Shadow Valley? I couldn't begin to tell you."

"Seriously?" I ask. "That's all you got out of her? Did you turn on the charm? I've never seen a woman who could resist the whole Greek god package you've got going on."

"Impervious," Matt says. "Hostile, in fact. I passed up the opportunity to test her knife skills, but as you saw, I have some moves she wasn't expecting."

"Possible opportunity and possible means, but no known motive," I conclude.

"The only reason to suspect her," Jake says, with exaggerated calm and a level stare, "is that Jill hired her and Maureen is prone to suspicion of Jill."

"Speaking of Jill," I begin, but Jake interrupts.

"We weren't speaking of Jill. We were—"

"You just mentioned her."

"If we could finish with Karin first? We don't even know for sure that Ida Mae was poisoned." He holds up a hand to stop me. "But even if she was, everyone in the Manor had access to any food or drink that Ida Mae consumed. We have absolutely no motive. Why would Karin want to kill that poor, inoffensive old woman?"

"Why would anybody?" Sophie asks.

"If you don't mind me saying so," Mac interjects, "there may not be a motive. The way that body was laid out . . . looks more like insanity than anything carefully premeditated."

"Except for the absence of evidence," Jake counters. "Somebody completely off their rocker is going to leave trace evidence behind."

"Which brings us back to Jill," I say.

Jake looks like he has a headache, which he probably does, but he writes Jill's name in his notebook.

"We already know she was involved in genetic meddling," I begin. "And she put snooper bugs in the lab."

"Which is a long way from murder," Jake argues. "Especially a murder as bizarre as this one."

"Can't imagine her dragging a corpse onto a table," Matt says.

"You're right, of course," I agree. "She'd get some poor deluded man to do it for her. Or pay him."

"We have no evidence and no motive," Jake protests.

"She may have ties to the Unit," I begin. Then stop. I have ties to the Unit. So does Matt. And so does somebody else. "Which brings us to Ellen."

Everybody reacts to this differently. Jake does an eye roll that makes it look like he's having a seizure. Mac looks fascinated. Sophie distracted. Matt's lips compress slightly, and his eyes wander off to inspect the ceiling.

"What on earth does that little woman have to do with anything?" Jake demands.

"Who is Ellen?" Mac asks.

"New resident," I say. "Crazy as a bedbug."

Unlike his demeanor when processing the crime scene, Mac seems to be enjoying himself. He grins at me. "Maybe she's a werewolf," he suggests. "Only pretending to be crazy. She could pay Ida Mae a visit. Slip a little poison into a shared nightcap. Then transition into animal form and drag her prey down the hallway and up onto the table using her superpowers, and then shift back to human and place the dish, signifying a meal is about to be served."

"Exactly," I say, even though he's laughing at me. "And then something drove her away from the feast before she could begin."

"Oh, come on, Maureen," he exclaims. "That's not even B movie–worthy. I'm disappointed in you."

Jake twitches.

"If we were dealing with some sort of shifter, there would be tooth marks in the fabric of Ida Mae's clothing and possibly on her body," Matt says, seriously. "Also, I've never seen a shifter capable of that kind of control. It would have fed—"

"There are other kinds of weres," I say meaningfully, letting this sink in. "They're not all wolves and bears. I left Ellen in my room with the doors all locked, and she somehow made it to the library, with the doors still locked."

"And now you've left her with a child and a defenseless old woman," Jake accuses. "What was she in jail for?"

I mumble my answer.

"Louder, would you?" he says.

"She was charged with attempting to murder her husband."

"Right. Of course she was." A grunt of pain escapes Jake as he rises from his chair. "I am going home to bed. And before you ask, no. I will not be investigating Ellen's family and friends. I suggest everybody get some sleep and wait to see what the evidence reveals. I also suggest that in the future, we do not leave children to supervise murderers."

"Accused murderers," I correct him. "Innocent until proven guilty. Wait a minute, would you? We really do need to talk about the Unit."

Matt shakes his head slightly, a warning in his eyes. But keeping Unit secrets and not cooperating fully with a team are partly responsible for Jake's brush with death and Sophie's near escape from the dark side. It's time to come clean about Charlie.

Jake's gaze snaps to mine, instantly wary. When I first told him about the Unit, I made him drive me halfway up a mountainside where no satellite tracker or bug would function.

"Ellen's here at the Manor because I'm working with the Unit, and they wanted her here," I say. The words feel like spitting out a handful of gravel, and the shocked silence that meets them would be an appropriate reaction to a sudden and unexpected self-evisceration.

"What, exactly, is the Unit?" Mac asks.

"The outfit responsible for creating the Medusa," Jake growls. "Government-sanctioned paranormal meddling, with a license to kill."

"I worked for them for years," I explain to Mac. "And then I got out. For whatever reason, they wanted Ellen placed here badly—very, very badly. Badly enough for Charlie to pay me a visit and drag me back into the fold."

"And you agreed? After everything? Thought you would have died first." Jake's shock hasn't landed in quite the right place yet, but I understand his reaction.

I stare straight at the wall, to avoid looking at either him or Matt, not wanting to tell them the rest of it.

"Oh, hell," Matt says. "What did he threaten you with, Maureen? You'd have rotted away in prison before you'd have agreed to anything Charlie suggested. Don't you lie to us."

"He had a lot of leverage." I keep my voice level. "His claims of a kinder and gentler Unit are all bullshit, in case anybody was wondering."

"You didn't make a deal with the devil to save my sorry ass, did you?" Matt queries. His tone is light, but there's a dark intensity in his eyes.

"Well, Charlie did say that he'd see you get the death penalty. He also made some veiled threats about Jake's life expectancy."

"That's what that cryptic phone call was all about. Knew you were up to something." Mac slams a massive hand on the table, rattling cups. Fortunately, I'm holding my coffee and not a drop is spilled.

"I confess I was going to hold out. Figured if Jake was safe, we'd have time to concoct a plan to spring Matt. But I was afraid they'd get to Jake while he was helpless, and I caved. Sorry, Matt."

"While we're all coming clean," Matt says. "I also had a visit from Charlie. He said he'd made Maureen an offer in exchange for my life, but she'd declined." He fidgets with his coffee cup for a minute, then raises his eyes again to meet mine. "He said your answer was that I deserved the death penalty for my part in what happened to Phil and your partner. Also, that you were released almost immediately."

Sophie glares at me. "It sounds exactly like the sort of thing Maureen would say."

She's right. Or at least it's the sort of thing I would have said before Matt tried to take the fall for me. Before I went soft and started trusting my team and letting myself care what happened to them.

I clear my throat. "Sounds like Charlie has tried to infiltrate the team and sow dissent. He's also exerted a lot of muscle to get Ellen installed at the Manor. So, like it or not, she's part of what's going on here, and so is the Unit."

"Perfect," Jake says. "We have a demented old woman planted at the Manor for some obscure reason, both Maureen and Matt are working for the Unit, and neither of you is supposed to let the other know. Have I got that right?"

"Right," I say.

"Yep," Matt agrees.

"What else do you know?"

"Nothing," Matt says. "I was told they'd be in contact but in the meantime to keep my mouth shut and pretend to know nothing. Not much of a pretense, as it turns out. Maureen?"

"Same."

"We're what, then—a reality show?" Jake says. "Got a bunch of assholes eating nachos and drinking beer while they watch us stumble around in blood and gore?"

"Technically, there hasn't been any gore," I protest. "Or even blood, for that matter."

Jake looks like he'd like to shoot me this time but only asks, "What now?"

"We investigate."

"Which means?"

"Best if the Unit doesn't know we've spilled to anybody, right?" Matt says. "Jake and Mac conduct a by-the-book investigation. And Maureen and Sophie and I do our thing."

"Which is?" Jake asks, sounding infinitely weary.

Poor man. It's more than just the fact that he's been wounded, or that we might be dealing with paranormals. It also goes against the grain to share information about a legal investigation with civilians. And, I suspect, it bothers him that he's not really the one in charge. None of which can be helped.

"Sophie is going to spend some time with Ida Mae's soul and see if she can get any more clues as to how she died. What do you need, Soph? Or is it too late, now that the body is gone?"

Sophie says nothing, but she wears an expression that, on anybody else, might be fear.

Matt leans forward. "What is it, Sophronia? You know something."

"I wasn't honest either. There's not just something weird about Ida Mae's soul. It's. . .missing? Only that's not quite right either," she says.

"It's what?" I stare at her. "Were you going to tell us at some point?"

"I wasn't sure what to say!" She crosses her arms defensively over her chest. "It's not missing-missing, like with that soul stealer. Ida Mae's soul still exists, but it's like—a ghost of a soul, maybe. I can't explain it better than that."

Sophie indecisive and insecure is more unsettling than when she's on a full paranormal rampage. My skin prickles into goosebumps as I remember the spirit storm that swirled through the Manor a few weeks back. "Is it contagious, do you think? Could it infect the other spirits that inhabit this place?"

Sophie shakes her head. "There aren't any here anymore. Except the library ghost. I took all the others across after you and Matt got arrested and Jake got. . ." Her voice quavers. She probably needs somebody to help her process what went down that night.

Too bad I'm useless as either a confidante or a comforter.

Jake, on the other hand, is a total softie when it comes to Sophronia. His eyes are misty and he walks over to put an arm around her shoulders, an act that I can see causes him physical pain. Sophie doesn't exactly lean into his comfort, but she doesn't pull away, either.

"You've done an amazing job of holding down the fort while we were all. . . er. . . out of commission," Jake says. "I don't think we've thanked you for that."

She laughs bitterly. "I let Jill lock me out of the Manor and turn the lab into. . .whatever this is. . .and I have no idea what happened to Ida Mae's soul and. . ." She glances at Matt, flushes, and adds, "Everything is all fucked up."

"At least it's not boring." All eyes turn to me and I realize I've said it out loud. "Look, Sophie. Think of it as a puzzle, or a challenge. You are the most perfect being in the world to deal with whatever is going on with Ida Mae's soul. Figure it out."

"What's my assignment?" Matt asks.

"You and Karin are glued at the hip."

"How about you fire her and I dig into her background

instead?" He moans, pitifully. "Never mind. I know. Easier to keep her here where we can see her."

"And Jill and Ellen?" Sophie asks.

"We are going to give Jill enough rope to hang herself. And I'm going to get to the bottom of what is going on with Ellen."

"Are we done?" Jake's gaze travels all of our faces. When nobody answers, he says, "Now I am really going home to bed."

Mac lumbers to his feet as Jake stalks toward the door. "Think I'll walk out with the sheriff. Try to stay out of trouble, Red." He nods, and I get the message that he'll see Jake safely out to his cruiser.

CHAPTER TEN

The night is disappointingly quiet. Ellen goes to bed without objection, no singing or kisses required. There is no midnight screaming and I sleep in my own bed undisturbed. Still, when I wake up, I feel uncharacteristically groggy and tired, which I blame on my time in jail.

I get up and start the coffeepot, which I'd had the foresight to load before crawling into bed. Anubis, who has claimed a spot at the foot of Ellen's bed, stretches and blinks his golden eyes at me before curling up and going back to sleep. Ellen doesn't even stir.

While the blessed liquid burbles into the carafe, I wake my brain by creating a list of questions around the murder. And then, with one unsmooth move, it all goes to hell. Unwilling to wait for the coffeemaker to finish, I take advantage of the sneak-a-cup feature. I've left the overhead lights off, so as not to disturb Ellen, working by the dim glow of the nightlight in the kitchenette. Maybe because it's dark, and maybe because I'm lost in thought, I overfill my mug and pour scalding coffee over my hand.

Reflex kicks in and my hand jerks violently, knocking over

the mug. Scalding coffee cascades over the counter toward me. My hand already burnt, I recoil to avoid further damage. My bad leg spasms with an intensity that nearly drops me. I stay on my feet but drop the carafe, which bounces loudly on the floor. Before I can replace it, the sneak-a-cup feature on the coffeepot times out and coffee starts flowing out of the machine with nothing to catch it.

The loud series of unfortunate events sends Anubis streaking off Ellen's bed and across the room, where he vanishes under my chair. The Ellen-shaped lump, however, doesn't so much as twitch.

Perhaps the poor creature has died in the night or had a stroke. Slowly, a sense of dread hollowing my chest, I approach the bed and draw back the covers.

Ellen isn't dead, or even ill. She's simply not there at all.

The lump is nothing more than two pillows tucked end to end under the covers.

This time, I know damn well I set the alarm on my door, and it would have awakened me if it went off. I stand there, blinking stupidly, holding the covers and staring at the pillows as if they're going to metamorphosize back into a frail old woman.

Of course, they don't.

Stepping away, I turn on all of the lights and systematically search the apartment, which takes approximately five seconds. It's not a large space. There is nowhere for even a small person to hide. She's not under the bed or in the bathroom. She's not on the balcony. She hasn't leaped or fallen to her death below.

Which leaves the secret passageway and, maybe, the lab.

My coffee-soaked shirt is cold and clammy against my skin. My burned hand throbs. I desperately need a jolt of caffeine. But I need to find Ellen, and I need to find her now. I also need to stay calm and not make stupid moves. I holster my new revolver. Buckle on the ankle sheath that holds a small knife. Secure the special flashlight invented by my old partner, Phil, to a quick-release carabiner hooked to a belt loop. For extra insurance, I grab the salt sprayer he created for managing unwieldy spirits.

Sophie can say what she will about the Manor being free of ghostly presences, but I don't trust spirits. They are deceptive, and adept at lurking unseen.

Anubis trails behind me as I make my slow way down the secret stairs. This is encouraging. The cat sees things invisible to my eyes and makes an effective early-warning system. Still, I'm uneasy and on high alert. No sign of Ellen on the stairs, or in the long hallway that leads to the lab, or in the lab itself. She's not in any of the little storage rooms. As far as I know, there are no doorways from here that lead elsewhere, but then, until a couple of weeks ago, we didn't know there was a tunnel leading from the official basement of the Manor out into a network covering miles of territory, with outlets leading to the funeral parlor, the Catholic church, and the cemetery. Other, as-of-yet undiscovered, passageways are probable. If Ellen has found her way down here, and if she found the tunnels, she could be anywhere.

Anubis is particularly enthralled with one small storage room. He crouches, the tip of his tail flicking, making a little clicking sound in this throat. When he leaps for the attack, at first I think he's after something invisible, but then I notice the small black body and scurrying legs.

"It's a spider," I say witheringly. "Let's go."

The cat pretends not to hear me, batting at the unfortunate arachnid with his paw.

"Would you give that up and come on?" I'm not leaving him down here, and he's a large and heavy cat who does not choose to be herded. Finally, I set the salt sprayer down to free my hands and scoop him up. He purrs and has the temerity to lick my face, as if I'm holding him because I want to. I do snuggle him for a minute longer than necessary, but not because I'm enjoying his blandishments. I snuggle him only to maintain an effective and polite working relationship. I do not want to be on the outs with a cat.

By the time I make it back into my suite, I'll admit that I'm in a mood. How can a small, elderly woman just disappear? And if she's with it enough to stuff pillows under the quilt, then she's not as demented as she wants us all to believe.

I'm on my creaky knees, wiping up coffee, when Jill taps at my door. I shout, "What the hell do you want?" without even pretending to get up and answer.

"I have something that belongs to you."

This day needs a serious do-over. I grab the counter and drag myself up to my feet, limp across the room, and fling the door open with so much force that it bangs against the wall.

"This better be important."

Jill has Ellen by the hand and drags her forward. Ellen smiles and asks, hopefully, "Tea?"

"Where on earth have you been?" I demand. "I've been looking all over for you."

Ellen tugs her hand free from Jill and wanders into my suite.

"You really should watch her better," Jill criticizes. "Letting her run loose in the Manor is irresponsible. You could at least lock—"

"Jill, I have another job for you." I smile at her as an idea floats into my mind.

"I am not scrubbing floors or cleaning toilets."

"Now, why ever would you think I would ask you to do that?"

She is suddenly intrigued with something on the ceiling. My eyes narrow with suspicion.

"Jill, what happened to the cleaning service?"

"They may have quit. You know how these agencies are. High turnover, unreliable—"

I'm already dialing the number for my contact. It's just past six a.m., but I'm sure he's up. If not, it's time for him to get up.

"Zak, it's Maureen," I say, the instant I hear breathing on the other end.

"Which Maureen?" he asks cautiously.

"Maureen at the Manor."

A moment of silence, during which Jill turns to leave and I grab her arm and yank her back, slamming the door and leaning against it.

"Oh," Zak says. "That Maureen. Can I help you with something? You do know it's, like, six a.m."

"I'm aware. Just checking where we're at with the cleaning service."

"Look, I don't want to be in the middle of this. You should talk to—"

"I want to talk to you, Zak. Just tell me what happened."

"What happened is, this job is hard enough without some bi —sorry, chick, I mean woman, watching every move we make and complaining about every fuck—sorry, freaking thing. You guys want somebody to lick the floors and hand-polish the bathroom thrones, you can find another service."

"Look, Zak. You know that wasn't me."

"Heard you were in lockup and the Manor isn't yours no more."

"You heard wrong. Could we possibly un-cancel the contract?"

"I dunno, Maureen. She—"

"You won't see her. I will meet you at the front doors personally and lock her in her room if I have to."

Silence follows.

"Well, Zak? I need an answer."

"Here's the thing. You were getting an old rate, being one of our first clients and all. The rates have gone up for new contracts."

"Draw it up. I'll sign off when you get here. Try not to make it highway robbery, would you, Zak? Being as none of this was my fault."

"Sure," he says. "See what I can do. We'll be up later this morning."

Jill is still evading my eyes when I hang up. "Nice work, Jill. Now. What I need for you to do today is track down one of those pressure-sensitive alarms for Ellen's mattress."

"What? This is not my job. I am not a warehouse worker."

"No, you're the woman who wants to run the Manor and agreed to take in a client we are not equipped to deal with. Ergo, you get to help solve the problem." There is absolutely no reason for Jill to know that I would have taken Ellen in if she hadn't. The responsibility angle is leverage I have no intention of giving up.

"While we're at it, maybe you—"

"I really need to go, now." Jill edges toward the door. "I can get dressed, *oui*? Have a shower. Before I care for the residents and watch Ellen, and search for this device."

"Before you go," I say, so pleasantly that Jill begins to visibly twitch. "How many people, exactly, are now aware that there is a secret passageway and a laboratory accessible through my suite?"

"I really must go. Please—"

"How many, Jill? Before we even begin to discuss all the shiny new equipment and what you think you're doing, exactly."

"Just the movers of my lab equipment. I swear it. And I swore them to secrecy. They will say nothing—why would they?"

"Maybe because a secret passageway and a lab beneath a retirement facility is a little unusual? You know, the sort of thing where you're at the bar with your other moving buddies, tossing back some cold brews, and one of them says, "Hey, you'll never guess what we stumbled over on a job today," and then your guys say, "Oh, man! We were in a fucking nursing home, and there's this totally secret door in a closet. We had to haul stuff that weighs literally a ton down these stairs, no elevator, and there's a freaking laboratory at the end of the hallway."

"They won't," Jill protests.

"Supposing they keep their mouths shut, which I consider unlikely, I know perfectly well you didn't clean and polish the lab yourself. So, who else has been down there?"

"A lab must be clean!" Jill squeaks. "Dust can ruin sensitive equipment."

"Which nobody asked you to take down there in the first place. What experiments are you running?"

She avoids that question and answers the previous one. Sort of. "I cleaned the equipment myself. And the lab."

I hold up my phone. "Shall I ask Zak?"

"I knew you would make a big deal of nothing. Yes, fine. Okay. I paid Zak to clean before the lab equipment was moved in. But after that, I swear I have dusted and damp-mopped myself."

"And then, let me guess. You were fine with him knowing the lab was there, but you don't want anybody to know about your lab equipment, so you bullied the workers until they quit so they wouldn't see what you were up to. Sound about right?"

"What does it matter?" she bursts out. "What is the point of a secret laboratory? I need a place to do my research and this is perfect but only because it's out of the way. You were supposed to remain in jail. . ." She stops, realizing what she's just said, then shrugs it off. "Why keep it a secret? Make money off of this. Charge people for tours. You could even pretend the tunnel is haunted, if you must be such a child, and make money for the Manor."

"Do you know what the word *secret* means?" I retort. "If people know about the passageways, they are no longer secret. Are you working with Charlie, Jill?"

"I don't know any Charlie."

"And the bugs in the lab. What was that all about?"

"You keep secrets from me. If I am to run the Manor, I need to know—"

"You're not running the Manor; you're doing a caregiver's job because you got rid of Cathy. Your attorney isn't going to find a problem with the will. It's my Manor. I run it. Do you understand?"

She opens her mouth but I shove her backward and slam the door between us. It occurs to me that it is possible to silence people. Jill could have an unfortunate accident, such as falling off her balcony. The movers might lose control of their vehicle. And Zak. . .damn it. I like Zak. And the movers are also innocent (probably, although few people truly are), and Jill is Phil's daughter. And I've lived almost sixty years without killing any humans, except in self-defense.

I abandon the fantasy and turn my focus to problems I can actually solve. First, I fit Ellen with a tracking device. I have a stash of such things, since you never know when you might need one. It only takes a few minutes to solder it onto the back of a silver cross and string it on a strong— but pretty—

chain. It will serve two purposes: protect her from some of the paras, and tell me where she is at any given moment.

She watches with mild interest or possibly feigned cluelessness.

"Pretty, isn't it?" I ask, holding it out to her. "Wouldn't you like to wear it?"

If she's playing me, this is the place where she will pitch a fit, pretend she's frightened, something, anything, to avoid putting on the necklace. But she smiles vacantly and allows me to fasten the chain around her neck. If she's play-acting, she's in for a surprise. The chain is too short to come off over her head, and I fasten it on with a tiny padlock. Anybody with some serious wire cutters can cut the thing off of her, of course, but otherwise it will stay in place.

I program the app in my secondary phone, the one I never

use for phone calls and don't carry unless I'm conducting a surveillance operation. I find it useful to let people believe that I'm a technological idiot, something they're inclined to assume anyway, given that I'm a woman of a certain age, so I carry a flip phone for regular use. My high-tech cell is more computer than phone and extremely useful. I have a number of flannel shirts with specially designed inner pockets to carry the thing, since I never encumber myself with a purse or a bag, both of which just scream to be stolen and are terribly inconvenient in any sort of altercation.

My next challenge is finding someone to watch a potentially dangerous old woman who may or may not be faking dementia while I go out and do some investigating. It really isn't a great idea for Jill to take Ellen into other residents' rooms, just in case she gets the impulse to try to smack somebody over the head. After struggling with my conscience, I again enlist Val and Gee—the only people who already know too much. They arrive together, knocking at my door at precisely five minutes to eight.

Val takes my hand in hers and says, earnestly, "All's fair in love and war."

This is not exactly confidence-inspiring.

Ellen is ensconced in my favorite chair, her body moving back and forth as if the chair is a rocker, which it's not. Her eyes are closed, and she's humming "Octopus's Garden" to herself. It's not a song that lends itself to humming, and the result is an annoying buzzing that has now been going on for an hour, ever since she finished her last cup of tea. Anubis lies across her lap, purring.

"Maybe this isn't such a good idea," I say.

"It'll be great," Gee says. "Don't you worry about a thing. Me and Val have got your back."

"Val and I," I correct her, absently, gathering my weapons. "Ellen might be dangerous. Be careful."

"You were going to show me what that thingy does," Gee reminds me.

"I will. Not now. Same instructions as last night. You will let me know about the smallest thing that seems wrong. Okay?"

"Yep. Got it."

I lock them in, then make my way downstairs where the true inconvenience of Karin presents itself. All I want is a go cup of Matt's coffee and a head start on breakfast. I have no intention of sitting through a meal with the herd. I've got things to do. Matt has always made me a quick breakfast to go on request. Karin has other ideas.

"There are rules," she says, glaring. "Random people cannot come into the kitchen. Food is delivered to the dining room."

"I am not a random person and you are possibly the most inflexible woman on the face of the planet," I say.

Her frame blocks the doorway and I duck to peer around her at the level of her waist, the least obstructive part of her. Matt shrugs, face and body language expressively conveying that having Karin still here is my idea, not his.

"Matt. Fix me up," I tell him, before standing straight and backing away so I can look Karin in the eyes without getting a crick in my neck. "Karin. Again. I own the Manor. I pay you. I make the rules."

"The rules of the kitchen are above your authority," she snarls. "Traitor," she flings at Matt, who has already poured a go mug and has begun toasting an English muffin.

"You will learn," he says, cracking an egg into a pan, "that the Rules of Maureen supersede all, even the rules of the kitchen."

Muttering to herself, Karin turns back to breaking eggs into a stainless steel bowl. Matt makes me a breakfast sandwich, wraps it in a napkin, and hands it to me with my coffee. Just inhaling the fragrance of the brew makes me feel capable of superhuman feats. "I'm so glad you're back," I say, taking the first scalding swallow.

"You just love me for my coffee." It sounds like a joke, but we both know there's an element of truth in what he says.

"Where are you off to?" he asks.

"A little of this, a little of that." I slip a folded piece of paper into his hand while Karin's back is turned. Even though I don't anticipate any trouble, one benefit to working with a team is that I can let somebody know where I'm headed, on the off chance that I don't come back.

———

The home where Ellen once lived is a singularity in a town like Shadow Valley, where the majority of homes are small and unassuming. A wrought-iron fence circles a large yard. The lawn is currently buried in snow, but the decorative bushes are sculpted and trimmed, and I'm willing to bet that no clover, dandelions, or bees would ever be allowed to sully the summer grass.

Greek-style pillars dominate a massive front porch, and two stone lions crouch at the top of the steps. The doorbell is set in an elaborate framework. When I push the button, it plays something that sounds like a pipe organ. A dog immediately sets up a frantic yapping, and an irritated male voice yells at it to be quiet. I ring the bell again, which results in more barking and more yelling. Finally, the door opens and I get my first look at Richard Ellis.

Before he even opens his mouth, I deduce some important facts about him. He is certainly not the one who does the yard work. He is also not accustomed to wrangling the ankle-biter shivering in his arms, although he may possibly take it for walks on perfectly lovely days when it is convenient for him to do so. He isn't familiar with cooking and cleaning, and probably doesn't know how to throw his own socks in the hamper.

"May I help you?" he inquires, in overly helpful tones that employ an accent that wants to be British but isn't.

"You can, as a matter of fact," I say, even though it's abundantly clear that the only help he wants to offer me is assistance in leaving his porch. "At least, you can if you are Richard Ellis and Ellen is your wife."

"I'm Richard Ellis the Third," he says, clearly hopeful that I've located the wrong Richard and Ellen Ellis, and am perhaps seeking a more plebeian version that lives on the other side of town.

"Perfect." I step past him into the house—no point waiting for an invitation that isn't going to come. "My name is Maureen Keslyn, and I'm the owner of the Manor where your wife is currently residing."

"She's out of jail?" His voice rises on the distasteful word. Since I'm proceeding through the entryway and down a high-ceilinged hall, I can't see his face, but the dog squeaks as if inadvertently squeezed.

"Ma'am? Ms. Keslyn?" His footsteps scurry behind me and I smile to myself. I'm pretty sure this man needs more scurrying in his life, and I'm happy to teach him how it's done.

I stop when I reach a large room with yet more pillars and a spiral staircase. "What a beautiful home you have!"

"Thank you. Now, Ms. Keslyn—"

"I need to ask you some questions about Ellen." I lower myself onto a chair that looks much older than any resident in the Manor, afraid that it's going to be every bit as uncomfortable as it looks. In truth, it's even more so, but I do my best to settle in and appear perfectly relaxed and intent on staying for a nice long visit.

"I don't suppose you have anything to drink? Tea, perhaps? It's cold outside." I make a show of shivering and rubbing my hands together. I'm not cold, and I don't like tea, but I do want to see what he will do.

"I don't. . ." he says. "I mean, it's not that I don't have tea. It's . . . I can't. . ." He sinks down onto another chair, the dog awkwardly in his lap, and confesses, "I've tried to make tea since she was arrested, but it always comes out terrible. Plus, I have no idea where the company tea tray is."

"Oh, for heaven's sake. Really? Put a tea bag in a mug and pour some boiling water over it. Surely, you can boil water."

He looks as aghast as if I've suggested roasting the dog for dinner, but wisely refrains from commenting. He clears his throat and asks, "Tea aside, how can I help you?"

I open my briefcase and pull out a clipboard and an intake form that I've brought for the sake of appearances. "We need to know more about Ellen's day-to-day functioning. Let's begin with mobility. Does she require any walking aids? Cane, walker, wheelchair?"

Poising my pen over the paper, I glance up at him expectantly.

"No," he says. "No, she was perfectly...why did nobody inform me that she'd been released?"

"What about daily activities? Does she require assistance with dressing, bathing? Bathroom activities?"

He flushes. "Ms. Keslyn, I don't quite—"

"There's no need to be embarrassed, Dick. I can call you Dick? It's common for elderly people to require some assistance in these areas. And the husband is the most—"

"No!" he bursts out. "No, to all of these things. Please don't call me Dick. Ellen is—was—completely functional. She cared for the house. She cooked, she cleaned, she walked the dog. Sure, she'd slowed down a little over the years but she. . ." His voice warbles and he pauses to swallow and control himself.

I keep my pen poised over the paper, gazing at him earnestly, not releasing the pressure. I suspect that his display of emotion is about the loss of the services his wife provided for him, rather than grief at her sudden decline, or heartbreak that she'd tried to kill him. I have absolutely no sympathy for his well-deserved and thoroughly insufficient suffering.

"What she may need now, I am at a complete loss to tell you," he goes on, looking martyred and brave. "Perhaps the jail could provide the information?"

"Suppose you tell me what happened, the day of the. . .attack."

"Is that really necessary?"

The dog yelps, and I'm sure he's pinched it again. I'm going to have to see what I can do to get the creature out of his clutches. Not that I like the shivering little beast, which looks more like a rat than a dog, but it still deserves better.

"Absolutely necessary. I must assess the level of risk to the other residents at the Manor."

"I can't believe they've just. . .let her out," he says, faintly. "You know, I really could use a cup of tea. I don't suppose you could . . . you know . . ."

I open my mouth to tell him that I most definitely could not, but on second thought I say, "Now, there's an idea. I'm sure a cup of tea would make this go more easily for both of us. Show me to the kitchen and I'll take care of this at once."

He gets to his feet in obvious relief, putting the dog down at last and letting it find its own way. It immediately sniffs at my ankles, pees on the carpet, and then follows hard on my heels as Dick leads me to the kitchen. There's an electric kettle on the counter, which tells me that if this man can't boil water, he is either an imbecile or a scumbag, and probably both.

"Fill it with water," I tell him, choosing to go with the former, "and then flip the ON switch. Now, where would she keep the tea and that tea tray you mentioned?"

Without waiting for an answer, I take the opportunity to open doors and check out cupboards. All are neatly organized and spotlessly clean. Medicines are in a cabinet by the sink, and I scan them, quickly, while he's filling the kettle. Most have his name on them and are generic prescriptions for blood pressure and cholesterol and prostate problems. There's also a little blue pill for a certain other difficulty he probably wouldn't want me to mention. There is only one prescription bottle for Ellen, and I slip it into my pocket.

Locating the tea and the teapot, I busy myself preparing for the hot water.

"Was she on any medications?" I ask, nonchalantly.

"Not a thing. She was perfectly healthy."

"You were going to tell me what happened the day she tried to kill you."

He slumps mournfully onto a stool next to the marble-topped breakfast bar. "I just don't understand what happened to her. Fifty years of marriage, and then all of a sudden she's trying to kill me."

"Walk me through the day," I suggest, pouring boiling water over the tea bags. If he's expecting me to do loose tea in a fancy press, he's got another think coming.

"It was an ordinary day. She was up before me, as she always is, making tea and fixing my breakfast. She seemed normal. I mean, she was dressed, her hair was combed, she'd put on makeup. After breakfast, I went to Spokane with friends. We went out for dinner, but I neglected to tell her, so she had prepared dinner for me and kept it in the oven.

"I thanked her and even apologized for my thoughtlessness. She seemed fine. Then I went to watch TV and drink a glass of port." He gestures at a sitting area separated from the kitchen area by a breakfast bar. It's furnished with two recliners, his and hers, an enormous ceiling-mounted TV, a coffee table, and an array of shelves holding books and knickknacks. A hallway leads from the far side to what looks like a study, from what I can see through the open door at the end. Two other doors on the left and right are closed.

"She was here in the kitchen," Dick continues, "putting away the food. Loudly, I thought at the time. Banging cupboard doors.

But I didn't want to complain, so I just turned up the volume on the TV."

He manages to sound virtuous and noble. I find my eyes searching the room for something I could smack him over the head with.

He goes on. "I heard her walk down the hallway to the laundry room and take the clothes out of the dryer. I assumed she was folding everything, maybe getting out the ironing board."

"Ironing your underwear, I suppose?" I ask. "Late at night, while you watch TV?"

Dick doesn't even recognize my sarcasm. "Cotton boxers, you know? You'd think they'd make them wrinkle-resistant. She called something to me, but it was the climax of the movie and I didn't hear what she said. Next thing I know, whack! Everything goes black and I wake up in the hospital."

"Cream?" I ask, pouring him a cup of tea. "Sugar?"

"No cream, one teaspoon."

I doctor his tea, wondering why Ellen didn't choose poison, which is slower and allows you to observe your victim thrashing in agony. Dick accepts the tea and makes a face that says it is not acceptable but he is too well bred to complain.

"But that's not really what happened, is it?" I lean forward and smile, confidentially. "You weren't really rendered instantly unconscious."

He sets his cup down hard, tea sloshing over the side. "Did she tell you that?" he demands.

I keep my gaze level and calm and wait for the pressure of silence to make him talk.

And of course, he does. He can't help it. "Fine. I saw lights flash in my head. I was dizzy and my vision was blurred, but I was able to tell Siri to call 911. The ambulance came. When I told the doctor what happened, they sent an officer to speak with me. They asked if I wanted to press charges and I said hell yes, I did. The woman had tried to kill me!

"They told me later that when they went to pick her up, she was sitting in my recliner, drinking a glass of wine and watching TV. She hadn't even folded the laundry."

"Pardon me, Dick, and I hope you won't take offense to me saying so, but this whole story is complete and utter bullshit."

He gasps. "I'm shocked that you would say such a thing!"

"And I'm shocked that you think I would believe such tripe. Now tell me: how long has Ellen had dementia? Days, weeks, years?"

"I have no idea what you are talking about."

"Your wife's state of mind, Richard. The fact that she's totally looney tunes. She is completely incapable of running a house of this size, either physically or emotionally. Did the police seriously buy this story from you?"

"Are you calling me a liar?" He pops up onto his feet as if yanked by strings, scowling ferociously. "I've been tolerant with your prying, but that is quite enough. Leave my house this minute."

"Perhaps you could give me some other names—friends who could corroborate your story?"

"I will give you until I count to ten. If you are still within the premises, I will call 911."

"Oh, very well, if you want to be a dick about it. Wait, you can't help being a Dick, can you?" My reluctance is only for show; I've already got everything I came for and am quite ready to go. I get to my feet and head for the door, slowly, deliberately pushing the man's buttons as much as possible without driving him to actually make that call.

Back in my Jag, I check the Ellen App, which shows her still in my suite. A text message to Gee comes back at once with *All's well. Me & Val playing Scrabble, Ellen singing some submarine song. Sophie stopped in. Morpheus is here on guard.*

Nothing from Jake or the others, so I assume everybody is working on their assignments and move to the second item on my investigation list: the county jail.

Even though I'm now on the right side of the law, with all charges dropped and my record cleared, it's not a place I'm excited about visiting.

"Can't stay away?" Smith's voice asks through the intercom in response to my buzz.

"I need to talk to Renny."

"Oh, come on, Maureen. You know the rules. It's not visiting hours."

"I'm not visiting. This is official business. FBI." I hold up my old Unit ID, the one with the FBI seal on it.

The door clicks and I step into a small waiting area. Cinderblock walls. Benches bolted to the floor. I shiver a little at the sensation of being locked in. There are only two ways out of this claustrophobic space: the door I just came through, which won't open until a deputy buzzes me out, and a heavily barred iron barrier that opens onto a narrow hallway.

Smith appears in this hallway a moment later and stands on the other side of the door. "Can I see that ID up close?"

I hold it up for her to examine.

"Things might have gone differently if you'd waved that around earlier," she says.

"Can't talk about that." I make my expression as secretive as possible, so maybe she'll think I was undercover the whole time. The truth is, the ID isn't exactly valid. Or maybe it is, since I'm back in the fold. In any case, I want her to believe I'm on official business.

She puts a key in the lock and holds the door while I walk through. I flinch involuntarily at the clang of metal behind me.

"Sure you don't want to check in, get a little R&R?" she queries. "You look tired."

"Ha. Ha."

She grins, cheerfully, ushering me into the consultation room. "Wait here. I'll bring her."

A few minutes later, the door opens again and admits Renny. She blinks rapidly when she sees me sitting at the table but doesn't otherwise miss a beat. "Couldn't stay away?" she asks, dropping into the chair across from me.

"I'll be outside," Smith says. "Buzz me when you're ready."

As soon as the door closes, Renny leans back, eyes narrowed suspiciously. "Did you bring me a smoke?"

"Hey, I'm lucky I got in. Wasn't about to risk contraband. I'll put money on your commissary."

"Fair enough. You miss me?"

"I missed you cheating at cards. Guess who was at the Manor when I got back?"

"Elvis?"

"Close. Ellen."

She looks at me blankly and I add, "Granny."

"No shit?"

"No shit. Listen, you were here when she was first booked, right? What was she like when she came in?"

"Damn, Maureen. So many inmates come and go. I've got a faulty memory."

"Likely to be helped by more money on your commissary?"

"Funny how that works, ain't it? Let's see. She was quiet when she first came in. Kept to herself, like we were all maybe beneath her."

"Tears? Hysterics?"

"Not her. Dry-eyed and alert. Looked like she'd just been to the beauty parlor for hair and makeup. Came in and sat down as calm and collected as if she was out for an afternoon tea. Feet and knees together, all prim and proper. I invited her to come over and play, figured a woman looked like that probably had plenty of money on the books and maybe I could get my hands on some of it.

"She said—and I remember this because it was unusual—'No, thank you, dear, I think I'll just observe a bit, until I understand how things are done here.'

"I thought it was hilarious! Laughed out loud. 'You want the lay of the land, Granny, just ask me,' I said. 'It's not so bad once you know how to get along.'

"'Oh,' she said. 'I don't think it's bad at all. Beautifully quiet, don't you think?' And then she just sat there, watching, soaking us all in, like, I dunno, like we were animals at the zoo and she was enjoying a pleasant afternoon."

"What on earth happened?" I ask.

Renny shrugs. Her fingers are tapping on the table, her knee jiggling up and down. "Not the first to go crazy in here."

"Was it gradual? Sudden?"

"How should I know? She wasn't my cellmate. I remember her coming in only because how she looked and acted. Not like the usual girls. Different. A change of pace. Then, next thing I noticed, we're all playing cards and she's trying to make doors in the walls and talking to herself." Renny's face takes on a look of cool calculation. "What's with all the questions?"

I shrug. "Something's not right, that's all. Did she have any medical problems, visitors that you know of?"

"Definitely gonna need another memory boost."

"Can't you do anything out of the goodness of your heart?"

"I can," she says. "But not when I've got the option of extortion. Humor me. What else have I got to do?"

"I'll donate a new deck of cards to the jail. All unmarked. How about that?"

"You wouldn't!"

I sit silent, holding her gaze.

"You would." She sighs. "Look, I honestly don't know

anything. Granny was on medical call a couple of times, but what surprise is that? What is she, a hundred? Got to have all sorts of health problems, right? Why people even bother to live past sixty, I haven't a clue."

"May you too be old someday," I say, getting up to push the buzzer.

"Hey, don't run off. Don't be so touchy."

I put my hand to my ear. "Sorry. Can't hear you. I'm dead."

Renny laughs. "You will never be old. It is kinda weird about Granny, I agree. How she just went cuckoo for cocoa puffs sort of overnight. If I do remember anything, I'll get a message out to you."

Smith opens the door and looks from one of us to the other. "What's all of this *message* business?"

"I was asking Renny if she remembered anything about Ellen," I say, casually, as if it's all an afterthought. "She's at the Manor now and I'm trying to get her. . .condition. . .under control."

"Is that where they placed her? I wondered about that. You sit right there, Renny. I'll be back for you." Smith slams the door, then leads me down the corridor that leads to the outside world.

"Don't suppose you remember anything about how Ellen was when she came in?" I ask.

"I booked her," Smith answers. "She was totally with it. When she first started acting crazy, I thought it was just that. . .an act. But it persisted. Anyway. Woman that age doesn't belong in here. Made me wonder what the husband is like."

"If I'd been married to him, I'd have tried to take him out years ago." I pause. "Listen, was she on any meds when she was here?"

Smith thinks for a minute before she answers. "I don't think so? Hang on; let me check."

We stop at the office, where she crosses to a desk in the back corner and pulls out a binder, flips through the pages, and stops to run her finger down one. "Nope. Not a thing. Why?"

"Seems like she might have been on an antidepressant at home."

"Hmmm." Smith's forehead puckers. "She said something when she first came in about needing her meds. But we called her doc and he said she wasn't on anything. Husband said the same. Anything else I can do for you?"

"Just get me out of here, would you? I don't know how you all live down here all the time."

"We're subterraneans. Stay out of trouble, now."

"I bet you say that to all the prisoners."

She laughs as she slams the door shut again, this time with me on the side of light and freedom, but with more questions than answers.

CHAPTER ELEVEN

Next on my Ellen agenda is the bottle of pills I took from the cupboard in her kitchen. It's of significant interest that both her husband and her doctor said she wasn't on any meds, and yet this bottle was sitting in the meticulously organized cupboard. The label says *Sertraline, 100 mg. Take one tablet two times daily.* When I open the bottle, it's half-full of round yellow tablets. I tip a few out into my palm. The imprint consists of the number 25, followed by a lowercase *s* with a backwards *r* underneath it. I pull up a pill identification site on my pocket computer but the imprint doesn't come up. According to the site, hundred-milligram Sertraline comes in an oblong tablet with the imprint *A-18*.

"Curiouser and curiouser," I say. "What kind of games are we playing, Ellen?"

I check the locator app again, which informs me that she has relocated from my suite to the basement. With prickles of apprehension running up and down my spine, I call Gee to read her the riot act for not notifying me that something is up, but she doesn't answer. Sophie doesn't answer either. Apprehension grows into foreboding and I head for home. My Jag isn't great in snow, but I push the speed limit anyway, fishtailing around the curves that lead up the mountain to the Manor.

When I walk through the door, the place seems empty. Nobody is in the office or the hallways. Everything is so quiet, the building could be uninhabited—or maybe it is now a haunted ruin, occupied only by the dead.

Pushing that disquieting image away, I half-run down the hallway and up the stairs, as fast as my damaged leg will let me.

My suite is locked but empty. A half-finished Scrabble game sits on the table, along with three empty mugs. Morpheus barks at me, sniffs the scent of foreign dog on my jeans, and then begins howling at the closet door. Anubis pokes his head out from under the couch and meows pitifully before retreating again, which is a very bad sign.

I open my closet, and sure enough, the door to the secret staircase is open. I'm already on the first step when I pause, debating the wisdom of waiting for backup. But Jake is miles away, hopefully resting, Sophie is already involved with whatever is going on, and Matt is, hopefully, with Karin. I don't want to leave her unsupervised.

Besides, I'm used to working alone. As a compromise, I send Matt a quick text: *New developments. Stand by. Check on me in 30 if I don't check in.*

Then I move my knife to my pocket. Check my revolver to make sure it's loaded and ready. Then I drag Morpheus to the outside of the closet and close the door between us; an excited dog is not conducive to stealth.

His howls and the occasional thud as he hurls himself against the door follow me down the staircase, gradually fading as I proceed along the passageway. When a low murmur of voices reaches my ears, I flatten my back against the wall and creep sideways, soundless, taking my time. My revolver is ready in one hand, my knife in the other.

And then the voices begin to chant, an ominous sound that

conjures up the image of another body laid out for death, this time on a gurney. A secret ritual. Sophie or Val or Gee bound and helpless. A knife instead of poison.

I speed my pace. A giggle breaks out, followed by shushing and more chanting.

Uttering a war cry, I swing around into the open doorway of the room the sound is coming from. I crouch, both knife and revolver ready for action.

Four robed figures stand in a circle, hands joined. Four startled faces turn toward me.

"Damn it, Maureen, now we'll have to start over," Sophie says. Her eyes are glowing green and her hair is drifting around as if there's a breeze, although there's not a breath of air moving down here.

"Will the circle be unbroken?" Val warbles. She looks like she always does, neat, intelligent, and classy, except for the melodramatic addition of a black robe.

"Hey, now Maureen can join us!" Gee crows. She is still wearing her baseball cap, her hair in a messy ponytail hanging out through the hole in the back. It makes an odd contrast with the robe, which is so long her hands are hidden by the sleeves, the fabric puddling around her feet on the floor.

Ellen, also draped in a robe, doesn't look at me at all, her eyes following the flickering shadows created by the four flaming torches set in the corners of the small room. At the center of the circle is an urn of some sort—black, with silvery stars painted on it. The stars glow in a way no paint should ever glow, and I feel the chill that indicates a supernatural presence. We are not alone.

"What the hell is this, Sophronia?"

"Research. Ida Mae's soul was too faint; I needed reinforcements so I could reach her."

I look at the urn and decide not to ask what's in it. "Do you really think it was wise to drag a child and Ellen into this?"

Sophie actually shuffles her feet a little at that, possibly feeling a little guilt, but says, defensively, "I needed Val in case we reach Ida Mae, so she could talk to her. Gee was there, and they were watching Ellen. They all know about the passage already—"

"But maybe don't need to be part of a seance."

"I'm not a child," Gee interjects, her eyes bright with excitement. "And it's too late, right? I'm already part of this. Harm could be done if we break the circle."

"This is not a haunted house at Disneyland," I say. "I want you out of here. Now. Scoot."

"Hand to the plow," Val murmurs, clutching the girl's hand tighter.

I dig around in my memory for the reference and come up with something Biblical about not turning back. Val's eyes on mine are serious and intense, reminding me that she is a powerful medium. I turn to Sophie, hoping for clarification.

"Is it really dangerous to send Gee out?"

"I'm not the medium," Sophie answers. "What do I know?"

There's a weird reverb to her voice and her eyes are still glowing.

I can feel the energy in the room, and it's not the kind I'd call Casper the Friendly Ghost.

I hate ghosts, even the so-called benign ones. All of my common sense says this is a very bad idea, but we do need information and even I can feel that something is trying to communicate.

Val releases Ellen and extends her free hand to me. I take it and reach for Ellen's. As the circle closes, I feel a jolt of energy. The torchlight shifts from yellow to blue; the shadows grow sharp-edged and solid. Where they flicker across my skin, they now have weight and texture. The temperature in the room drops dramatically. The urn at the center of our circle glows blue, and a faintly silvery smoke wafts from its open mouth.

Sophronia no longer looks human. Her eyes glow green, her black hair swirls around her. Val's eyes are closed, her face vacant, trancelike. Ellen blinks rapidly, her eyes darting from one face to another, then to the torches and the shadows and back again.

"Cool," Gee whispers.

The silvery mist from the urn rises in a thin spiral, like smoke, but with a seeking, questioning quality, as if it has sentience. It drifts around the circle, exploring. I feel a brush of vivid cold against my face, then watch it drift past Ellen without touching her. It winds tendrils around Gee's throat and brushes up against her cheek. She giggles, and it moves on, hovering in front of Sophie, who blows at it, as if it's smoke, and her breath carries it across the circle to Val.

Val opens her mouth and the thing swirls in between her lips and down her throat, like water down the drain. Val's eyes snap open, and it's easy to see that whatever is looking out of her body, it's no longer Val.

I'm also pretty sure it's not Ida Mae.

Ida Mae was mild-mannered and pleasantly confused. Ditzy. Cheerfully forgetful. The kind of woman who always had cookies for everybody's grandchildren and stopped in the street to pat passing dogs but had no idea what time it was or what day it was. She was always searching for her keys and even managed to misplace her walker a time or two, wandering off without it and then sitting down on the nearest flat surface, laughing and exhausted, saying, "How on earth did I manage that?"

But whatever it is that is now looking out of Val's eyes is cold and cunning. The temperature has dropped even further. The shadows seem to creep along the floor toward us, then between our feet and into the center of the circle, and I see that they're not shadows at all but spiders. Thousands of spiders, all different sizes and shapes, scuttling along as if moved by one mind.

They gather until the entire circle is filled with them and

then go still. Waiting. Something emerges from the mouth of the urn, and at first I think it's another bit of that silvery smoke. But then I see that it's a jointed, hairy leg, followed by another, and then an arachnid body as big as my head squeezes out and crouches on top of the urn. Silver hairs cover its body. Its cluster of eyes glow ruby red.

I'm not bothered by spiders, in general, but this thing is too big and too intelligent by far. The host of smaller spiders lower their bodies to the floor, as if bowing.

She—I have no way of knowing, but I'm certain it's a she—crawls down the side of the urn. The spiders clear a path for her, every one of them turning to face her as she moves, straight across the circle to Val. I look to Sophie for guidance but her eyes are closed. The giant silver spider crawls onto Val's foot, then begins to ascend her robe.

This can't be good, I'm sure. I try to call out a warning but my lips won't move. My hands feel welded to the hands on either side.

The spider continues to climb, its feet making little scratching noises in the silence. It pauses when it reaches the neckline of the robe, and taps at Val's skin with its first pair of legs.

A shiver goes through me as it climbs onto her neck and up over the angle of her jaw, half-obscuring her face. Again, I try to call out, but can't summon a sound.

The spider's front legs tap on Val's bottom lip. She opens her mouth. Horror curdles my blood.

And then a voice declares, "I don't think so."

Gee drops the hands she's holding, darts forward, grasps the spider in both hands, stuffs it back into the urn, then seals the opening with a stoneware stopper.

The silence that follows is broken by a shriek from Ellen.

Spiders scatter, scuttling toward the corners, no longer moving as one.

Val doubles over, making choking, gagging noises. A column of smoke wisps out of her mouth. She begins to shiver, violently.

I find that I'm able to move, and my first action is to brush my body from shoulders to feet, an impulse I'm unable to control.

"Super cool!" Gee exclaims.

"Cool?" I stare at her. "Seriously? I don't think that's exactly what this was. Everybody okay? Sophie?"

Sophie's eyes are still closed, her face wearing a look of concentration. After a long moment, she sighs deeply, and her face relaxes. Her eyes open. They are no longer glowing, but they look unfocused and distant, as if she's still seeing things that I can't see.

"Well," she says, "that was unexpected."

Gee crosses to Val and puts her arms around her waist. Val hugs her back.

"*Charlotte's Web*," she says, looking from me to Sophie and back again.

"Charlotte's what?" Gee asks.

"It's a kid's book," I tell her. "A talking spider and a pig named Wilbur."

"I hate talking-animal stories. They're stupid."

"This one happens to be a classic. Do you understand what happened there, Val?" I ask. She shakes her head, eyes wide.

"Val needs to eat," Gee says. "This sort of thing burns tons of calories. Let's go find a snack."

"Really, Gee? You aren't freaked out at all?" Sophie asks, her voice almost, but not quite, normal. "Me, personally? I do not like spiders."

"I love 'em, ordinarily," Gee says, cheerfully. "I have a pet tarantula. His name is Cuddles. Because he's furry. But that sucker? She was absolutely evil. I wanted to crunch her, but I don't think she would have crunched. Did I do the right thing?"

"You did awesome. You are now my personal heroine."

"Soph?" I ask. "Are we safe?"

She looks drained and exhausted. "For now," she says. "I think." And then she sways on her feet and I run to catch her, managing just to break her fall and ease her limp body to the floor.

Finally, Gee squeals with appropriate fear. "Is she okay?"

"She's breathing normally; her pulse is steady. But she looks like she hasn't slept or eaten in a week." It's true. Sophronia's unconscious face looks almost skeletal, the skin pulled tight over her bones.

"Val too," Gee says. I look up at Val and see that her face, too, is etched with lines of fatigue, and that she's still shivering uncontrollably.

Perfect. Everyone is falling apart around me. Cell phones don't work down here, so I grab the walkie. "Matt? Come in, Matt."

There's a crackle of static and then Matt's voice, "What's up, Maureen?"

"Staff meeting," I say, code in case he's with Karin. "You're late."

"On my way."

I look up at Val, who looks like she's aged twenty years in the space of a few minutes. "Are you okay to walk up?"

She nods, and smiles at Gee, who has a steadying arm wrapped around her waist. "Wind beneath my wings."

"Good. Gee, take her up to my suite and find her something to eat, would you? And open the door for Matt."

For once, Gee doesn't argue. "Got it," she says. "Let's go, Val."

They shuffle out of the room, leaving me with the unconscious girl, the urn, the flickering torchlight, and Ellen. The latter stands precisely where we left her, unmoving, barely even blinking, which does nothing for my peace of mind. I keep feeling the phantom touch of something crawling on my arms, in my hair. I'm almost sure they are imaginary, but I can't stop brushing myself off, expecting to feel creepy legs and soft bodies.

As far as I can see in the dark room, the spiders have all vanished. When I flip the electric switch on the wall, nothing happens. No surprise there. We keep the lights in the hallway operational, but the bulbs in these other rooms haven't been replaced in years.

Matt arrives within what is probably five minutes but feels like an hour. He crouches on the other side of Sophronia, his face taut with worry.

"What happened?"

"Weird-ass seance with Val. When it ended, Sophie looked exhausted and then she just. . .Well. Here we are. I couldn't carry her."

Matt doesn't seem to even hear me. He strokes Sophronia's hair, calls her name. "Soph, come back from wherever you are." His voice is coaxing and cajoling at first. When she doesn't respond, he barks an order that would do a drill sergeant proud.

"Sophronia. Come back at once."

Her eyelids flicker and open. "Matt," she whispers. "You came for me."

He clears his throat and lays one hand over her cheek. "I thought you'd gone too far." They gaze into each other's eyes in a way that can only mean trouble.

"I'm sure she's fine," I say brusquely. "Care to explain, Sophie?"

She winds herself up into a sitting posture, managing to look both very young and very old in the way she moves. She retrieves her hand from Matt's and bends her head, screening her face behind a fall of hair.

"Anybody want to tell me what is going on here?" Matt demands sharply. "Val doesn't look much better. Morpheus is freaking out and Anubis was howling under the couch."

"Need time to find words," Sophie croaks.

Matt rises gracefully to his feet and reaches a hand down to her. She lets him help her up, her eyes still on his face. And then she drops his hand as if it's suddenly burned her, straightens her spine and says, "I said I was fine. I do not require babysitting." Then she turns her back and stalks out, ignoring both of us. If she were a cat, her tail would be puffed and her fur standing straight on end.

"What did I do?" Matt asks, bewildered.

"It's what you didn't do."

"I don't—"

"Never mind, Matt. If you'd give me a hand up, I'd accept it." Not that I can't get up by myself, of course. But his ego may need soothing, and men do like to feel strong and needed.

He lifts me to my feet, politely ignoring the audible creaking of several of my joints. "Did I tell you I'm glad you're back?" I ask, adjusting my clothing and checking my weapons.

"Are you sure?"

"Positive."

"Right," he says, clearly still distracted and maybe a little snarly. "Who do I watch now? Karin or Sophie?"

I'm torn but in the end decide to give the girl the space she needs and trust she's okay. "Karin, I guess."

"What about the urn?"

"Leave that where it is." I shudder in memory. "Soph will have to secure it somehow."

"Want to tell me what happened down here?"

"Seance, apparently. Trying to summon Ida Mae. I have no idea what was supposed to be in that urn, but what emerged from it was an oversized spider. And the room was covered with her. . .minions."

"That's not at all creepy," he says. There's a distant quality to his voice.

Ellen stands where we left her. I unzip the robe she's wearing.

Matt lingers, as if he has something to say but doesn't know how to say it.

"Look," I say, while I undress Ellen as if she's a mannequin, "I was going to get you out of jail. I just thought there would be a better method than selling my soul to the Unit."

"What, oh, that?" He extinguishes one of the torches, moves on to the second. "No worries. Saying no to Charlie is a skill I wish I'd learned years ago."

I drop the robe on top of the others and lead Ellen out into the corridor. Anubis is waiting at the bottom of the stairs. He winds around my ankles in a way that is likely to be the death of both of us, until Matt scoops him up and carries him. When we enter the suite, Morpheus dances around us, barking with delight, begging to be patted.

Val sits on the couch, eating cheese and crackers.

"Where has that infernal child got to?" I demand, looking around to see no sign of Gee.

"Patience is a virtue," Val says, primly.

At that moment, Gee bursts into the room, out of breath, her cheeks flushed. An industrial-sized mayonnaise jar is clutched in both hands.

"Where have you been, and where did you get that?" I ask.

"The new cook." She stops and looks uncertainly at Matt. "Or sub-cook? Anyway. That woman in the kitchen with the yellow hair."

"Karin?" Matt blinks as if Gee's suddenly sprouted an extra arm out of her forehead.

"I told her I needed it for a science project. A spider habitat. She said she hated spiders and to make sure I kept them secure."

She drops the jar on the table and pulls out a series of salt shakers from the front pocket of her hoodie, setting them out in a line.

"I hope you're going to put those back in the dining room," Matt says.

"Of course." Wide, innocent eyes make it clear that she has no such intentions.

"The mayonnaise jar?" I prompt, getting back to the heart of the matter.

"Don't you wish you could have gotten a better look at that spider?" she asks. "I mean, so you could observe it. Study it. You can't see it when it's in the urn."

"There is no jar that will contain that creature."

"What if I put a ring of salt around it? And maybe salt on the lid? I mean, it was a ghost spider, right? I didn't even know they existed! And ghosts don't like to pass through salt. And—"

"Let me be clear." I make my voice as menacing as possible. "You are not to be trapping creepy things in jars or invoking spirits or doing any such thing. You will definitely not go through that door in my closet. Ever, for any reason, unless I give you explicit permission. You will certainly not deliberately make contact with that arachnid. If something unusual appears —and I mean anything so small as a wisp of a breeze that feels out of place—you will message me immediately and stay out of its way. Do you understand me?"

"But what if we're attacked? What if something creepy-crawly starts moving across the floor toward Val. . ." She demonstrates, lifting her feet with exaggerated slowness, her hands at her shoulders in claw form. "And there's not time to wait for you? I could—"

"You could all stand on the furniture. But you know what? Let's eliminate the possibility. You need to go home. And don't try the waterworks on me like you did earlier with Jake."

"I'm staying overnight at Val's again," Gee replies, setting the jar on the counter. "My parents are gone, remember? I can't stay home alone. Do you have a nail? Something I can make holes in this lid with?"

"Gee—"

Children are not my strong point. Not having any was one of my better life achievements.

Matt laughs. "All right, then. I'm back to Karin; much easier than what you've got going on here. Don't strangle the child, Maureen."

"How did you know what I was thinking?"

"I can read your face." He hands me an armful of purring cat and asks, "I don't suppose you've got a knife I could borrow? They confiscated mine when they booked me, and I haven't had time to secure another. Kitchen knives are a little unwieldy to carry around."

"Sorry, they took mine, too. I'm already using my backup."

"Carving knife it is, then," he says cheerfully. He heads for the door, then turns back and says, with the sort of seriousness that makes my skin crawl a little, "Be careful, would you?"

I lock the door of my suite securely behind him, return to the closet, and make sure the secret door is closed and locked. Ellen and Val and Gee are now all three seated in a line on the sofa, staring at me. I drag a bag of salt out of my cupboard and pour a line in front of the secret door, and another in front of the closet.

Then I turn to survey the troublemakers on my sofa. "Can I trust you three to actually stay put?"

"We're hungry," Gee says. "Especially Val. We will need sustenance."

"Right." I hand her the radio and show her how to use it. "I'll ask Matt to run some food up for you. Do not open the door for anybody else. Lock it behind him when he leaves. Understood?"

Two heads nod. Ellen is staring at something on the ceiling that my eyes are unable to see.

My phone rings. It's an unknown number, but I answer and am totally unsurprised when Charlie's voice comes on.

"Are you alone?"

"Thanks to you, I am no longer ever alone," I snap.

"Good."

"Tell me what the hell is going on!" I order, but the phone is already dead. I hit redial and get a "this number is not in service" message.

I start swearing, remember Gee, and bite my tongue. I memorized the number on the business card he gave me, the one that read, *Charles Livingstone, attorney-at-law*, with a bogus address. But the phone number ought to be legit, since he wanted me to call him. I dial, and it rings for a long time before a woman's voice comes on, professional to the point of robotic. "Transformal Dry Cleaners. This is Mallory. How can I help you?"

"Put Charlie on."

"I'm sorry," the voice repeats. "This is Transformal Dry Cleaners. You must have a wrong number." And the phone clicks off.

I call back.

"Transformal Dry Cleaners. How can I help you?" the same voice says.

"Hey, Mallory. This is Maureen Keslyn and I demand to talk to Charlie."

"I'm terribly sorry, ma'am, but I don't know any Charlie."

"Just tell him to call me back." I thumb off the phone, thinking longingly of the days of slamming down receivers.

Three pairs of eyes stare at me. "Dead end to the Unit," I say. "I'm off to try another angle to find out what Charlie is up to. Stay safe."

CHAPTER TWELVE

Shadow Valley Pharmacy & Sundries was once an unassuming but essential business that did exactly as the first half of its name promised: sold prescriptions, over-the-counter medications, and other medical supplies. Recently, its founder died of old age, and the daughter who inherited it aspires to what she considers greater things. The store is now painted a garish shade of yellow, closer to fake cheese than sunshine, and is bedecked with yard flags and windsocks. The windows display T-shirts sporting cartoon renderings of surprised-looking sheep and slogans like *I Survived Shadow Valley*. I know for a fact that at least two of these shirts have sold, because my ex and his new woman once showed up at the Manor wearing them.

Because of Christmas, current choices include sheep with reindeer horns, a flock of sheep pulling a sleigh, and a few random penguins. As I walk in the front door, a Santa nearly as big as I am starts singing "Santa Claus is Coming to Town" in a key that is in direct conflict with the anything-but-peaceful rendition of "Silent Night" blaring through the overhead speakers.

The woman behind the counter puts down the paperback

she's reading and looks at me the way Anubis does when I open a can of cat food. Most likely she thinks I'm an out-of-season tourist since she knows everybody in town and my face is unfamiliar. I ignore her. I am not buying a coffee mug or a windchime or a T-shirt just because she desperately wants me to.

Keeping my eyes focused on the pharmacy counter nearly hidden by all of the fuss and furbelows hung from the ceiling, I navigate past the impulse buys and stop in front of the sign that says INCOMING PRESCRIPTIONS. A stoop-shouldered, snowy-haired man glances up over old-timey wire-rimmed spectacles. He looks so much like a Norman Rockwell painting that I think for a minute he's window dressing for the store, but then he sets aside the prescription bottle he's filling and walks to the counter.

"I don't believe we've filled for you before," he says. His name tag reads *Bert, Pharmacist*. No *pharmacist assistant* nonsense for this store.

"Actually, Bert, I need help with a bit of a mystery."

He lights up. "Nothing I love better. Let me guess. You found some loose pills in the bottom of your purse and you can't remember what they are."

"Exactly! How did you guess?" I'd meant to actually tell him who I am, and that the mystery pills belong to a resident, but this is easier.

"Women and their purses," he says. "Happens more than you'd think. Before you accuse me of misogyny, men are worse, only they tend to combine all of their pills in one old bottle that has a label on it for something they stopped taking years ago. Let's see what you've got."

Fortunately for the veracity of my story, I've left Ellen's pill bottle in the glove compartment of my Jag, and have brought in a single tablet, sequestered in a baggie.

Bert lifts it to the light, turning it this way and that, then smiles at me radiantly. "A true mystery. I have no idea what this might be. Would you give me a few minutes?" He leans forward and whispers, conspiratorially, "April over there will have her day made should you choose to buy something. You are not a T-shirt candidate, I can tell, but maybe a coffee mug."

I stay where I am. So does he. Getting the message that information is going to come at the price of buying a gewgaw of some kind, I betake myself off to the floridly encumbered shelves where I can still watch Bert's process.

The coffee mugs are not something I would choose to drink out of, given pretty much any other option. There is one rather horrifying cheap ceramic affair shaped like a hollowed skull, with ink that has accidentally bled into the eye sockets. A red smear, probably meant to be blood, stains the grinning mouth. *Shadow Valley Got the Best of Me* is emblazoned on the inside.

With a glance at Bert, who frowns at the computer and then starts flipping through the pages of a thick book, I carry the mug to the cash register. April clasps her hands at her breast. "Oh, you've chosen the death mug. How fun! A gift, yes? Would you like balloons to go with that? Is it a birthday? We can do an entire balloon bouquet."

Bert glances in our direction, as if he's overheard not only April's words but my unspoken reaction, and I summon up a smile and agree to the balloon bouquet. "Not a birthday, though. I don't suppose you have any 'I'm glad you didn't die' balloons?"

"No, but we do have some I Walked Through Shadow Valley ones. They have fluffy sheep on them. Kind of a take-off on the twenty-third psalm, you know? Even though I walk through the valley of the shadow?"

"I'm familiar," I say, watching Bert, who has shuffled off to a corner and picked up yet another book. "Fix me up. That will be perfect."

April digs around behind the counter and fits the first balloon over the helium tank, inflating a large mylar monstrosity to its full garish glory. "See?" she asks.

And yes, I do see. By the time she's done inflating all of the balloons and tying them together with red and black ribbon, Bert has gone back to the computer. I pay an astonishing price for my items and walk back to the pharmacy counter, wrangling a floating balloon cluster that wants to catch on various fragile items. I picture wiping out a whole row and having to pay the You Break It You Buy It price for things that should never have existed in the first place.

Bert meets me at the counter, all traces of his smile vanished.

"What kind of games are you playing, young lady?"

Nobody has called me young in a number of years but I can see from his expression that smiling in response was a bad decision. "I thought we were playing 'tell me what pill this is.'"

"This pill, as I think you well know, is not on any list or in any directory. It has certainly not been approved by the FDA and is not even in the FDA tracker."

"I don't understand."

"You have been wasting my time."

"Look. Bert. Let me level with you."

"Too late for that, missy."

"But I bought a mug *and* the balloons," I protest. "At least just listen."

Curiosity, or maybe my purchases, takes the edge off his annoyance. He's still not smiling, but at least he's listening.

"I'm Maureen Keslyn. I run the Manor."

"So, *that's* who you are," he says, as if it explains everything.

"I have a new resident who is a bit of a mystery. She appears to have dementia, but her husband claims she was perfectly normal up until a few weeks ago. He told me this pill was an antidepressant but I couldn't find it on an online pill finder. So, I wanted to know what she's taking."

"Why didn't you just tell me that?"

I shrug. "I was going to, but then you suggested the whole bottom-of-the-purse routine and I went with it."

Bert relents. "I did kinda hand that one to you. All right.

Here's what I can tell you. Whatever it is, it's either an experimental or black-market drug. That imprint isn't registered anywhere in the public domain."

"But what might it be?"

"Anything from a recreational drug to a cancer treatment to a vitamin. I'd need to see a chemical analysis to tell you more. Your resident may be part of a research study."

I pocket the pill. "Interesting. Thanks for your help."

"If I might make a suggestion," Bert suggests. "If she is part of a research study, you should find out what. It could mean life and death."

"Agreed. I will get on that immediately."

"Good luck!" Bert says, like he means it. "I'd love to know what you discover."

I wave, corralling wayward balloons all the way out of the store.

When I get to my car, I run into a whole new problem, this one of my own making. No matter where I put the balloons, they are in the way, blocking the rearview mirror or the windshield. Driving anywhere with them floating around will put lives in danger.

Also, I'm hungry and need more coffee, and I suddenly have an inspired idea.

Jake answers on the second ring, his tone abrupt. "What?"

"Meet me at House of Joe. I have information."

"What time?"

"I'm already there." This is a bit of an exaggeration, but it's only two blocks away, a distance I can easily walk before Jake can get here.

"On my way," he says.

I tread carefully on the icy sidewalk, feeling the balloons tug at me with every gust of winter wind, making it feel like I'm about to have lift-off. When I get to the door of the café, there's another struggle as several of the balloons make it clear that their preference is to remain outside rather than in, but one of the other patrons comes over to help me and, finally, my aeronautical sidekicks and I are inside where it's warm and everything smells like coffee and bacon.

There's an empty table by the window, and I sink gratefully into a chair. Pammi, the waitress, comes over with menus, laughing at my purchases. "I see April got her claws in you. Swear to God, that place is a tourist trap in the fullest sense of the words. Except, of course, you're not a tourist. Your usual?"

"Coffee for now. The sheriff will be joining me."

"Ooooh." She bats her eyelashes. "Isn't he just a tall drink of water? Wait. Didn't I hear something about the two of you?" She gasps, pausing in the act of pouring my coffee. "You shot him!" Her voice drops confidentially. "Tell me. Was it a lover's quarrel? Did he cheat on you? And how did you get out of jail already?"

The small-town gossip mill has apparently been busy, and this is as good a place as any to begin shifting the story. "Actually, I was shooting at a bad guy and the sheriff got in the way. Which is why I'm not heading for death row and am sitting here waiting to drink coffee."

Pammi takes the hint and fills my cup. "Got you. But still. You did shoot the sheriff and you almost killed him, and now here you are meeting over coffee and whatever. It's romantic, isn't it?"

"What's romantic?" Jake growls. Pammi, intent on her story, completely missed him walking in. Now she startles and flushes, clutching the coffee carafe to her heart.

Fortunately for her, the balloons distract Jake, his expression moving from surprise to appropriate disgust at the general tackiness of the display. He sits down in the chair across from me, eyebrows raised almost to his hairline. "I see you've been to the pharmacy." He draws one of the balloons down to eye level and then releases it so it pops back up, tugging at the black ribbon that holds it.

"These are for you," I say, gesturing expansively. "As is this."

He unwraps the mug I hand him, running his fingers over it as if he can't quite believe it's real.

"Coffee, please," he says to Pammi. "And a cheeseburger."

"Same for me," I tell her. She fills Jake's cup and nearly runs for the kitchen.

"No rabbit food and orange juice?"

"Learned my lesson," he says. "Life is short."

"Which is why I've gone to great time and expense and difficulty to buy you this gift that says I'm glad you didn't die." To my absolute shock and dismay, my throat closes over those last two words.

"Allergies," I say, grabbing a napkin and blotting at my eyes.

"If I didn't know better, I'd think you really meant it," Jake says. "Not the allergies. The other."

Our eyes meet and hold and my heart beats a little faster. "You do know I was saving you from a fate worse than death."

"I do know it." He sounds like he, too, has allergies, and attempts to cough into his napkin. When he speaks, he's all business again.

"You have something to tell me?"

"You do know how to sweet-talk a woman. I should warn you that you're not going to like it."

"Look," he says. He takes his time stirring cream into his coffee. Drinks. And then goes on. "Every time the paranormal comes up. Every time the Unit gets mentioned. What do you think that does to me? How do you think it feels knowing that I was a dupe that got used years ago by those people? It's like they're sucking me back in, over and over again. I hate that."

"You're not the Lone Ranger on that, Jake." My voice is sharper than I meant it to be, edged with my own guilt, my own anger at Charlie and the Unit's games. I touch his hand to let him know it's not him I'm pissed at. "The balance of power is on their side at the moment. So for now, we dance. And we let them think we're all on board. Once we've got everybody safe, then we regroup. And we take those motherfuckers down."

Pammi brings our plates and he stops talking to take a big bite. I wait, but he says nothing. He wipes grease off his chin and swallows coffee before he finally says, "Let me hear it."

"I have information about Ellen."

He stops with his burger halfway to his mouth. "Maureen. That poor unfortunate woman is not our murderer."

"Maybe not. But she does have some connection to the Unit. Here's what I found out so far. According to her husband and people at the jail, she was sharp as a tack when she was arrested."

"You've been interviewing people? I thought you—"

"Very normal for a facility to need information about a new resident who is unable to supply it herself. Calm down. You'll hurt your ribs." I take a bite and savor it before continuing. "She vanished from my room again last night, even though all the locks were set. And she rigged the bed to make it look like she was still in it. My alarm never went off."

"Or maybe you are not infallible and slept a little more soundly than you thought. And maybe Ellen was clear enough when she was arrested but deteriorated rapidly in jail under the force of grief and guilt and sensory deprivation."

I wave my burger at him and go on as if he hasn't interrupted. "Her husband said she's not taking any medications, and her doctor concurs. But there was a bottle of antidepressants in the cupboard with her name on it."

"Not exactly a sign of conspiracy," Jake says. "Maybe she had a different doctor. People do all kinds of strange things around their mental health."

"Until we discover that what's in the bottle isn't an antidepressant and isn't even on the FDA's radar. The pharmacist says it's likely some kind of experimental drug. Also, Charlie called to check on her, refused to tell me anything, and when I called back, the person who answered claimed that she hadn't the least inkling of his existence."

Jake gets it now. I can see the pieces coming together, his expression sharpening into a clear focus. "All right. Let's say that she is involved with the Unit, she's on an experimental medication, and she can walk through doors without opening them. All of this still has nothing to do with what happened to Ida Mae."

"I don't like coincidences, Jake. And where the Unit is involved? Trust me. There are no coincidences. Also, there's more."

"About Ellen?"

"No. This is about Sophie and Val and Gee."

"They're suspects now?"

"No. At least, I don't think so."

He sighs, shoving back his plate with his food half-eaten. "Apparently, our suspects are a couple of old ladies, a sixth-grader, and Sophronia. Oh, and Jill. And three terrified seniors who discovered the body. And the interim cook. Where is Ellen, by the way? If she's such a sinister force of darkness."

"Being babysat by another sinister force of darkness."

He stares at me blankly. My appetite has been stimulated rather than suppressed by this conversation, and I finish my own food and draw his plate over to start work on his fries. "You not eating this?"

"Maureen, where is Ellen?"

"I left her with Gee and Val. And Morpheus. Sophie is keeping an eye out."

"All perfectly safe and secure, then," he snarks.

"Look—I can see where Ellen is." I show him the tracker on my phone. "Right in my suite where she's supposed to be."

"And maybe the other two have been murdered and she's feasting on their souls."

"You're the one who was discounting her as a suspect. Here." I dial Gee's cell and she answers right away.

"All's well," she says. "Matt brought us pizza. We're playing Scrabble. You can *trust* me, for God's sake."

"See?" I tell Jake as I hang up. "Are you ready to hear the rest of what I need to tell you?"

"Just as soon as I remind you that locking a resident into a room is illegal. That tracking a resident is also illegal."

"Are you going to arrest me, officer?"

Jake's jaw tightens. "What were you going to tell me?"

I decide to hold off a bit on the Ghost Spider Seance. There's something we need to do before he demands to go back to the Manor and hook Gee up with Child Protective Services.

So instead, I say, "We need to investigate Karin."

Jake drops his head into his hands and rubs his temples. "Why, exactly? Other than that Jill hired her?"

"If it makes you feel better, let's just say it's so that we can rule her out. Come on; let's get moving. I'll pay."

Jake gets up and begins to walk away from the table. I call him back. "Don't forget your balloons."

____

CHAPTER THIRTEEN

____

Jake drives while I anchor the balloons to my side of the vehicle, although a stray does escape me once or twice and get in the way of his rearview mirror. When we arrive at Karin's building, the address of which I lifted earlier from her personnel files back at the Manor, Jake removes a knife from a holster and methodically and efficiently slashes every last one of them.

"See if I give you gifts again."

"Spare me," he says. And then, "You know you can't just break into her apartment, Maureen."

"Maybe she left the door open."

Karin occupies one of the ground-floor units of a fourplex at the edge of town. Across the street is a wide-open field, and beyond that, white-peaked mountains in the distance. An oak tree stands tall in the middle of the snow-covered yard, which is marked with a wide variety of paw prints, large and small, presumably from cats and neighborhood dogs. None of them are werewolf-sized, but that doesn't mean anything.

I walk to the front porch and ring the doorbell, knowing that Karin is not going to answer, because she's at work. But maybe we'll be lucky and she has a roommate. There's no sound from

inside. The place is locked up tight and the windows are all shut-
tered. If I hadn't brought Jake and my tools hadn't been confiscated, I could pick the lock and have a quick look around.
Fortunately, both of these problems can be easily remedied, and
I'll just come back later.

"Well?" Jake asks, blissfully ignorant about my future plans,
"Did you gain valuable information?"

"I got the landlord's phone number." I snap a picture of a
FOR RENT sign in the window of the neighboring apartment.

"We are not going to ask him to let you into your long-lost
friend's apartment so you can retrieve your best pair of shoes for
your cousin's funeral," Jake says.

"Of course not! I'm shocked that you'd suggest such a thing.
I don't even have a best pair of shoes. Or any friends. Do you
know me at all?"

"Maureen," he growls, and I laugh.

"Lighten up, Jake. Talking to the landlord is well within the
scope of your investigation. You are going to just casually ask the
landlord some questions about Karin as a tenant. Routine questioning because she works at the Manor and there's been an
incident."

"I don't really need you telling me my job," he says.

"Of course not. I just thought you'd prefer it to me barging in
and asking questions outside my purview."

A quick search on my not-flip phone gives me a name and
address to match the phone number: KD Kar and Kollision
Services. The tag line, *We Kare for your Kar*, with its egregiously
misused *K*'s, makes me shudder. Jake, grumbling under his
breath, is already driving.

"I haven't told you where we're going yet."

He snorts. "Don't you know I'm the sheriff and I own this
town? Not the first time I've visited that fourplex, and I've had
several conversations with Kurt."

While Jake is busy driving and swearing, I check on the

whereabouts of Ellen. According to the app, she is still in my suite, where she belongs. A text to Gee results in the message: *You can TRUST ME,* accompanied by eye-roll and frowny-face emojis.

Jake turns off the pavement and onto a rutted road that winds around the edge of an empty lot and ends in front of a large metal building with a collection of cars haphazardly parked in front of it. Some have obviously been in collisions with deer or other cars, their hoods and fenders crumpled, windows cracked or missing.

A man in blue coveralls stands in front of the building, smoking a cigarette. "Hey, Jake," he says, as we walk up. "One of my tenants in trouble again?"

"Just some routine questions this time," Jake says, not looking at me. "About your newest tenant."

"Is this to do with that business up at the Manor? Either of you want a smoke?"

He holds out a pack of cigarettes. Jake shakes his head. "I quit. But I'm sure Maureen here would be grateful."

Kurt passes me the smokes and then lights me up, along with a new one for himself while he's at it.

"Tell us what you know about Karin," Jake says, casually.

"Don't know much. Only that she's got a chip on her shoulder big enough to sink a ship." Kurt Jensen shoves his glasses up higher on his nose so that the heavily smudged lenses obscure his mud-colored eyes. "Not very many people wanting to rent in Shadow Valley, or I'd have sent her packing the day she came to see the apartment."

"Did she give references? Previous landlord, that sort of thing?" Jake, who came along on this mission about as eagerly as a toddler goes to the dentist, can't resist asking questions now that he's here. From his glance at me, I suspect he's asking them to prove that we're on a wild-goose chase rather than to uncover evidence that confirms Karin as a likely suspect.

But I'm not after geese; I'm hunting something cannier and much more dangerous. I've seen my share of shifters, and Karin fits the profile. Law-abiding enough in human form, maybe, but with a fondness for meat and an intolerance for societal norms.

"Previous landlord is a landlady," Kurt corrects. "Post Falls, Idaho. She says this Karin was always on time with her rent, but the damage deposit was withheld when she moved."

"Property destruction?" Jake asks, with another sidelong glance, which I return with total innocence.

"Cleanup," Kurt exclaims. "Feathers, if you can believe it. Place was full of black feathers. Under the bed and such. And a red stain on the carpet that Karin *said* was wine but the landlady doubted."

"And what do *you* think?" I ask, before Jake can return to boring fact-checking-type questions.

"Me?" Kurt shoves his glasses up again, fingers slipping from his greasy skin onto the lenses and leaving new smudges. He leans forward and lowers his voice. "What I think is sacrifice. Like a chicken or some such."

"Oh, come now," Jake objects. "It's a big leap from a few feathers and a stain to blood sacrifice. Maybe a pillow got torn and maybe she did spill wine. Both common occurrences."

"Maybe my eyes are bad, but my hearing is good," Kurt says. "And I'm telling you I've heard bird noises in the apartment on multiple occasions. Clucking sounds, not like sparrows or something small. When I knocked, nobody answered. It's against our tenant agreement for her to have chickens in the apartment, so of course I checked. Not a bird to be seen, but feathers under the bed."

"What about spiders?" I ask, casually.

"Spiders?" Kurt repeats.

"You know. More of them than you'd expect. Enough to call in an exterminator."

He shakes his head. "Nothing like that."

"Could we get the number for the previous landlady, do you think?"

Kurt shrugs. "I guess. Hang on a sec." He walks into the shop and comes out a moment later with a stained and crumpled manila folder.

"Let's see, now." He opens it, balancing it on the palm of one hand and running a grease-stained index finger down a sheet of paper inside. "Here we go." He reads off a number and Jake jots it down in his notebook.

"Anything else I can do you for?"

"Just let me know if anything else seems out of order, would you, Kurt?"

"You got it, Sheriff. Happy to be of service to the law."

"See?" Jake says, once we're back in the car. "Feathers. Chicken sacrifices. That's what you get when you start a witch hunt."

"Mmmm."

He gives an exasperated sigh, winces, and says, "Out with it. What's up with the spider question? You know something you're not telling me."

Before I can get the words out, static comes up on the radio. "Sheriff, this is control."

"Jake here."

"We've got a 10-54 up at the Manor."

"On my way."

Jake concentrates on driving, full lights and sirens, and I concentrate on trying to figure out which resident is dead this time. Gee doesn't answer my call, and when I consult my app, Ellen is on the move toward the game room.

Matt answers on the first ring and fills me in without wasting any time. "Containing the scene. In Sylvia's room—another weird one. Come straight up."

CHAPTER FOURTEEN

Jill is in the office, sitting behind my desk, pouting. The instant she sees us, she springs to her feet and launches into a tirade. "Matt marched me in here, basically at gunpoint, and told me to stay. To stay! As if I am a dog. Can you tell him—"

"Just stay where you are Jill. He's trying to contain a crime scene and you are a suspect."

"But—"

"Sit, Jill. Stay."

Leaving her sputtering incomprehensible curses in French, I trot a few steps in an attempt to catch up with Jake. Given that he's recently had a collapsed lung and his ribs cracked open, he's a little easier to keep up with than he was before I shot him. For once, I don't quibble about the elevator. A spider hangs on a web in the upper right corner, but it does nothing other than watch me as intently as I watch it.

On the second floor, we wade through a congested traffic of walkers and slow-moving bodies who all consider themselves too old to be told what to do.

"Hey, Maureen, are you going to evacuate us again?" Dan asks. It's a justified question. Given back-to-back murders, resident safety is in question and Dan is one of the sharper knives in the drawer. Of course, the last time I tried to evacuate the Manor for safety reasons, most of the residents refused to leave.

"If you would all please go either to your rooms or to the game room and wait, I will fill you in as soon as I know anything." I raise my voice to carry and I know they've heard me. Nobody moves. Jake, standing in the door of Sylvia's room where Matt has cleared a space for him, turns around and turns the request into a legal and authoritative command.

"Clear the hallway. Go directly to your rooms and stay there. A deputy will be around to collect statements."

For a long moment nobody moves, and I wonder if we'll have a mutiny, but the dam of resistance breaks and they turn and flow down the hallway, only to jam up again at the elevator. I cram into the entrance of Sylvia's room with Jake and Matt.

Sylvia sits upright in her recliner, eyes wide open and staring at nothing. A fork is clutched in her left hand, a steak knife in her right. In front of her is a TV tray, laid out with a bright yellow mat, a plate, glass, and a small vase of fresh flowers. She looks like a posed figure in a wax museum.

"Have you taken photos?" Jake barks.

"Not my area of expertise," Matt replies. "I was mostly busy guarding the door. Nobody has been in this room, to my knowledge, other than Jill."

"Who found the body," I say, uneasily.

"Who found the body," Matt confirms. "Apparently, she came to see if Sylvia had taken her meds and found her in this condition. Jill claims not to have entered the room and that she called 911 immediately before coming to find me in the kitchen."

"What time?" I ask, before Jake can do so. "Also, where is Karin?"

"I left her in the kitchen."

All three of us exchange glances, and Matt adds, "I have watched her every minute up until now. I had to take a pee break but did so when she was taking her own lunch break and was out of the kitchen. Also, I installed a camera and I have checked the footage. She did not enter the kitchen while I was out. So, I can't see when she'd have an opportunity to poison food. Plus, she'd have to be very specific to target only one resident and leave the others untouched."

"Supposing they are untouched," Jake says, seriously. "What if it is poison and there's some sort of delayed reaction?"

"That's a terrifying idea," Matt responds. "No new word from the tox lab?"

"They're still checking." This is a new voice, Mac's, and I slip into the room and slide along the wall to make room for him in the doorway.

"What in the fiery inferno is this now?" he asks, obviously not expecting an answer. "And who all has been in this room?"

"Nobody that we know. Jill discovered the body but says she didn't go in."

"That one does get around, doesn't she?" he says. "Stand out of the way so I can get some pictures."

"Full rigor," Mac says, a few minutes later as he examines the body. "Been dead six to twelve hours, probably."

Jake steps out of the room and I hear him on the radio, calling for backup.

"We're securing the Manor," he says, when he returns. "Nobody in, nobody out, except for law enforcement. Maureen, track down Ellen and keep Jill contained until I can interview her. Matt, keep an eye on Karin. And when Sophronia shows up—"

"What about me?" Sophie pops into the room like a genie who has been summoned, taking in the scene with a face full of dark foreboding.

"I was going to say turn her back at the door," Jake says. "Being as she's not law enforcement and this is a coroner's case."

"I'm here already," she says, unnecessarily, approaching the body with footsteps slow and soft, as if she fears she'll disturb its rest and send it into zombie mode.

"Don't you touch my body," Mac barks, but her hand is already on the dead woman's forehead.

"Stop calling her a body. She's still Sylvia. I think." Those last two words do not inspire confidence.

"Same as Ida Mae?" I ask.

Sophie nods. "It's like. . .an echo of her soul. But it's so faint, I can't get a feel for it."

I have more questions for her, but it might be better if Jake doesn't hear them right now. Besides, the little dot on my Ellen App indicates that she is now in the library, and I really need to check on her and on Gee and Val. "Come on, Sophie, you're with me."

She startles, then comes back as if from very far away, her eyes dreamy and half-focused. She tosses her hair and responds, "Fine. Mac is going to kick me out of here anyway."

"Damn right I am," Mac says. "We need a forensics team to clear this scene."

Jake looks from me to Sophie and back again. "Why do I have the feeling there's something you're not telling me?"

"Because there's something we're not telling you. Do your lawman thing, then come find me and I'll fill you in." Before he can push it, I grab Sophie's arm and tug her out into the hall. "Come on. Let's go."

As soon as we're out of ear shot, I ask, "What are you not telling me?"

"Nothing you don't already know."

"Anything new with that. . .thing. . .that came out of the urn?"

She shudders. The hair on the back of my neck stands up and prickles run down my spine. It takes an awful lot to make Sophie shudder.

"It's contained. For now. I think."

"You sure?"

"No, I'm not sure. What do you want from me?" she demands. "It's not like there's a self-help book out there, *Ghost Spiders for Dummies* or whatever. I've never even dreamed a thing like that might exist."

"Listen, Soph. I know you've got a lot to handle, and I don't know another teenager that would be able to take in everything you've had thrown at you in the last few weeks."

"I'm the only teenager you know," she snarks. "Admit it."

"Fine. You're right. I don't know another *person* who would have been able to take in everything you've had thrown at you in the last few weeks and cope with it as well as you have."

"Maybe I'm not actually coping," she says.

I stop walking, grab her arm, and make her look at me. "You are walking, talking, at least reasonably sane, and haven't sucked the soul out of anybody recently. Me, for example. Right now, while I'm annoying the hell out of you."

Her eyes flare with that weird glow and I know I've guessed right about that particular temptation. I let go of her arm and start walking again. "Maybe you can't figure out this particular problem. But if anybody can, it's you."

She falls into step beside me, and just before we reach the library door, she mutters, so low I barely catch the words, "Thanks for the vote of confidence. I guess."

CHAPTER FIFTEEN

Ellen is in the library, exactly as my tracker app indicates. Gee and Val are with her. All three sit so still and silent, they might as well be statues. Their eyes are rolled upward, apparently focused on the ceiling. I check to make sure that they are breathing and not the latest murder victims.

I shiver as the unmistakable chill in the air finds its way through my clothing and into my bones.

"Just the library ghost," Sophie says. "Nothing to worry about. She's as old as the hills and completely harmless."

Our voices snap the others out of their trance. Ellen looks vaguely interested and a little quizzical. Val smiles, calmly, as if we've found her supervising Gee's homework. Gee bounces in her chair, her face brimming with excitement. "I can see her!" she squeals. "This is so cool. I can now truthfully say that I've seen a ghost. Which is, like, the most awesome thing ever. You can see her too, right, Maureen?"

"Nope. Can't see her, don't want to see her." But for the first time ever, I actually feel like I've been left off the guest list for a party that I kind of want to go to. Apparently, even Ellen can see the damn thing. Which is interesting information to store away for later.

Sophie slides into the seat beside Gee. "What's up? Medium lessons? Also, is she talking to you guys or just floating around looking annoyed because we're disturbing her space?"

"Her name is Veronica," Gee announces. "But she hasn't told us anything else yet."

"Is this really a good idea?" I ask Val. "Encouraging Gee like this, I mean."

"When the student is ready." She smiles at me.

"The teacher will come," I finish, with a sigh.

"Wish I had somebody to teach me about all the soul stuff," Sophie says. "Gee's lucky she's got Val."

"Has Ellen been with you the whole time?" I ask, skipping directly to the most salient point. Everything else can wait.

"Yep. We came in here so I could work on homework. And then Veronica floated in."

Val nods assent.

"All right. Well." I clear my throat. "There's been another. . .incident."

"A murder, you mean," Sophie says. When I glare at her, she adds, "What? Don't try and sugarcoat things for Gee. She's too smart for that."

I clear my throat. "All right. There's been another murder."

"For real?" Gee's eyes are wide with fascination and excitement, and completely devoid of the fear that ought to be there. Val looks worried. She lays her hand on my wrist and says, earnestly, "*Charlotte's Web.*"

"You keep saying that. I get that it must be important, but I'm missing the connection, other than Charlotte was a spider and wrote messages in her web to save Wilbur. What does that have to do with anything?"

Val slaps both hands on the table in frustration. "What a tangled web we weave. Danger, Will Robinson."

"I know that first one!" Sophie interjects. "When first we practice to deceive."

"Messages and lies and danger," I say. "We've already figured that much out. Listen. It's not safe for you to be here, Gee, not to mention that you did not stay in my room like I so very clearly told you to. If you really don't have anywhere else to go, we need to call social services for an emergency placement."

"Oh, my God. You wouldn't!" Gee exclaims.

"Et tu Brute?" Val asks.

"That is, like, the worst idea ever," Sophie chimes in. "I can't believe those words just crossed your lips."

Even Ellen glares at me.

"Listen. People. I should have done this immediately after Ida Mae was killed. Now two residents have been murdered. There's a very nasty spider thing that is not securely contained. I can't trust Gee to stay where I put her, and whatever the rest of you may believe, she is a *child*."

"Like foster care wouldn't be danger?" Gee wails. "Haven't you heard the stories? Kids beaten, starved, shoved in cages. . ."

"Nobody's going to put you in a cage. Except maybe me. You've been watching too much *Law and Order*," I object, but there is a knot of uneasiness in my stomach. Foster care is not something I'd wish on any kid, even temporarily. "Are you sure we can't get in touch with your parents?"

"They're on a cruise," she says. "You can try to call, for all the good it will do you."

"Number."

She gives it to me. I dial, and after a couple of rings a woman answers, a clamor of voices and Caribbean music loud in the background.

"Hi, is this the mother of Guinevere?"

"Depends who is asking." The words are slurred, and a trill of laughter follows.

"This is Maureen Keslyn. I run Shadow Valley Manor. Your daughter is here with one of my residents."

"That's right. Staying with Val."

"*Was* staying with Val," I say. "We've had a murder here. It's not safe for your daughter and we need another place for her to stay."

"Oh, my God," the voice squawks. "Val was murdered? Ben, Val was murdered."

A male voice comes on the phone. "Well, that's a pickle," he says. "Is there another resident there that would keep an eye on her?"

"No, there is not! First of all, the Manor is not your babysitting service. And even if it were, we may have a serial killer on the loose and it's not safe for your child to stay here."

"Probably natural causes," Gee's father says.

"Pardon me?"

"Your resident. Natural causes. They're all old, right? Old people die."

"This was not natural causes. Definitely murder. Possibly a serial killer, as I said."

A surge of laughter and a shout almost deafen me and I move the phone away from my ear. "Sorry," the woman's voice comes back on. "We're at a bar and there's a shot challenge going on. What were you saying?"

I shout into the phone. "There's a serial killer at work in the Manor and Guinevere needs another place to stay."

"Oh, good," Gee's mother says brightly. "If it's a serial killer, Gee's safe, then, right? Those creepos always have a type, which is what? Old women?"

Gee, who I know can hear every word of this conversation, has begun kicking the leg of her chair, a rhythmic thudding in a different time signature than the music blaring in the background of the phone call.

"She can't stay here," I enunciate. "We're locking down the Manor."

"Well, just send her home, then. She is very self-sufficient. Could you maybe just lend her a little grocery money?"

"Don't you think she's a little young for that?" A burst of laughter covers the response. "You need to come home," I shout.

"I'm afraid that's impossible. We're in Barbados. Won't be home until next week. Oh, battery is dying. . ." The line goes dead, either because the phone actually died or because the woman hung up on me.

"Told you," Gee says. There's an uncharacteristic darkness in her eyes and her shoulders are slumped.

"You can stay with a friend, then. Give me a name."

"Don't have any," Gee says.

"Then I have to call social services."

Sophie takes the phone from my hand before I can search out the number. "Think, Maureen," she says. "That's a terrible idea."

"I'll run away," Gee says.

"Give me back my phone."

"You know she will." Sophie holds the phone behind her back. "And once she's in the system, she's there for a long time."

"Good. Maybe her parents will be forced to behave."

"Not likely," Sophie snorts. "But it's not like they beat her or whatever. I grew up with Lysander. It wasn't great, but at least he didn't get in the way of me being. . .whatever it is I am. You want to subject Gee to all of the counseling and brainwashing that's going to come at her when they find out what she can see and do?"

Val nods, vigorously, and wraps both arms around Gee. All three of them stare at me defiantly. "She's safer here," Sophie continues, seeing the crack in my resolve and pressing her advantage. "Besides, what makes you think that spider thing couldn't follow her? And then she'd be on her own with nobody to protect her."

Gee peels herself away from Val, runs over to me, and flings both arms around my waist. Tipping her head back, she looks up at me and says, "Please. Don't do this to me. Please. I'll be so good. I swear."

I've never once in my life been hugged by a child. It's very disconcerting and suddenly difficult to think clearly. I clear my throat. "I don't think you're capable of staying out of trouble for five minutes."

"Val needs me!" she says. "What if something came for her? She couldn't even ask for help."

Val nods.

"I'll stay with both of them as much as I can," Sophie pleads. "Don't do this, Maureen."

"Oh, all right. You can stay. For now. But take one more step out of line and—"

"Yay! You're the best!" Gee squeezes me even tighter around the middle and presses her face against my chest. I find myself patting her back, and there's an unfamiliar warmth in the vicinity of my heart. I clear my throat and detach myself.

"Go back to Val's room and stay there. Don't open the door, unless it's Matt or the sheriff. Or me. Take Ellen with you and watch her. She might be dangerous. Understood?"

Gee salutes. "Aye, aye, Captain."

"Sophie, can you walk them back and make sure they lock the door?"

"Aye, aye, Captain."

"You are all incorrigible."

Even though I know better, I leave them all there and go in search of a deputy to drive me back into town to pick up my car.

CHAPTER SIXTEEN

Dinner is loud and more than usually chaotic. The residents are used to buffet-style self-service, but Karin has insisted that she and Matt stand behind the steam table and dish up all the plates. The residents are not exactly speedy, and a lot of them use walkers or canes, so the line seems to be barely moving. If Karin were going to drop poison into somebody's food, this would be the time, and between keeping an eye on her hands and maintaining a facade of charm in the face of her constant hostility, Matt wants nothing more than to retreat to his room and seek oblivion with a bottle of whiskey.

The line of hungry residents complains at top volume about the delay, and about the lockdown, even though they've all been ruled out as potential suspects and given the opportunity to vacate the premises. Jake has lectured them about safety. Maureen has offered to arrange rides to the airport or to one of Shadow Valley's three motels. Nobody wanted to leave. The truth is, they are enjoying the excitement. They perked up like this a couple of weeks ago, when the spirit storm happened—and he guesses they are animated and excited by the promise of something other than the same old boring routine.

"Is it safe to eat?" Dan asks, holding out his plate and waiting for Matt to load him up with roast beef and mashed potatoes. "Rumor is that the others have been poisoned."

"We're confident the food was not poisoned," Matt says, in a carrying voice, even though he has his lingering suspicions.

"How confident?" Julia calls out, from where her wheelchair is parked at the table. She gestures at Sophie and Gee, sitting in the chairs once occupied by Sylvia and Ida Mae. "A lot of empty chairs, all from the same table."

Chuck, who was first in line and has almost emptied his plate, rubs his pronounced belly and booms, "Anybody doesn't want their share, pass it over. Worse ways to die than eating."

Karin walks over just then with a plate for Julia, and he pats her lower back, dangerously close to her butt. As his wandering hand slides downward, Karin whirls around to face him. "Keep your hands to yourself, you ridiculous buffoon!" She hurls the plate onto the floor at her feet, sending potatoes and gravy and shards of stoneware flying everywhere. "You dare to suggest I would serve spoiled food? Or poison residents on purpose?"

"Oh, for God's sake," Ginny says, her voice even more dignified and cultured than usual. "Must we be subjected to such displays by the help?"

"I'll need a new plate." Julia wrinkles her nose and wheels her chair back a little, peering down at the globules of potatoes and gravy on her shoes.

"The help?" Karin bellows. "Did she refer to me as *the help?*" Even Ginny flinches and quails before her wrath. "I am a chef. I am a graduate of the Culinary Institute of America. I have worked in five-star restaurants. Now here I am, creating slop for the likes of you, and *you dare*—you dare to dismiss me, to accuse me, like so? It is. . .it is. . ."

Her face crumples and she bursts into a loud, keening wail. The residents hold their collective breath, eyes wide. They lean forward as a single unit, eyes glued to the entertainment unfolding in their midst.

Matt sees an opportunity. An emotional breakdown is always a doorway for confidences. He lays a comforting hand on Karin's quaking shoulder. "Always with the unappreciative idiots," he murmurs into her ear. "That's the way of it, isn't it?"

He tenses as she turns toward him, prepared for anything from a fist to a knife. Instead, she tries to bury her face in his shoulder. She's as tall as he is, so her tear wet face presses, instead, against his neck and his ear. Although he'd honestly much rather engage in a knife fight, he puts his arm around her shoulders and guides her toward the doorway, the residents watching in fascinated horror. He glances back over his shoulder at Maureen, but she's already stepped behind the table and has taken over serving out the food. Sophronia is cleaning up the mess on the floor.

"Show is over, people. Watch where you walk," Sophie says.

"All I ever wanted to do was be a chef," Karin sobs. Matt steers her past the kitchen, which is equipped with too many potential weapons. Knives. Frying pans. Rolling pin. Meat tenderizer.

He thinks he could take Karin in a fight but his job is to get information from her, not bludgeon her into unconsciousness.

"Everything was against me realizing my dream from the beginning," Karin sobs. "My parents think McDonalds is fine dining. They think pâté is something for cats."

"There, there," Matt says. Her guides her into the office and tries to seat her in one of the chairs. She's too distraught to be seated and paces the room instead.

"Look at me!" she proclaims, thumping her chest with both hands. "Do I look like a chef? I am cursed to be in this body."

"It doesn't matter how you look, if you have the skills," Matt tries.

Karin laughs, wildly, tears streaming down her face.

"You think? But of course you do. You are handsome and charming. Everyone wants a handsome, charming chef. Me? 'Go work in a carnival, Karin. Roast an ox. You will make a million.' This was said to me!" Another explosion of wild weeping follows. She tears at her hair with both hands, the coiled braid unwinding like a snake over her shoulders.

Matt glances up to see Sophronia standing in the doorway, looking young and beautiful and vulnerable, if he discounts the death blazing in her eyes. Surely, she'll understand what he's doing, that it's all work. There's not time to worry about her and her feelings, and he turns his attention back to Karin.

"You're the graduate of an acclaimed chef academy. Surely, there are restaurants who would look past your appearance. Unless. . ." He lets his voice drift into silence.

"Unless what?" she shrieks. "What are you suggesting?"

He shrugs. "Perhaps displays like this have contributed to your difficulty?"

"This?" She laughs, wildly. "Have you seen a true master chef in the kitchen? No, of course not; you are nothing but a cook. They rage! They proclaim their unreasonable demands. And it's all 'Yes, chef. No, chef. Of course, chef.' But not for me!"

Matt has, in fact, observed the reign of terror of an egotistical chef in the kitchen, but he doesn't mention that. He takes a step closer to Karin, gazing deeply into her eyes, keeping his hand close to the sheathed knife hanging from his belt. "Perhaps there's something else. Something unfair. Uncontrollable. An unfortunate condition brought on by extreme emotion."

Karin shakes her head and backs away. Her eyes are locked on his, desperate, and he knows his guess is right. Just a little more pressure, and she'll break.

"It's happened more than once, hasn't it? Your employers don't talk about it, because they don't want to believe it. Instead, they come up with other stories about why they've had to let you go."

"It's not fair!" she cries. "I don't know why it happens. Or how. It just—"

"When was the first time?" Matt asks, his voice syrupy with sympathy. He feels a twist of guilt at playing her. Life can't have been easy for her. But it's his job to find out what she is.

"On my thirteenth birthday. In the locker room at school. I was changing into gym clothes, and a group of girls made fun of my body. I should go to the boys' room, they said. Too much muscle. Too tall. No breasts. I screamed at them. I wanted to hurt them. I—"

"Tore out their throats?" Matt pushes. "Mauled them beyond repair?"

Karin shudders. "I wanted to."

"Poor baby," Sophronia says, lounging into the office and leaning against Maureen's desk. "Like you're the only misfit. You want to know what the girls said about me?"

Rage flashes in Karin's eyes. "You couldn't begin to know. Look at you. Beautiful. The men desire you. You think I don't see the way this one looks at you?" She glares at Matt.

"But the boys didn't desire *you*, did they, Karin?" he goads. "They made fun of you. The girls taunted you. You wanted to tear them apart, so you became a monster so you could. And it happens still, whenever you're jealous. And nobody wants a monster in the kitchen."

Karin shrieks and lunges toward him. He's ready. Knees bent, knife out, braced to meet an onslaught that never comes. An inhuman sound strangles in her throat. Her body twists and warps and shifts. Black feathers sprout on her cheeks and arms, and then the top of her head, replacing the yellow hair. Her nose becomes a beak. Her hands disappear and her arms morph into wings.

She shrinks, growing smaller and smaller, until he sees nothing but empty clothing, thrashing about on the office floor.

Matt stands frozen in his fighting stance as a raven struggles free from the mound of clothing. It croaks, sadly, and half-hops, half-flutters up onto Maureen's desk.

"Oh, shit," Sophronia says. Her eyes are wide with horror and pity. "I'm sorry," she whispers, maybe to him but he thinks to the raven, and then she glides away. He wants to follow her, to hold her and comfort her and—yes, he'll admit that he desperately wants to kiss her.

If he didn't have a job to do, maybe he would run after her, even though she's only eighteen and he knows it's a bad idea. But responsibility comes first. He calls Maureen on the radio. "In the office. I think you need to see this."

"On my way."

When she arrives a few minutes later, Matt watches her calmly take in the large raven perched on the back of her chair. The heap of clothing on the floor. Her eyebrows go up, but other than that, she shows no surprise and says, directly to the raven, "At least you aren't a chicken."

The raven glares at her and *kronk*s in a way that sounds like avian profanity.

"I was expecting a wolf," Matt says. "The whole Viking thing, you know? Although I couldn't see the link to the murders. Now I guess she's in the clear."

"Not at all," Maureen says. "More of a suspect now than ever." The raven flaps its wings, lifts into the air, and makes a dive at her head. She ducks and draws her revolver.

Matt remembers his glimpse of Maureen dead, the black bird perched on her chest. An icy chill runs down his spine. "Karin," he shouts. "Here."

Unthinking, he holds out a hand. With a whirring of wings, she lands on his arm, her claws digging through the fabric of his sleeve into his flesh.

"Care to explain why she's still a suspect?" he asks.

"The question has always been who could get in and out through that open window."

Understanding dawns. "Fly in, shift back to human, inject the victim with some arcane poison, or put it in her food, position her when she's dead, and then shift and fly back out the window. If she has that kind of control."

The raven shuffles sideways on his forearm, radiating annoyance.

"Exactly," Maureen confirms. "Karin is certainly strong enough to subdue an elderly woman and to drag a body up on the table. And she had access to the food."

The raven squawks angrily.

"What now?" Matt asks.

"Can we talk. . . privately?"

Maureen bends over and picks up Karin's apron from the floor. Before either he or Karin can react, she throws it over the bird and grabs her, ignoring the angry squawking. Crossing the room, she nods at the door to the storage closet. "Open that, would you, Matt? Pardon us for the rudeness, Karin, but we'll need to confine you for a moment." She deposits the struggling raven in the closet and slams the door, then drags Matt out of the office and into the hallway.

"You'll have to keep her with you. Twenty-four-seven."

"Maureen. I can't take her into the kitchen. Health and sanitary reasons aside, she might be our poisoner."

"She'll probably shift back in the morning. If she doesn't, fix her a perch, keep her out of the food. She can't hurt anybody in raven form, and the health department won't know unless we tell them."

Matt wipes perspiration off his face with the back of his arm. "And now?" he asks.

"Take her to your room."

Matt feels the heat rising to his face. "What if she. . .shifts in the night?" He pictures Karin in his room, naked, and adds, his voice rising, "Hell, no. That's not happening."

"You're man enough to handle her," Maureen says, with the

sort of grin that makes him think maybe death by raven would be fitting for her.

"Remember she's still got ears and might remember everything when she shifts back. Watch her closely. Be careful what you say in front of her and let me know when she shifts."

"Or we could just kill her now," he says. "While she's a raven."

"That thought is beneath you," Maureen says in a glacial tone. "If she needs killing, you'll do it like a man—while she's human. Not while she's defenseless."

She's right. Probably. He hasn't told her about his vision, because he doesn't trust it. When he was young and stupid, he used to try to change what he saw in his visions, only to have his own actions cause the disaster. It's best to stay alert, watch and be ready, and act when the time comes.

When he opens the closet door to let Karin out, she flaps up onto his shoulder and pecks him, sharply, on the cheek.

"Ow!" His hand goes to his face. "You drew blood, you unnatural beast. I'm not the one who locked you up."

She *kronk*s, thoughtfully this time, and he wonders if she's plotting her revenge.

CHAPTER SEVENTEEN

Thanks to Matt's avian complication, I get stuck with kitchen cleanup, but it's not time wasted. I use the time spent washing dishes, wiping down tables, and sweeping the floor to think things over. There are a number of clues to follow up and questions to be answered, but I have two pressing concerns that need to be dealt with immediately: Sophie and Jill.

Sophie went after Matt and Karin when they left the dining room, but she wasn't in the office when I got there. She's not answering my texts. Neither is Jill, who didn't come down to dinner. Sophie frequently chooses not to respond to texts, so her behavior isn't alarming. Jill, on the other hand, has never skipped dinner, and I'm certain that she's up to something.

When I'm done with my chores, I hold out my hand to Ellen, who has waited patiently and quietly so long as I kept her supplied with tea. "Let's go find Jill, shall we?"

She comes with me willingly, no singing or coaxing required.

Jill doesn't respond to my knock, so I pick the lock with my new kit and let myself and Ellen in.

"Another one?" Jill slurs. She's sprawled on her sofa with a bottle in one hand, the back of the other resting on her forehead in a dramatic gesture of despair. Her hair straggles down from her updo, her makeup is smeared, her clothing wrinkled.

"Another what?" I ask.

"Body. Murder."

"Were you expecting another one?"

"Why else are you here?" Her face crumples and her voice wavers. "What is with this place, Maureen? Why did Phil buy it? What did he even want with it?"

"The question is, what do you want with it?" I hurl back, fighting off an attack of sympathy. I know full well she's an actress. And she's drunk. I cross the room and take the bottle from her hand, taking a healthy swallow before pouring the rest down the sink.

"Because it was his," she says, which is what she's insisted all along and what I've never believed.

"What really happened in Sylvia's room?" I ask.

Jill tries to glare, but her eyes won't focus. "You have no heart. I have no idea what my father saw in you."

"I believe he was attracted to my heartlessness. Now. What time did you discover the body?" A vision of Sophie's disapproving face flickers through my mind and I rephrase. "Sylvia. What time did you discover Sylvia? And you can drop the accent. I already know it isn't real."

She sighs. "The sheriff already asked me that. He grilled me, Maureen. Like a common criminal. Like a *suspect*."

"You *are* a suspect. Please be so good as to answer this for me. It's important."

"Sometime after lunch. Twelve thirty, maybe? She didn't come down to eat. I am responsible, doing Cathy's job, yes? So, I went to check on her and found. . ." She shudders. "So, is there? Another body?"

It occurs to me that her state of intoxication is conducive to interrogation, but only if she doesn't actually pass out. I shift my strategy. "No, there is not another body. I'm here because I actually need your help."

She blinks up at me. "I'm already helping."

"You need coffee for this. Come with me."

Slowly, she wobbles up onto her feet, grabbing my shoulder to keep her balance. It takes a ridiculous amount of time to herd both her and Ellen out into the hall and then into my suite. Jill immediately stumbles over to my favorite chair and flops bonelessly into it.

"What time is it?" she asks.

"Just past eight. You missed dinner."

"Wasn't hungry. Not after seeing that. . ." She squeezes out a few tears, the prologue to another bout of dramatic sobbing, then curses instead, as Anubis leaps into her lap and begins kneading, claws digging through her skirt.

Ellen cruises around the perimeter of the suite while I turn the lights on in the kitchenette and start the coffeepot.

"Can you put a splash of scotch in that?" Jill asks.

"I think you've had enough. Besides, last time you got into my scotch, you vomited all over my floor. And I need you sober."

Ellen drifts over to peer at the filling coffeepot. "Tea?" she inquires.

"You are going to float away on all that tea. But okay. Whatever you want."

I put the kettle on and turn just in time to see her walk across the room, put her hands against the wall, and walk right through it.

"Holy mother of God," Jill exclaims, crossing herself and entirely forgetting that she's supposed to swear in French. "I'm drunker than I thought."

My first reaction is a breath of relief. At least Ellen didn't shift into a spider and scuttle through the crack underneath the door. But she could still be the killer, and she could be anywhere, doing anything, right this minute.

By the time I undo all of my locks and look out into the hall, Ellen is nowhere to be seen.

"Am I dreaming or hallucinating?" Jill leans against the door-jamb, staring blearily one way and then the other.

"Unfortunately, neither." I retrace my steps for my phone and check the tracking app. "She's in your suite."

"But my door is locked."

"Yeah, doors and walls don't seem to be much of a barrier. Now she's headed downstairs."

There's a secret staircase in Jill's suite, identical to the one in mine except for one crucial difference: it opens into a public access basement that houses storage lockers and the water heater. I happen to know, however, that in the floor of the public area, there is a hidden trapdoor that leads down into a warren of subterranean passageways. If Ellen finds that, she could go anywhere.

"We must stop her." Jill rises to her feet, flinging her arms out in a stage-appropriate gesture, then loses her balance and falls back into the chair. "The floor keeps moving," she complains.

"Give me your key."

I fidget as she fumbles in her pocket, finally coming up with the key. Then I leave her there, moving as fast as my leg will let me, harboring images of Ellen sneaking up on ordinary citizens in Shadow Valley and smacking them over the head or poisoning them with some obscure substance. But when I reach the base-ment, she's just standing still, looking lost and confused, as if she has no idea how she got there.

"Hey, you," I say, in my most coaxing voice. "Come back upstairs and let's get you that cup of tea." I hold out my hand.

"Door," she says. "Must find the door."

"There's no door here. Come on. Let's have tea." I edge closer to her, not wanting to spook her with sudden movements.

She sighs. "I like tea."

"I know you do. Come on, now."

Ellen takes my hand. The two of us creak up the stairs, one slow step at a time. I lead her out of Jill's suite and back into mine.

Five minutes later, the three of us resemble a reenactment of Alice's mad tea party. Jill huddles in my chair, clutching a mug of coffee as if it's a lifeline to reality. Ellen, settled on the couch, is humming snatches of "Yellow Submarine." Anubis leaps up beside her and insinuates himself into her lap.

"So, that really happened, then." Jill waves at the wall and then at Ellen. "Are you sure I can't have another drink?"

I lean forward, dropping my voice to a confidential tone that is almost a whisper. "Can I trust you?"

"I am the soul of discretion."

I give her a withering look. "See, that's exactly the sort of thing that is a problem. You expect me to believe you."

"I'm working for no one. On the soul of my father, I swear it. We both loved him, you and I. This is a sacred oath. He would wish for there to be peace between us, would he not?"

It's a touching little speech, complete with an appropriate quaver in her voice and moisture in her eyes, but I'm still not buying. She might be drunk, but she's still a liar. Even if she's not working for the Unit, she's already proven that she can't keep her mouth shut.

"Not sure whether you loved or hated your father," I say. "And his soul has gone beyond the realm of caring what we are to each other."

"How shall I swear, then?" She flings her hands outward. One of them is still holding her mug, and a wave of coffee sprays out onto the sofa and the floor. "How will I ever persuade you that I mean no harm?"

"Don't even bother to try. You've tried to kill me. You've tried to take over my Manor."

She opens her mouth but I keep talking before she can get any words out. "It doesn't matter. I'll admit that I need you enough that I'll have to trust you even though it's beyond all the pales of reason. I need you to have a look at Ellen's DNA. You can do that, right, with all the fancy equipment you now have down in my lab?"

"I could. Of course. It is my specialty," she says, with great dignity.

Despite the fact that she's thoroughly inebriated, her eyes turn toward Ellen with a focused enthusiasm that is eerily similar to an expression I've seen plenty of times on her father's face. That look means that all fires of curiosity and purpose have been ignited, and that no loyalty or emotion will stand in her way.

I lean forward. "First, tell me what Charlie told you when he called about Ellen."

"Charlie?" She tries to sound innocent, but her eyes waver and fall when I stare her down.

"Jill. I know you're connected to the Unit somehow. What did he tell you, what did he promise you?"

She shakes her head and lays a finger over her lips. "It's a secret."

"You want to be next?" I ask. "Found lying on your table in your nightdress? You want Matt and Jake and the others to see you like that?"

"Stop!" She tries to cover her ears but can't figure out what to do about the mug. "It won't happen to me. He said—"

"What? What did he say?"

"He talked about my work. He knew of all of the experiments, about the Genesis project, about what I am qualified to do but never have the opportunity—"

"And he promised you Ellen as a research subject."

Jill says nothing, but her expression tells me everything.

"Well?" I persist.

"Well, what?"

"What have you found out, then?"

Again, she presses a finger to her lips, then mimes locking them and throwing away a key.

"Look, it's no big secret, is it? I already know there's been some kind of genetic meddling. You might as well tell me what you've been able to discover. I know you've already analyzed her DNA. How could you resist? All that fabulous equipment. Your intelligence and skill. And opportunity. You had access to her and the lab while I was in jail. Tell me what you know."

She can't help herself, not when it comes to her passion. "Well, of course I can't explain it to you, really. You wouldn't understand anything about DNA and what it does."

"I know it contains the genetic blueprint for all that we physically are. I know that genes can be turned on and off. That they can be spliced and mutated. Skip the technical language and just give me the general gist of the thing."

"I'm not done analyzing it yet," she says. "But there has been what you would call splicing, or grafting, maybe. She looks so normal, but some of her DNA isn't human."

"Normal except that walking-through-walls bit. What kind of DNA is it?"

"I don't know. I've compared it with the DNA profiles that I have in my system—several kinds of shifters, mermaid, soul stealer, vampire. It doesn't match any of them."

"Anything about it that explains her walking through walls?"

"I don't know what sort of creature has that ability. But it makes a sort of sense."

"How?"

"Her DNA is. . .unstable. I took a second sample after the first one, because it was so unusual. And the second one was different from the first."

"Different how? I mean, isn't DNA constant?"

"Normally."

"What does this even mean? Can you stop being cryptic and talk like a human?"

She shrugs. "Nothing was normal about her DNA to start with. So, maybe what was done is coming undone? I need much more time to study this."

"Listen, there's another thing. Ellen was on an experimental medication before she was arrested. She's been off it ever since. Could that cause some sort of unraveling?"

"It's possible. Maybe some sort of stabilizer. If I had access to the medication, I could run a chemical analysis and tell you more."

"Well, you're in luck." I dig the pill bottle out of my pocket.

Ellen reaches for it. "Medicine," she says.

"Not now," I tell her, passing the bottle to Jill.

"Sertraline?" she asks. "An antidepressant."

"Which she is not prescribed. And which it isn't."

Jill opens the bottle and taps a pill out into her hand, holding it up to the light. "So very interesting," she murmurs.

"According to the local pharmacist, it's an unknown imprint. He assumes this is an experimental drug of some kind. That she's part of a research study."

I watch Jill for any hint that she knows about the research study or recognizes the imprint, but she's focused on the pill as if genuinely curious.

"Let us see what is in it. That will tell us much." She meets my eyes and suddenly remembers that we're not exactly friendly colleagues. "If I may? I will need to go to the lab."

I hesitate, not about the lab but because of the spider thing that must still be lurking downstairs. Much as it would be convenient and so much easier if Jill were to die suddenly and inexplicably, she's still a human being. Besides, I need her. I barely restrain a shudder, not so much at the memory of the ghost spider as at the scurrying of all of the smaller spiders who had gathered to adore it. How much danger is Jill in if I let her go down to the lab alone?

"You don't trust me!" she pouts, wrongly interpreting my silence.

"I don't," I agree, "but that's not the problem. There may be an unruly ghost down there."

Jill tosses her head disdainfully. "Pfft. I am not afraid of ghosts. If you are, then age has weakened you."

I should tell her the exact nature of said ghost and about the spiders, but her comment and the way she is looking at me dispel all of my guilt about putting her at risk.

"Maybe morning would be better," I suggest.

"In the morning, I have Cathy's work to do," she says with great dignity. "Tonight, I shall do my own work."

She can walk an almost straight line by now. The salt in front of the closet door doesn't even slow her down, and she's already descending the stairs before guilt catches up with me and I call her back. "Here. Take this. In case."

I hold out the salt sprayer.

"So very *Ghostbusters*," she sniffs.

"Your father made it. For self-protection. Take it."

"Oh, very well." She climbs back up and takes it from me.

I watch her go with an uneasiness in my gut that I usually pay attention to. This time, I choose to ignore it. She's an adult and she's been warned. Sort of. And I'm pretty sure she's a Unit agent. She can take care of herself.

CHAPTER EIGHTEEN

Ellen is yawning and I'll admit that I've begun entertaining fantasies about my own bed, but I need to check in with my team before I sleep. I call Matt, who informs me that Karin is still a raven and that he is not, under any circumstances, taking her to his bedroom. He'll be camping out in the game room, thank you very much. No, he has not seen Sophie since she witnessed Karin's transformation.

I call Sophie again, and this time she answers. "Back off, Maureen. I've been doing research, which would go more smoothly if I wasn't interrupted every thirty seconds by somebody trying to call or text me. I am not ten and you are not my mother."

"You could just answer when I message you. We do have a murderer and a spider thing loose in the Manor."

"I'd noticed," she says, scathingly. "I'm now with Val and Gee. We are all alive and none of us is the murderer. If I need you, I'll call. Satisfied?"

"Was that so very difficult?" I ask.

She hangs up.

I call Jake next. He sounds about two steps away from death's door and is also irritable.

"Can it wait?" he asks.

"I was just checking on you."

"Well, I *was* sleeping, which was quite delightful. Do you mind if I do it again?"

I refrain from giving him the same spiel I gave Sophie and hang up. I ought to inform him about Karin turning into a raven, and that Gee is spending the night, and that Jill is looking into Ellen's DNA, but the man needs at least one night of solid sleep. I tuck Ellen into bed, making sure the new pressure-sensitive alarm I've installed on her mattress is working and will alert me if she gets out of bed, and take a tour of the Manor. All is quiet. Matt swears at me when I shine a flashlight into the game room. Karin's raven eyes reflect the light.

The only person I encounter is a deputy, not Garrity but an older woman, seasoned and on top of things, who will patrol the Manor throughout the night and watch for any sign of trouble.

There is nothing else that can be done before morning except check in with Jill. Ellen is definitely in her bed, asleep and snoring. I leave her there and make my way down to the lab. My footsteps quicken as I pass the doorway of the room where the spider seance happened. The door is closed and nothing moves. I aim my flashlight up at the ceiling and into dim corners but see no sign of spiders, large or small.

Jill is intently peering into a microscope and doesn't even hear me enter until I call her name. Then she swivels around, rotates her shoulders, and cracks her neck. "Perfect," she says. "I have results."

"Do tell."

"The chemical compounds are. . ." She spouts a long string of gibberish and smiles loftily at my blank expression. "Of course, you wouldn't know. The purpose of this drug, I would guess, is to turn certain genes on or off."

"A medication can do that?"

"There are several approved by the FDA. And many more under research. We are barred by people's *ethics* from making true progress."

I ignore the bitterness of her inflection on the word *ethics* and keep to the point. "This drug could be something that helps keep her altered DNA stable?"

"You could put it that way. I am unsure yet of anything. I must continue to study her DNA. About the pills—I think perhaps you should give them to her."

"But you're not completely sure what they are or what they do?"

Jill shrugs. "There is no certainty, not without talking to her research team."

"Can you? Do you have access to Charlie?" I almost hold my breath, hoping for an affirmative. I want very much to find a way to have words with the man.

But Jill shakes her head. "He said that he would contact me. Which he hasn't done."

"All right. Well. You're done for tonight."

"I am not done. There is so much more to learn and—"

"Tomorrow. Let's go."

"Oh, fine." She sighs heavily and turns away from her microscope. I suspect her capitulation has more to do with the beginnings of a hangover and a need to pee than anything else, but I'll take what I can get. I walk her back to her room, caught up in uncharacteristic indecision. Do I give Ellen the medication or not? Will it clear up her thought processes? And if it does, will it turn her into an unstoppable killing machine? What is Charlie's game, sending her to the Manor and telling Jill to do research? If the Unit is behind her genetic alteration and the research study with the medication, wouldn't he make sure she had a supply?

Something that has been nagging at me from my conversation with Ellen's husband floats to the surface. He and I need to talk again—another thing that will have to wait for morning. For now, I'm going to play a hunch. After Jill is safely behind her own door, I fill a glass with water and carry it and one of the pills to Ellen's bed.

"Wake up; I have your medicine," I say.

Her eyes flutter open. "Medicine," she says, sitting up and holding out her hand. She swallows the pill, then snuggles back into the blankets with a contented little sigh. I check to make sure all of my alarms are set, and crawl, at last, into my own bed.

Few things in my life have felt so good as stretching out my weary limbs on the beautifully soft mattress. Mind you, bare limbs against the coolness of clean sheets would have been better, but I remain fully dressed, just in case. Almost immediately, I drift off into well-earned slumber. I'm in the middle of a dream in which a congregation of ravens is feasting on an infestation of spiders, when a noise startles me wide awake.

I'm out of bed with my revolver in hand before I realize it's only my phone.

"You need to come," Sophie says, when I answer. "Library. Now."

She hangs up before I can ask questions. Sophie isn't one to cry wolf, so I check on Ellen, making sure that she is really in the bed. She is sound asleep, still snoring softly. I hate to leave her alone, but there's nothing for it. I slip into my shoes and out into the hallway, locking the door behind me, for all the good it will do.

The library is lit only by candlelight. Sophie stands just inside the door, watching silently. Gee and Val sit directly across from each other at the library table, their hands linked. Flames from seven thin white tapers illuminate their faces, three to their right, three to their left, one on the table between them. A scent of burning herbs and spices fills my nostrils. The temperature is glacial and I wish I'd thought to bring a jacket.

"Spirit of books and secrets, you who inhabit this space, we ask you to speak to us," Gee intones. "By the powers of darkness and light, I call you. Our ears are open. We have need of what knowledge you may impart."

A faint blue glow appears in the corner as Gee speaks, spreading into a vaguely human-shaped form. The temperature drops another degree and I clench my muscles tight to stop myself from shivering.

Val's body stiffens and jerks. And then she speaks, in a voice definitely not her own. "I like to be seen. I like to be heard. Ask me."

Gee, irrepressible as always, wriggles in her seat with excitement, "What can you tell us about the recent deaths?"

The blue light trembles, dissipating and coalescing, and the voice says, through Val, "I ask for your protection."

"But you're already dead!" Gee exclaims, not having been educated in seance etiquette. Even I know that spirits don't appreciate having their deadness pointed out to them.

This one takes no offense, although she's every bit as cryptic as the infernal things always are.

"Exactly," it says, through Val's lips. And then, "Ask."

"Right," Gee says, forgetting all about trying to sound mysterious and talking to the thing like it's totally normal to have this conversation. "Val said you probably couldn't volunteer information. What do you know about the murders?"

"Two have died. Two still live."

"Dang, this is harder than I thought." Gee chews on her lower lip. "Who killed them, then?"

"The Queen is hungry," the voice that is not Val's says, resonating annoyingly, as if the library is an echo chamber instead of a carpeted space with four walls of books.

"Can't you just give me, like, a real answer?" Gee complains.

"I answer as I can," the voice says. "Time is short. My edges grow thin. Ask."

The blue light is fading and flickering. It takes a lot of energy for a spirit to manifest and speak, and after this, it will likely be days before we could summon it again. I disapprove of this seance and would have stopped it if I could, but since it's already underway, I whisper, "Gee. Ask if there have been any clandestine meetings at night recently."

Gee's head jerks toward the sound of my voice and then turns back toward Val. "Have there been any nighttime meetings?"

The spirit sighs, and the response is barely above a whisper.

"Here they have gathered to feed the Queen. One naysayer, dead by denial. One holding back what is rightfully offered. One foolish, giving offense."

The last words are uttered so low, I step closer to hear them. The blue glow fades and goes out. Val's head falls forward on her chest. The candles sink low.

Gee lets go of Val's hands and opens her eyes, bouncing out of her seat and scratching her belly. "I've been itching since forever and didn't dare," she announces. And then: "She didn't tell us anything! I suck at this."

"You did great. Nobody can get details out of a ghost." Sophie puts her hands on Val's shoulders and whispers, "Come back to us, Val."

Val stirs. Her head comes up and her eyes flicker open.

"Sophie's right. Spirits never say anything straight out, Gee." I flip the light switch, blinking against the sudden brightness. "They can't ever just tell you what you need to know, and you can't trust what they do tell you."

"It's not their fault," Sophie says defensively. "They do the best they can."

Val opens her hands, turning them palms up, her face asking the questions she's unable to articulate. As the medium, I know she won't remember any of the words that came out of her mouth.

"We'll write it all down for you, Val," I say. "Right now, actually, before we forget. Soph?"

She nods, reaches for the notebook and pen lying ready on the table, and begins to write.

"We did get some useful information," she says. "At least three people have been meeting at night, probably right here in the library, since I've never seen this spirit anywhere else."

"I had my suspicions that Chuck and Sylvia and Ginny were out of bed and up to something the night Ida Mae was killed," I muse. "She said two dead, and two still live. I'm assuming the dead she referred to are Ida Mae and Sylvia. So, we know who the other two are."

"Also, who is the Queen?" Sophie asks. "And how are they feeding her?"

"*Charlotte's Web.*" Val's voice is dark with foreboding.

"Val, for the love of Thoth, can you find a way to explain that better?" Sophie snaps. "Charlotte was a nice spider. A self-sacrificing spider. She loved Wilbur."

"I'm so glad I haven't read this book," Gee says. "It sounds really stupid."

"What does the library ghost want protection from?" I ask. "Shouldn't she be beyond any harm?"

"Listen to them, the children of the night," Val says.

I stare at her, drawing blanks.

"*Dracula,*" Sophie says.

"Vampires? That doesn't fit."

Val slaps her palms on the table in frustration. "The river flows uphill."

"Anybody?" I ask.

Sophie shrugs. Gee says, "*Dracula* was cool."

Tears gather in Val's eyes. She looks exhausted. The woman is in her eighties. It's midnight, she's just served as conduit for a spirit, and now she can't communicate something that she knows.

"It's okay, Val," I say. "You need food and sleep. It's been a big night already. Gee, vampires are not cool. They are ugly and evil and they smell horrible. They definitely do not sparkle. Do you understand me? All vampires get staked on sight. Also, leave that ghost-spider thing alone."

"Whatever."

She doesn't look convinced, which worries me. She's exactly the sort of child who will have to experience everything herself rather than listen to those older and wiser. She reminds me rather too much of myself.

"Come on. Let's get Val back to bed. Gee, tomorrow, I am finding some place for you to be outside the Manor, even if it's the circus or wherever kids run away to. Do you understand?"

"We'll see," Gee says, as cryptic as if she's been taking lessons from the ghost. Which I guess she has. But she helps Val to her feet. Sophie gets on the other side, and the two of them support her out of the library and toward her room.

CHAPTER NINETEEN

Ellen is still asleep when I get back to the suite, but my planned night of blissful slumber is ruined. I keep jolting awake with a sense that I've missed something important. I replay Jill's findings, Charlie's meddling, Karin's shift to raven form, and my visit to Ellen's husband over and over in my head. By the time daylight breaks, I know I need to have another conversation with Dick, and this time I'm taking Ellen with me.

She's awake early, and I get us both dressed and off before breakfast. I have a sense that Dick is not an early riser and I want to catch him off guard. I watch Ellen carefully as I pull into the driveway, but she gives no sign that she's aware of her surroundings. Even when we walk up the sidewalk to the house, she trails along quietly, just as she does in the Manor.

I position her out of sight of the security camera, and she stays where I put her. When I ring the doorbell, there's an immediate explosion of dog barking but no human response. By the third time I push the button, the dog is in a frenzy. I can hear him dashing back and forth, claws clattering and scratching on the hardwood. Finally, a voice shouts, "Just shut up already, would you?" And then there's the sound of footsteps and the door swings open.

Dick is in a dressing gown and pajamas, his hair disordered. There are lines on his face from a CPAP machine. He's trying to maintain his well-bred persona, but the outrage of being dragged from his bed at this hour is clearly visible in both his expression and his tone.

"Do you have any idea of the time?"

"You don't mind if we come in, do you, Dick?" I ask, cheerfully. "Ellen and I have some questions for you."

He gapes as he finally notices her. "You can't bring her here."

"Do you have a restraining order?"

"No, but—"

"Well then. It's her house, too, you know."

The dog meanwhile dances around Ellen's legs, barking up a storm. "Lucy!" she crows, bending down and lifting the exuberant creature into her arms. The dog wiggles and squirms and tries to lick her whole face at once.

"She tried to kill me!" Dick protests.

"Did she?" I ask. "Are you absolutely sure about that?"

He glances desperately from me to Ellen and back again. Still holding the dog, she brushes past him into the house and I follow.

"She can't be here," Dick tries again, grabbing at my arm. "I didn't think I needed a restraining order. Because. . .because—"

"Because she was all safely locked up?" I wither him with a look that has warned off much braver men. "And yet here she is. Shall we sit? Did you want to make us some tea?"

"No, I don't want to make tea. I want to go back to bed. I'm going to call the police right now and—"

"You're not, though. You're going to tell us what really happened the night Ellen supposedly assaulted you." I flash my FBI badge at him, and the blood drains from his face.

Ellen has already settled into a chair with the dog in her lap.

I deliberately make myself comfortable in Dick's recliner and smile at him, brightly. "You look unwell. Maybe you should sit down? And then tell me again about the night your wife tried to kill you."

He sits awkwardly on the edge of a chair. "How many times do we have to cover this territory? I gave my statement to the deputies. I'm seeing a counselor, for goodness sake. Post-traumatic stress."

"Humor me. Just recount what happened."

"Suppose you ask her?" he snaps.

"Now, Dick. That's ridiculous, as you know. Suppose you just do what I've asked, and then we'll go away."

He sighs, heavily. "Anything to get you out of here. Ellen was doing laundry. I was sitting here watching TV. She coshed me over the head with a sock full of rocks and then I woke up in the hospital. Like I told you. Like I told the deputy. Like I told everybody."

"Suppose you tell it in more detail? Your wife was doing laundry. . ."

"And then she hit me over the head."

"You didn't see her walking toward you, wielding this weapon?"

"I was watching TV. I didn't see anything. She hit me from behind."

"You didn't notice her walking down the hall?"

"Maybe. I don't know. I wasn't paying attention. And then she got behind me and tried to kill me."

"What about the sock?" I ask.

"I don't understand."

"Describe the sock for me."

"I really don't see where this is going."

"Just tell me about the sock, Dick."

"It was an ordinary black sock. Like I usually wear."

"And are you missing any socks, Dick? You know, one orphan sock in the laundry? An incomplete pair?"

His brow furrows. "Why does that matter?"

"I don't think it was one of your socks, Dick. And I don't believe it was your wife that smacked you with it."

"That's ridiculous!" he protests. "There was no evidence of a break-in. Nobody here but the two of us."

"Dick. Think very carefully now," I say gently. "Have you rearranged the furniture since the incident in question?"

"No. Why would I do that?"

"Well, because right now, you can't see the TV from your favorite chair without twisting your neck sideways. You know what I think? I think you've moved the chair."

"This is ridiculous."

"I think the chair was right here." I get up and drag it to a point where it faces the television, which is mounted to the ceiling. There are scuff marks on the hardwood floor that line up perfectly.

"Come sit here, would you, please?"

"I don't see—"

"Humor me."

His jaw is now clamped so tightly, the cords in his scrawny neck stand out. "No," he says.

"All right. Suit yourself. I'll just be you." I settle into the chair, recline it, put my feet up. "Okay. I'm you. I'm settled here, watching TV while my wife slaves away. She walks down the hall toward me, carrying a weaponized sock. She passes right under the television, so I really can't help but see her. And she can't get around behind me, because reclined like this, I'm too close to that credenza."

Dick swallows. He licks his lips. But he says nothing.

"She's not the one who hit you. And I think maybe you know that. Maybe you were visited in the hospital, by somebody who told you what to say. Maybe they threatened you. Maybe they offered you money."

"No." He shakes his head. "No. She did it."

Ellen, the dog now curled in her lap, has her head tilted to one side, a puzzled expression on her face, as if she's trying to interpret a foreign language. He glances at her and then away. He has collapsed in on himself, looking old and frightened and lost enough to almost soften my heart.

Almost.

I remind myself of the things he said the last time I talked to him, of all the ways he has taken his wife for granted and of the travesty he has capitulated to.

"You deprived her of a medication that literally keeps her from falling apart. You let her go to jail. What did they threaten you with?"

"I don't know what you're talking about."

"Liar," Ellen says. For just an instant, her face looks focused, but in the blink of an eye, she's lost and confused once more.

"I found her medicine last time I was here," I say. "I know what it's for and what it does. The real murderer here is you for keeping it from her."

"An antidepressant," he protests, rallying. "One little prescription! How was I to know it would make her go crazy if she stopped taking it? They said—"

He breaks off, realizing his mistake.

"*They* who, Dick?"

He stubbornly refuses to say anything.

"But it's not an antidepressant. Maybe you didn't know that. I'll give you the benefit of the doubt on that one. But it was rather convenient, didn't you think? Ellen sliding suddenly into dementia so she couldn't say what really happened? And you were content to just leave her there, in jail, with her brain turning into mush, for your own comfort and safety. Isn't that right? What did they promise you for your lie?"

"My life," he whispers.

"And what did you need to do for your safety?"

"Just say she did it. That Ellen snapped and hit me. They said no one would know. That there would be no real investigation." He begins blubbering, tears cascading down his cheeks. "I'm sorry. I was frightened. I—"

"You're pathetic." I return the recliner to an upright position and get to my feet. "Come, Ellen, let's go."

She gets to her feet, still holding the dog.

Realization dawns on Dick's face. "You have to protect me. They'll know you were here. They'll know—"

"I don't think you deserve protection."

I'm about to tell Ellen to put the dog down, but I can't stomach leaving the obnoxious little creature here with this man. Dick trails behind us to the door, pleading. "Don't you have an obligation? To protect life?"

"Human life, yes," I tell him. "You don't qualify."

"Please, don't do this. They'll know. They'll come for me."

His voice follows us out to the car. Ellen climbs in and settles the dog on her lap without so much as a glance in his direction. When we drive away, he's standing in the driveway in his dressing gown, shedding tears that he should have wept for what was happening to his wife.

CHAPTER TWENTY

Halfway back to the Manor, the door alarm in my pocket starts buzzing. Damn it. Somebody has entered my suite. I step on the gas, and my Jag fishtails on the icy road. Ellen squeals. The dog yaps. The ruckus makes it hard to concentrate, but it doesn't take much thinking to suspect that the culprit is Jill.

To my surprise, when we walk into the Manor, she is sitting in the office, in my chair, doing something at the computer.

"Is that a *dog*?" She wrinkles her nose at the furry creature squirming in Ellen's arms.

"More or less. And you get to watch it and Ellen."

"I don't do dogs."

"Cathy would have done it, and you are now Cathy."

"But I have to check on residents!"

"Figure it out." Without waiting for her assent, I head down the hallway, moving as fast as I can. Ellen may not be entirely safe with Jill, but the option is better than exposing her to whatever or whoever might be waiting in my suite. If the intruder is dangerous, the last thing I need is a clueless old woman and a yap dog underfoot.

I pause in the hallway outside my door, scanning for any sign of danger. Nothing out of order to be seen or heard or smelled. The door is unlocked. I turn the knob, then kick the door open with my foot, a movement I know I'm going to pay for later, and slam my body back against the wall in the hallway, revolver in hand, ready to fire. There's no sound, and I risk peeking around the door frame.

An overnight bag rests on my couch, open. The bathroom door is closed. Water is running in the shower. I catch a whiff of shampoo-scented steam. Leaving the door open, I cross to the sofa and dig into the bag. A long black skirt and a black knit top. A makeup case containing black mascara, black kohl eyeliner. Which explains everything.

"What the hell, Sophie!" I shout through the bathroom door.

"Can't hear you; I'm in the shower!" she shouts back.

A few minutes later, she floats out of the bathroom on a cloud of steam.

"You do know the meaning of *emergency keys*, I presume," I say witheringly.

"Trust me, this was an emergency. Both Gee and Val needed the bathroom in Val's room. Where's Ellen?"

"Since I assumed there was an intruder in my room, I left her with Jill in the office. Everything okay with Val and Gee?"

"That child never stops talking! When can I go home?"

"Have you figured out what's going on with Ida Mae and Sylvia's souls?"

She plunks down on the sofa and starts combing through her long hair. "This isn't like anything I've ever experienced, Maureen. I can't reach them."

"This whole case is bizarre," I agree, starting the coffeemaker. I have unfortunately missed breakfast and Matt's coffee. Speaking of which, I haven't checked in with Matt this morning.

"Is Karin still a raven?" I ask.

Sophie snort-laughs. "Matt is so not happy. He put her on a

perch in the dining room and introduced her as his new pet. The residents were all crooning over her, and some of them tried to pet her."

"Did she hurt anybody?"

"Only the people who actually touched her. Drew blood twice, and then they all backed off."

The radio crackles and Jill's voice comes on. "Maureen. Oh, my God. Send help."

"What's happened? What did she do?"

"It's Chuck!" Her voice is shrill with panic. Visions of Ellen shifting into some ghastly, monstrous beast and mauling Chuck flash through my brain.

"Jill. Where are you?"

"Chuck's room. Hurry. It's horrible. And . . . Oh, God. Just come now."

With a regretful look at my coffeepot, which has just begun to emit a tantalizing aroma, I head for Chuck's room, Sophie right on my heels.

Chuck lies on his back in the middle of the floor, eyes staring up at the ceiling, both hands pressed against his belly. "Hurts," he moans.

Jill's face is ashen. Ellen is nowhere to be seen. "Maureen. Thank God you're here. He's so hot. And he's . . . stiff. And he's . . . you know . . . puked." She says the last word as if it's the worst thing that could actually happen to a person.

"Chuck," I say, lowering myself to my knees. "Can you hear me?"

His eyes roll back in his head but the lids don't close. Not good. "Sophie, call 911, would you?"

"What is it?" Jill wails. "Is it contagious? Oh, dear God, what if it's the plague?" She heads for the sink and begins scrubbing her hands.

"Chuck," I call again. "What happened?" There's an angry red swelling on the side of his face and another on his hand. I try to move one of his hands from his belly so I can have a look, but Jill's right: he's stiff as a board. Without warning, he begins to convulse, his back arching, limbs thrashing.

Matt appears in the doorway, the raven perched on his shoulder, Ellen behind him with Lucy in her arms. He calmly takes in Chuck, thrashing and moaning like a beached whale, Sophronia and me on our knees beside him, Cathy scrubbing furiously at the sink.

"Ellen, stay," he says, entering the room. To my great surprise, she obeys.

Matt bends down to get a closer look at Chuck. "That's not good."

"How long for that ambulance, Soph?" I ask.

"They said twenty minutes."

We all look at each other. Too long. I feel helpless and angry. Chuck is a misogynistic, handsy son of a bitch, but he's *my* misogynistic, handsy son of a bitch. If anybody is going to kill him, it will be me.

"These swellings look like bites or stings, don't you think?" Matt queries. "Mosquitoes on steroids."

"Um, Maureen?" Jill says, from the corner where she has retreated after washing her hands.

I ignore her.

"Maureen!" she repeats, with more urgency. And then she screams and bounces out of the corner as if she's on springs. Part of the shadow seems to move with her, separating into individual little blots of black cascading over the toes of her shoes. She stomps her feet, swatting at her legs, screaming at the top of her lungs.

Matt dashes over to help, which is brave but stupid, because whatever it is will just swarm him, too. I unlock the carabiner that holds Phil's flashlight on my belt loop. "Close your eyes. Both of you. Sophie, stay put." Matt moves behind Jill, holding her around the waist with one arm and covering her eyes with his free hand, squeezing his own eyes shut. For once, Sophie does as she's told. I turn on the special flashlight, whispering a prayer to Phil on the other side. *Let this work.*

Wherever I aim the beam, little black bodies drop onto the floor, twitch, and curl in on themselves.

"Come out into the light," I command, and Matt shoves Jill forward. Bits of shadow scurry back into the corners. I swipe at my own hair and shoulders even though I'm pretty sure nothing is crawling on me. Sophie does the same. Jill turns into Matt's arms, sobbing against his chest.

The raven stalks over to the black things on the floor, cocks her head to one side, then darts her beak forward and swallows. I nudge her aside with one foot and bend down to look more closely. Spiders. Only, they're not ordinary spiders. The flashlight only harms certain paranormal creatures, which means we have a problem. I feel a shiver at my center, looking at all of those legs, curled up in death. The raven continues her feasting.

"Spiders? Is that what happened to. . .to. . ." Jill breaks out of Matt's arms and runs for the door.

I beat her there and block her.

"Let me go," she wails. "Get out of my way."

I put my hands on her shoulders and shake her. "You can go. But you will take Ellen with you. You hear me? Remember your training."

She is wild and frenzied, in a total panic, and I fully expect her to knock me over and gallop away. But her eyes focus. She nods. I step out of the doorway and she walks through, grabs Ellen's arm, and drags her off down the hallway.

When I turn back to the room, Sophie is bending down to pick up and examine one of the spiders. Matt takes it from her hand. "That's so weird. Spiders don't usually attack. Or congregate in colonies. I wonder why they went after Chuck."

Footsteps in the hall, along with the sound of wheels, signal the appearance of the ambulance crew and all questions of the why and wherefore are put aside in a flurry of medical activity.

"Black widow bites," I tell the young man who is assessing Chuck. It's not like telling him the truth will help at this point.

"Ma'am," he replies. "Contrary to abundant myths, black widows seldom bite and only when disturbed. And the bites are seldom lethal to—"

I hate being either ma'amed or condescended to, but there's no time to put him in his place. "Did you need to see the evidence?" I gesture to the spider bodies all over the floor. "The place was crawling with them when we entered and they attacked us."

The EMT gulps, all of the confidence going out of him. His partner radios the hospital for instructions.

When Chuck has been transferred onto a stretcher and rolled away, we follow. I lock and close the door behind us.

"Nobody goes back into this room without full body covering and gloves."

"You think this is connected to Ida Mae and Sylvia?" Matt asks.

"Well, he is one of the witnesses, but the other victims didn't have bites." I think uneasily about the seance, and the giant ghostly spider, and what Sophie has said about the souls of the deceased.

"Was Chuck at breakfast?" I ask.

"He was. He seemed perfectly fine then."

"Could you start checking rooms? Look for evidence of spiders; make sure the other residents are okay. I'll start with Ginny."

Matt salutes lightly. "On it." Sophie follows him with her eyes as he strides away with the raven on his shoulder, but before she can go after him, I say, "You're with me. I need you." Really, I need to ask her some pointed questions.

To my surprise, she complies without an argument, and we head for Ginny's room. I call Jake on the way.

"Please don't tell me what you're going to tell me," he says, picking up on the second ring.

"Nobody's dead. But the ambulance has just carted Chuck off for treatment of multiple black widow spider bites."

Silence. And then: "Black widows don't generally attack. And certainly not in numbers."

I wait for him to draw his own conclusions.

"Damn it, Maureen. I'm going to regret this. Why Chuck? And is Ginny okay?"

"Checking on her now."

A gusty sigh wafts into the phone, followed by a string of expletives that impresses even me. "I'm on my way."

"Stand back," I order Sophie when I knock on Ginny's door.

"Might I ask who is out there?" Ginny, like Dick, has had a "you there" to answer doors for most of her life.

"It's Maureen. I need to talk to you."

The door opens and Ginny looks out at us, cool and smooth and unrattled. "What can I do for you?" She's wearing a cashmere sweater and a skirt, there's a string of perfect pearls around her neck, her makeup is flawlessly applied.

"There's been another event."

"Oh, dear. Another death?"

"No. Not yet at least, but they just took Chuck away in an ambulance. Could we please come in?"

"I don't see why you'd need to. Thank you for notifying me, but—"

"Sylvia and Chuck have both been attacked, Ginny. I really do need to ask you some questions. It seems that the three of you may have seen something you weren't meant to see."

For the first time, Ginny's composure cracks. I see a flicker of emotion beneath the surface, but it's only for an instant, gone before I have time to read it. "Well, you'd better come in, then. Tell me what happened to Chuck?"

She sinks down into a chair and gestures toward an antique fainting couch. "Sit, if you like."

Sophie sits. I take the opportunity to look around the room. Ginny is completely self-sufficient and rather reserved, and I've never had a reason to enter her space. It matches her. Polished, cultured, every item speaking of wealth. I'd be willing to bet that the paintings on the wall are originals, even the small Monet strategically hung where a wall sconce perfectly complements the play of light and shadow. The furniture is all antique and in immaculate condition. Everything is scrupulously neat and spotless.

Not a spider to be seen.

"Chuck was suffering from a burning fever, abdominal pain, and convulsions," I answer, not mentioning the spiders.

"Where was he found?" she asks, revealing symptoms of distress by patting hair that is not in any danger of straying from its appointed order. "Have you considered it might be poison?"

"The sheriff's department is investigating all angles."

As if summoned by my words, there's a tap at the door, and Jake's voice calls out, "Sheriff."

"You might as well come in," Ginny calls back. "Let's make it a party, shall we?"

Jake opens the door. "Well, isn't this cozy," he says. "Maureen, I'm certain you're just here in your capacity as mistress of the Manor, checking on the well-being of your resident. Because you certainly would not be interviewing witnesses."

I make my eyes wide and innocent. "Of course. I was worried about Ginny, especially since both Chuck and Sylvia have been smitten."

"I assure you that I will take all safety precautions, although I can't begin to imagine why anybody would want to harm me," Ginny says. "But in case it is poison, I do think perhaps I don't wish to eat anything I haven't prepared for myself until this is cleared up." Her eyes alight on Sophie. "Perhaps you could do some shopping for me, my dear. I'll make a list."

"I'm not a delivery girl," Sophie protests, but nobody is listening.

"Would you tell me about discovering Ida Mae's body one more time?" I ask. "Just in case we've overlooked a detail."

"Something I might have seen that would make the killer want to eliminate me, you mean? I can't imagine. Plus, I've already told it all to the sheriff."

"Tell us again," Jake says. "And then Sophronia here will go on that grocery run."

Ginny waves a hand, heavy with diamonds, in a gesture that clearly means "Sometimes, you must humor the less intelligent," and says, "All right. What do you want to know?"

"Just tell me again about finding the body."

"She's still Ida Mae," Sophie objects. "You wouldn't want to be called 'the body.'

"I was in my room, sleeping, when I heard Sylvia screaming," Ginny says, ignoring the comment. "As I've explained before."

"And your first impulse was to run directly toward the screams?" Sophie asks. "You're here all safe and warm in bed, and the first thing you do is unlock the door and run to see what they're all about?"

Jake and I exchange glances. A glimmer of an idea flickers in my brain. What the library ghost communicated through Val makes me very interested in exactly where Ginny was and what she was doing.

"Unless you weren't in your room," I say. "Unless maybe you were already out and about."

"Now, why would I be out of my room at that ungodly hour? In my nightclothes? Some sort of tryst with the likes of Chuck?" Her face attempts to prune into distaste, but her botoxed forehead is not getting in on the act.

"Exactly that. Maybe you were in his room and the two of you came down together."

"Or all three of them were . . . trysting," Sophie says. "And their . . . activities . . ." She shudders, clearly imagining wrinkled skin and creaking joints in a ménage à trois of horror. ". . . gave them an appetite, so they all trooped down to the kitchen together."

Not being eighteen, the idea of a little sexual indulgence between consenting seniors doesn't bother me at all, but the image of any woman in general, and Ginny in particular, consorting with Chuck does twisty things to my stomach.

"How dare you imply such a thing!" Ginny points an elegant finger at Sophie. "As if I would allow myself to be pawed by that . . . that . . ."

"Plebeian pig?" I suggest, noting that she's not denying the idea of a threesome.

The regal facade shatters and her face flushes with outrage. "Get out. I will not sit here in my own room and listen to your demeaning inferences."

"What about those groceries?" Sophie is all innocence. "Did you want to make me a list?"

"Get. Out!"

"The Plebeian Pig is dead," Jake says, not budging from his place by the door. "He died in the emergency room."

Ginny pales and sinks back into her chair. "Oh, dear."

"Please do consider that telling us what really happened that night might save your life," Jake continues. "If you notice any heightened arachnid activity in your room, I suggest you notify me at once."

A quiver runs through her, a moment of indecision, and I think maybe there's something she's going to tell us. But it passes. She gets up and opens the door, pointing into the hall.

As soon as the door closes behind us, Sophie makes a gagging sound. "I need to bleach my mind. Do you think that they really . . . Is it even possible?"

"People do have sex past their twenties," I retort, carefully not glancing at Jake.

"That is just so gross."

"Says the girl who likes to hang out with dead people. Speaking of which, it's rather more concerning that Chuck is now one of those dead people." I pull out my Ellen tracking app and consult it. She is still safely in the office; hopefully, Jill is still with her.

"Well, I'll see you two later. I'm off to do things," Sophie says, speeding her steps.

"What things?" Jake asks, his tone deceptively pleasant.

"Oh, you know. Things." Sophie's attempt at the innocent act is worse than mine.

Jake scowls. "You are not to go off investigating on your own. Do you hear me?"

"Whatever," Sophie says. "I'm *researching*, if that's okay with you."

I have a pretty good idea what kind of research she's planning, and I'm certain Jake would not approve. I'll admit to my own misgivings, but the truth is that she's much better equipped to protect herself than any of the rest of us are to do it for her. So, I let her go and focus on my own problem at hand. There are a few things Jake needs to know, and I'm the one who is going to have to tell him.

CHAPTER TWENTY-ONE

"Let's talk in my suite, shall we?"

Jake makes a sound that I take as assent, and we proceed down the hall and up the stairs without a word. Only when we're safely behind my door, closed and locked, does he say anything.

"You don't really believe they had a midnight tea party in their jammies?" he asks.

"Ginny didn't exactly deny the allegation, did she? What if Sophie's right about some sort of sexual liaison?"

Jake shudders. "Surely not. I mean, Ginny and Chuck? I'm with Sophie—that's an image that requires brain bleach."

"Agreed. But Ginny is lying about something."

"Maybe I could be readmitted to the hospital," Jake says, thoughtfully. "A nice quiet bed. A respirator."

"And somebody from the Unit unplugging you in your sleep." I hand him a mug of coffee and wait until he's settled in a chair and has had a swallow or two before I say, casually, "Gee spent the night, by the way."

He slams his mug down on the coffee table. "She spent the night—here?"

"Well, not here, precisely. In Val's room."

"Let me clarify," Jake growls. "An innocent minor spent the night in the Manor, where we have someone—or something—on a killing spree."

"She may be a minor, but innocent she is not."

"Maureen, this is the most irresponsible behavior I've heard of in a long time. What the hell were you thinking?"

"I took precautions. Sophie stayed with them and—"

"Sophie. God in heaven grant me mercy."

"Look. I tried to send her home. Gee claims she has nowhere to go. I spoke with her parents. They're on a cruise and have no intention of coming back early. I threatened to call child protective services. Gee threatened to run away. She'd do it, too. You know she would. I figured she'd probably be safe enough with Sophie. And Val." I leave out the bit about the seance in the library. There are things Jake doesn't need to know. It's not like the ghost provided any practical information.

"Perfect," he says. "The child is under the protection of an eighty-year-old woman who can't communicate and a teenager that can kill without a weapon. What could possibly go wrong?"

"Also—"

Jake groans. "I don't want to hear it."

"No? I thought you'd want to be completely up to date on the evidence."

"Evidence? Yes. What you're about to tell me? Not so much. But we might as well get this over with."

"Ellen's DNA has been tampered with."

"You spoke with Charlie, then?"

"As if! That asshole is saying nothing. Jill has looked at Ellen's DNA and—"

"Jill." Jake sets his mug back down and presses both hands to his forehead. "Is she off your suspect list now? Because it hasn't escaped my notice that she's discovered two of the victims."

"Nobody is off my list, but she's moved down it. Look, genetic research is her one true thing. She's passionate about it.

She said Ellen's DNA has been altered, that it seems to be unstable. Also, she analyzed the chemical makeup of the medication I found at Ellen's house. Some sort of psychotropic compound, probably. I've started giving the pills to her. To Ellen, I mean."

"Of course you have. Why wouldn't you? Any other small but shocking details you'd like to share?" he asks, jaws clamped so tightly, it's surprising any words can get through.

"Nothing important." I should probably tell him that Karin is a raven, but I'm worried about the effect the news will have on his health.

"Oh, good," he says. And then he says nothing else, just sits there, quietly, drinking coffee, as if it's an ordinary morning and he hasn't a care in the world. I'm a little worried that I've broken him.

"What's your next step in the investigation?" I ask, with my best impression of a submissive subordinate awaiting direction.

Jake laughs, which is more alarming than his silence. "Just so I'm clear, even though we really have no evidence at all, you suspect some collusion between Karin and Ellen, with potential involvement from Ginny, Chuck, and Sylvia? And that Jill might somehow be involved, but not to worry because she's more concerned with her research?"

"All I'm saying is that all of those people either know—or, in the case of Chuck and Sylvia, knew—something they aren't telling, or they are hiding something, or they aren't—or weren't—who or what they claim to be."

"Don't try to tell me that Ginny is a vampire in disguise. I am not buying it."

"We're not dealing with a vampire, Jake. Either some bizarre shifter or an entity entirely outside of my experience."

"Great," he says. "Absolutely fantastic. Any chance an exterminator is in order?" he asks, hopefully. "Like maybe this spider infestation is terrifying but normal?"

I consider that and shake my head. "We don't want to anger

that . . . thing. Not until I'm sure Sophie's figured out how to contain it."

"Whatever you say, boss." His gaze lingers on my face, and I feel my breath quicken with expectation. We're alone, for the first time in forever. Maybe—

"God help me. What did I do to deserve you?" he says, and it's not in an *I must have done something good* tone. At all. He swallows the rest of his coffee and slams down the mug.

"Where are you off to?" I ask as he gets to his feet.

"I'm off to see that Gee went to school. And if she didn't, I will drag her out of this building and take her somewhere safe."

He's right. I know he's right, but I hate the feeling of being censured, even more so because I know I deserve it.

"I'll go with you," I say, half-expecting him to tell me he doesn't want my company or my help ever again. He shrugs and heads for the door without a backward glance.

"Suit yourself."

Which I choose to take as an invitation.

CHAPTER TWENTY-TWO

As it turns out, Gee has not gone to school. She opens Val's door at Jake's knock, but only enough to peer out at us. "Maureen. Jake. Isn't it kind of early?"

It's not exactly a welcoming greeting, and her eyes look shifty. She's up to something.

"Why are you not in school?" Jake demands.

"Christmas holidays! No school until next year!"

"How about you open the door so we can come in?" he says. He's phrased it like a question, but the words are clearly a command.

"We're not dressed," Gee protests.

"You're up to something," I say, out of patience. "Get out of the way."

I lean my weight against the door and it slams open.

"I wish you hadn't done that," Gee says, and there's a note in her voice, a flatness of intonation that is all wrong. Obviously, everything is not okay.

Val still sits on the sofa. Or at least I presume the mummy-like bundle on the couch, almost entirely wrapped in spider webbing, is Val.

"Holy shit," Jake says.

I plunge into the room. "Val, are you okay?"

"Stop right there or she dies," Gee orders in that off-kilter voice. It's a voice that means what it says. Remembering Chuck, I stop short.

Val's dark eyes flicker toward me. "Will you walk into my parlor?" she asks. I catch the warning in the reference, an old poem about a spider and a fly. At that instant, Jake flicks the switch and I realize all of the warnings have come too late.

The entire expanse of ceiling is thickly festooned with spider webs. Hundreds of arachnid bodies cling there, silent, waiting. I shudder at the sense of so many eyes watching.

"They won't hurt you," Gee says. She holds out her hand. A spider descends toward her, lengthening its tether and landing on her palm. "Unless I tell them to. Go on back up now." She lifts her hand and the spider ascends toward the ceiling.

"How long has this been going on?" I ask.

"The time is out of joint," Val says, or at least I think she says. The webbing over her mouth doesn't make for clear communication.

"O cursèd spite, that ever I was born to set it right," Jake finishes. "Gee, come here," he says.

She shakes her head. "I can't."

"Old too soon, and wise too late," Val says.

Jake steps into the room, reaching for her. "Gee. Let's get you safe. Then we'll worry about Val."

The child retreats from his reaching hand. "You need to go."

The spiders begin to move in a coordinated wave that flows across the ceiling and down the walls.

"Will that flashlight contraption work on them?" Jake gasps as spiders scurry over our shoes, begin the ascent of our pant legs.

As I reach for the weapon, Gee screams, as if in pain. "Don't do that! She'll kill me." She backs into the center of the room and sinks down into a nest of blankets on the floor, where I assume she's been sleeping.

"The lights are too bright. Turn them off," she says.

Jake complies, and in the dimness that follows I see it: Gee's mayonnaise jar, and inside it the spider, radiating an infernal blue light. Gee lifts the jar to her chest and removes the lid.

"Oh, shit! Too late!" Sophie's voice says from the doorway.

"Do not come in here, whatever you do," I order, unable to tear my eyes away from the scene of horror unfolding before me.

The spider emerges from the open mouth of the jar and crawls up the girl's arm, over her shoulder, coming to a stop on top of her head.

"She's hungry," Gee says. Her expression is blank, her voice toneless. "She's agreed to leave me and Val alone. For now. She wants a . . ." She pauses, as if listening, swallows hard, and adds, "A willing sacrifice."

I finger Phil's flashlight. If I can take out the ghost spider directly, then maybe the others will scatter. But the thing apparently also has supernatural intelligence.

"Put it down!" Gee squeals, in her own voice. "She says if you try to kill her, she'll consume me. And Val. And she says if you don't bring her something else to eat by midnight, then . . . she'll . . . You've got to help us."

"What exactly do you eat?" Sophie asks.

My own voice seems to have deserted me. I'm not sure how this monstrosity kills or what the elaborate staging of the bodies is all about, but I'm sure she's responsible for our string of deaths.

"My hunger grows." Gee's lips move, but the voice isn't hers. It is cold, implacable, alien. "Go now, unless you wish to volunteer."

The spiders retreat, descending my pant legs and forming a circle around my feet. I feel an odd sensation of fatigue, as if an invisible something is leaching my vitality. Grabbing Jake's arm, I drag him backward through the doorway, slamming the door between us and the living nightmare within.

"You can't just leave them there like that!" Sophie's eyes glow green. She lunges for the door, but I grab her arm and hold her back.

"Listen to me. We have no choice right now. Didn't you feel it? That thing was siphoning energy. That's how they died."

Jake nods, his face deathly pale. "I felt it."

Sophie's eyes go wide. "She consumed their souls. That's why there's only a wisp of anything left. Oh, my God. This is all my fault!" She looks at me, a pleading expression on her face. "I slept here last night, on the couch. I didn't see any spiders. They were fine when I left! I didn't know Gee had that thing in the jar until I went to the basement just now and found the stoneware broken and got suspicious. Oh, God. I did this."

I put my hands on both of her shoulders and give her a good shake. "If it's anybody's fault, it's mine, but blame isn't going to save them. We have to figure this out. How did she even get to that thing? She would have had to go through my suite."

Sophie wrings her hands and says, again, "My fault. If they die, I killed them."

Understanding dawns. "While the door was unlocked and you were in the shower."

"I'm sorry, Maureen. I didn't—"

"You couldn't have seen this coming. Go find Matt. Fill him in. Meeting in my suite."

She sprints for the stairs. Jake rubs his hand across his lips, and I see that he's shaking. I tug at him. "Come on. Let's go."

"We can't leave them like that."

"We have no choice. We can't help them if we're dead." I get him moving, then radio Jill.

"Go back to the office now, and take Ellen."

"But I haven't finished. We are just—"

"Just go. Stay in the middle of the hallways. Do not enter the elevator. When you get to the office, turn on every light. Understood?"

"Got it. On my way."

"Tell me you have a plan," Jake says. "Because, to tell you the truth, I've got nothing."

"Get a deputy to guard Val's room so nobody accidentally goes in there. We'll discuss our options as a team."

I dial Charlie's number. Again, a female voice answers, with "Transformal Dry Cleaning; we clean up your spills."

"Dry cleaning, my ass," I say. "Let me talk to Charlie."

"I'm sorry, ma'am. There is no Charlie—"

"Listen to me. You find Charlie. You tell him to contact Maureen within fifteen minutes or I will begin spilling Unit secrets on the internet. I don't imagine the public will be thrilled about paranormal and human DNA experiments involving teenage girls. I don't imagine the public will be happy to know that the Unit even exists. And if I were to mention the Medusa—"

"Ma'am. This is a dry cleaning—"

"Fifteen minutes."

I hang up and drag Jake toward the front office. The phone rings before we reach the stairs.

"Don't ever manipulate me like that again," Charlie's voice threatens in my ear.

"Then please do let me know where and how to contact you. I have a child in danger here, and I want answers. Now."

"Ellen harmed a child?"

"What I have is a giant glowing arachnid that is responsible for a massive spider infestation and is currently possessing a twelve-year-old girl."

"That's not good."

"You think? I want this fixed, Charlie, and I want it fixed now. People are dead here."

"You asking for my help, Maureen?"

"I'm asking you to clean up the mess you made in my Manor."

"Your spider problem, while it sounds fascinating, has nothing to do with either me or the Unit. Don't call me again."

"Don't you dare hang up on— Damn it. Damn it, damn it, damn it."

I allow myself the luxury of imagining beating the obnoxious little man with a very big stick and then putting a bullet in him. Which is pleasurable but not exactly helpful. Neither rage nor panic make for good problem-solving, so I discipline myself back to a place of calm.

Jill and Ellen are waiting in the office. The little dog in Ellen's lap yips at Jake and then growls ferociously.

"What's happened?" Jill demands. "I wasn't done with my rounds."

Ellen's eyes focus on my face. I'm just wondering whether I see intelligence and deliberation when she goes unfocused again and whispers, "Tea?"

"The spider infestation is more of a problem than I thought. The two of you are safer here in the office. Maybe you could work on putting out an ad for Cathy's replacement? And make Ellen some tea."

A rebellious expression emerges on Jill's face and I stare it down. "You want to help, so help."

"No." Jill and I both startle at this word emerging firm and clear from Ellen's lips. "I can help."

Ellen hums a few bars of "Octopus's Garden." I look at her, at Jill, at Jake, and succumb to the inevitable. Our team meeting has just become complicated.

CHAPTER TWENTY-THREE

Matt and Sophronia are waiting in the hallway outside my suite. The raven cocks her head and *kronk*s inquiringly at Jake. The dog yaps at her. She ruffles her feathers and clacks her beak, and the dog tries to burrow under Ellen's blouse.

"Sorry, Maureen. I had to bring her," Matt says.

"Never mind. At this point, you might as well."

"Do I want to know why Matt has acquired a raven?" Jake asks.

"That is Karin," I answer. "There was an incident."

"Of course there was," he says. "And Jill and Ellen and. . .Karin. . .are joining our meeting why, again?"

"Good question. You'll get your answer in a minute." I unlock the door and everybody troops in. Ellen's dog struggles down out of her arms and chases after Anubis, who arches his back and hisses, then charges. There's a chaos of teeth and claws and yelping dog before Sophie dives into the mix and separates them.

"Bad kitty," she says, picking up a cat that any cautious mortal would never had dared to touch. His ears are back and he's growling deep in his throat, but Sophie pats him, murmuring baby talk as if he's a harmless kitten.

Jill, as usual, claims my favorite chair. Matt and Sophie settle onto the couch, the cat in her lap. Jake pulls over a chair from the table. I install Ellen next to Sophie, then settle myself on the remaining kitchen chair.

"Are we really talking in front of Jill?" Sophie demands. "And Karin?"

"Not sweeping for bugs?" Jake asks.

"The time for secrets is over," I tell them. "There are at least three people in this room, plus a raven, who might be ears for the Unit. I don't trust Jill, and Jill doesn't trust Sophie. Nobody trusts Karin. As for Ellen, I don't know if she's a victim or a weapon or neither. I don't give a rat's ass anymore about who is listening or who trusts whom. All I care about is that we rescue Gee and Val and figure out how to kill that monstrosity of a spider. And if any one of you is in league with that thing and helping it kill, then I swear to you I will find you out and you will get what's coming to you. Are we understood?"

The raven *kronk*s. The dog yips. The cat growls.

Nobody in human form objects, so I plow ahead. "First, let's talk about Ellen."

All eyes turn in her direction.

"Tea?" she inquires, politely.

"I'll make her some." Matt gets up, carefully dislodging the parts of Anubis that have spilled over onto his lap.

Jake, for once, doesn't dismiss the idea of Ellen. He gets out his notebook and pen, flicks to a new page and asks, "What about her?"

"First off, she didn't actually try to kill her husband. That was the Unit's doing."

"And you know this, how?" Jake asks.

"Her husband lied. He said she came up behind him and hit him over the head. If he was sitting in his chair, watching TV as he said he was, he would have seen her coming; plus, it would have taken some serious maneuvering for her to get behind him and she wouldn't have had room to swing."

"And of course the only other possible alternative is the Unit," Jake says, bitterly. "I suppose she was framed?"

"Exactly. The question is why. It seems a very complicated way of getting her into the Manor. Jill has studied her DNA—"

"Wait, we trust Jill now?" Sophie asks.

"Hey," Jill protests. "I have been nothing but helpful with this—"

"Save your breath, Jill. Why don't you tell the others about Ellen's DNA."

This is her favorite topic and she shifts trajectory without drawing a breath, launching into a complicated explanation of Ellen's DNA, followed by a chemical analysis of the medication Ellen is taking.

Faces are glazing over, so I intervene. "Long story short, Ellen did not try to kill her husband, the Unit wanted her up here at the Manor, she can walk through walls, her DNA has been tampered with, and she's taking an experimental medication, presumably created by the Unit. The question is whether she is in league with the Queen Spider."

"Well, that clears things up," Jake says. His pen stopped moving long ago.

All eyes in the room rest on Ellen, who sits quietly drinking her tea, looking back at us. Her eyes appear somewhat focused and she says, quietly, "Hate spiders. More medicine. Please?"

When I hesitate, Jill says, "It does seem to be helping."

Ellen nods.

It does seem to be helping; the only question is whether a clearer Ellen is a good thing or not. There's only one way to find out, so I go fetch her another tablet, and she swallows it down with her tea while I continue laying out my questions to the team.

"Next, there's Karin. Is she a hapless shifter who happened

to take this job because it was available? Or is she also connected to the murders in some way? Interestingly enough, Jill, who discovered two of the bodies, is also the one who hired Karin."

"I resent that," Jill protests.

"You did hire her," Jake says, thoughtfully. "Maybe you could tell us about that? Only, for the love of God, make it short."

Jill pouts. "After Matthew and Maureen were arrested, it was up to somebody to save the residents of the Manor from starvation and neglect—"

"Single-handedly, of course," Sophie says, eyeing Jill in the same way Anubis is eyeing the little dog, who has dared to stick his head out from under the chair where she is hiding. "I could have helped. I even know people in town and could have located a cook who was not a raven."

"You are dangerous and should never be allowed near these helpless senior citizens," Jill begins.

Sophie's eyes begin to flare. Matt lays a hand on her shoulder. I glare at Jill and she subsides, smoothing her hair and her dignity before continuing. "Karin was not a raven when I hired her. I called the employment center, and hers was the first name they sent me. She has a degree from a recognized culinary school."

"And one assumes her background check and references were in order," Jake comments.

Jill bristles. "There was no time for these things! The residents were hungry. What was I to do, feed them myself?" When nobody answers, that she begins talking to herself in French. I recognize a few swear words and assume that what is incomprehensible is more of the same.

I raise my voice to be heard over top of hers. "Karin is a shifter. As a raven, she could easily have flown in and out of the open kitchen window. As a human, she is strong enough to lift a body up onto a table. We know that she has a difficult personality and her landlord had concerns. The killings started after she came here."

"Maureen, duck!" Matt shouts.

I obey, instinctively wrapping my arms around my head. I hear the rush of wings, feel the wind of the big bird's passing, right where my head was an instant ago. More wings, more wind, and then a heavy weight on my back, sharp claws digging through my shirt.

"Karin!" Matt snaps. "No! Bad raven!"

A commotion of beating wings and cursing follows. The dog is yapping, Anubis is yowling. The weight lifts.

"Settle down," Matt's voice says, "Or I will wring your neck and feed you to Anubis."

I dare to look up. Black feathers drift through the air. Matt has the raven by the legs and neck. Anubis sits at his feet, tail twitching, making little clicking noises, eyes glued to the raven. The raven has eyes only for Matt, who looks uncharacteristically shaken, his face white to the lips.

"Try not to antagonize her," he says.

I sit up and extract a feather from my hair. "Easy, Matt. She's a bird, not a bullet."

The raven glares at me and I glare back. Anubis crouches, tail lashing side to side, ready to spring.

Jake clears his throat. "Perhaps I might add some information, if we're done with the drama. Do you need to lock that creature up somewhere, Matt?"

"I'd rather keep her where I can see her."

"Suit yourself. Here's what we know about Karin. Unlike Jill, I did do a background check. She is the adopted daughter of a couple who once lived in Shadow Valley but have since moved to Portland." His eyes meet mine with an expression I can't decipher until he continues. "There is no record of her birth. She was found abandoned on the steps of a church in Newport."

"That's awfully close to Shadow Valley," Matt says.

"She was an experiment," Sophie breathes.

Jake clears his throat and shifts his weight. "Given her approximate age, she may be one of the human/paranormal babies created here when the Unit was doing research in our lab. Possibly one that I. . ." His voice trails away into silence, and I supply the word for him.

"Rescued, Jake. Or tried to, anyway." He looks miserable, and I know the poor man feels guilty and responsible for an action taken when he was young and caught up in a situation he couldn't possibly have understood.

"In any case," I say, "if she was our murderer, in her human form she'd be killing with knives, I'd think. As a raven, she'd be pecking out eyeballs."

The raven's wings start flapping again.

"Behave," Matt reminds her, and she settles.

I go on. "The question is whether the Unit knows about Karin and planted her here, and whether she is in alliance with the spider."

"She was with me when Chuck was attacked," Matt points out.

"Is what happened to Chuck even the same thing that happened to Ida Mae and Sylvia?" Sophie asks. "They weren't bitten by spiders." She scoops up Anubis, who is trying to climb Matt to get at the raven. "There's also the information Gee got from the library seance," she says. "We should talk about that."

"Which seance would this be, now?" Jake asks, his voice dangerously soft, his eyes pinning me to my chair.

Sophie glances at me. "Oops. I guess you didn't know about that."

"I guess not. Maureen? Care to explain?"

"There wasn't exactly a lot of helpful information," I say, deliberately misunderstanding his question. "Spirits are notoriously unclear about everything when they choose to speak. Sophie wrote down what the library ghost said through Val. Just a minute." I flip through my notebook to the page. "Here we go. '*Here they have gathered to feed the Queen. One naysayer, dead by denial. One holding back what is rightfully offered. One foolish, giving offense.*'"

"Well, if anybody is going to give offense, that would be Chuck," Matt says. "But there are two others referenced?"

"I'd guess that one of them is Ida Mae," I say. "*One naysayer, dead by denial.* That would be her. And then Sylvia would be the one to hold back what was rightfully offered."

"Unless it's Ginny," Jake says. "In which case she's in danger. I don't suppose anybody knows what the bit about feeding the Queen means?"

"You felt that, didn't you?" I ask him. "She feeds on souls."

"But how? And why those particular people? How do we kill her? Who else is at risk?"

I glance down at my notebook and scan through my notes. "Val knows something, I think, that she can't tell us. She keeps going on about *Charlotte's Web*, which doesn't really make any sense. I mean, yes, it's a book about a spider, but it's also about friendship and self-sacrifice."

"Maybe Val feels a bond with Charlotte," Jill suggests. "Charlotte can't speak and has to work hard to send a message. Using other people's words, you know?"

This is unexpectedly insightful, coming from Jill, and we all stare at her in surprise. Stranger things have happened than Jill having a moment of empathy, and I go back to my notes.

"Here's another phrase of Val's that I jotted down but couldn't place. '*Listen to them, the children of the night.*' Anybody?"

"*Dracula*," Sophie says, promptly.

"Vampires? On top of this spider thing? I'm admitting myself back to the hospital," Jake mutters.

"A soul vampire," Sophie says. "But what was that about voluntary sacrifices? And we still don't know how to kill her."

"Vampires are easy to kill," I say. "A stake through the heart."

"A little hard to pull off when the thing is sitting on Gee's head and can mind-control a horde of spiders," Matt says.

"Where is Chuck's body?" Sophie asks. "Please tell me he hasn't been sent to Spokane yet."

"In the hospital morgue, far as I know," Jake answers.

She puts down the cat and gets to her feet. "Well, that's where I'm going. To check in on Chuck's soul and see if it's like the others."

"Matt and Karin are going with you," I say.

Sophie nods, and the three of them head out, the raven once again riding on Matt's shoulder.

Jake heaves himself up to his feet. "I need to have another chat with Ginny. Maureen, you'd better come along."

"And me?" Jill asks. "What do I do?"

"Stay here with Ellen."

She pouts but doesn't argue. I take this as a sign of some sort of guilt, but I can't take Ellen with me, so I hush my misgivings as Jake and I head out to interrogate Ginny.

———

"Go away." Ginny sounds petulant and querulous, not like her usual controlled and imperious self.

Jake knocks again. "Sheriff Callahan here. I have some more questions for you."

"I've already answered all of your questions."

"I have more. Your life is at risk, Ginny. Let me help you."

"We could bring the Queen down here and loose her under your door," I threaten. "She says she's hungry." Jake glares at me.

The door swings open. "What kind of nonsense are you talking? I have no idea what you mean by any of that."

Ginny is wearing her usual sweater and skirt, strands of pearls, stockings and shoes. Either her makeup is flawless or her skin is ridiculously smooth and glowing for a woman her age. Maybe she actually *is* a vampire.

I dismiss the idea immediately--she's clearly reflected in the mirror hung at the far side of the room. And she'd have to see herself in it in order to get her makeup on. So, that's one theory down.

She stares at us, cool, calm, her nose wrinkling delicately. "Anything I can do to help, of course, but I can't see how."

"If we could just come in and talk," Jake says calmly. "It's possible that you know something that you don't realize you know. It happens often with witnesses. And, again, your own safety is at stake."

He smiles, all smooth tact and charm. His request is so very reasonable, nonthreatening. She can't turn him down without looking like she's hiding something. Jake seals the deal by playing up his already-visible fatigue and pain. "I could really use the opportunity to sit down for a moment. Would you mind terribly if I came in to continue this chat?"

"Of course. I appreciate all you are doing to protect me and solve these heinous crimes." Ginny steps away from the door and seats herself in an uncomfortable-looking chair, feet and knees properly together, hands folded in her lap. Jake lowers himself gingerly onto an antique that appears too fragile to hold his weight. I stay on my feet.

Looking around the elegant, expensive room, I wonder, not for the first time, why Ginny is at the Manor. Surely, she could afford a nice house, or at least a condo with a maid and maybe a doorman.

"Please tell me one more time about the events of the night Ida Mae was murdered," Jake requests. "I know we've been over this several times, but there may be some small detail you've overlooked."

"I was sleeping when I heard the screaming—"

"Are you sure?" Jake interrupts. "Before he died, Chuck told a nurse that you and he and Sylvia were together in the library when the screaming began."

A whole new respect for Jake warms my heart at this statement, which is an outright lie. Unless, I think in dismay, it's the truth and he's kept it from me.

"The poor man was obviously delirious," Ginny says. "A fever like that, the poison from so many spider bites." She shivers.

I move around the room, looking at Ginny's belongings. She follows me with her eyes, mouth tightening in disapproval.

"Chuck seemed quite lucid for just a moment prior to his death," Jake says, "Some kind of exclusive health club meeting was what he said."

"And you believe this ridiculous story? It's nearly as farfetched and insulting as that Sophronia creature's suggestion that there was some improper sexual tryst going on. As if I would fraternize with a man like Chuck, God rest his soul. I must say, Sheriff, I do not appreciate the implication that I am lying. And must that woman touch my things?"

"That woman can expel you from the Manor pretty much on a whim," I say, picking up a photograph in an ornate frame and studying it. Ginny and two other women stand together in front of a nondescript building, their arms around each other's shoulders. Something about the photograph tugs at a loose thread in my mind, a familiarity, a dissonance.

"Somebody is lying." Jake's affable charm is gone. "I'm beginning to wonder if it's you."

Ginny sniffs disdainfully. "I refuse to be insulted like this, here in my own room. If you have cause to arrest me, arrest me." She holds her hands out toward him, dramatically. "You should be ashamed of yourself. Bullying a victim in this way."

"Being a witness doesn't make you a victim," I clarify helpfully, still trying to make sense of the photograph. "It's often the murderer who supposedly discovers the body, right, Jake?"

"It does happen," he says.

I cross the room and slouch down into a chair, looking as insolent as possible, and wave the photo at her. "Who are these people?"

"Friends. Would you mind putting that down?"

Without looking up at her, I say offhandedly, "Charlie confirmed the midnight meetings in the library."

"Charlie is a liar."

Now I look up, my eyes drilling into hers. "So, you do know Charlie."

"Of course I knew him. He sat at my table. It was impossible to avoid being groped by the man."

Jake's eyes sharpen. "You said Charlie. Not Chuck. And you used the present tense."

Ginny waves a hand dismissively. "Charles, Charlie, Chuck. Call him what you will, not to speak ill of the dead, but he was a lewd buffoon and a liar. A terrible liar, I'll admit, but still a liar. Now get out!"

"I'd like to search your room," Jake says.

"Get out. And put that picture down."

I cross the room and put the frame back where I found it. I've been working on removing the back while we've been talking, and it's a simple matter to slip out the photo and hide it under my shirt while Jake holds Ginny's attention.

"I can get a warrant," I hear him saying.

"You do that. And I'll call my lawyer while I wait."

"Listen," he says. "If you know anything, you need to tell us now. There are lives in danger. One of them is a child."

"That has nothing to do with me," she says. "I can't help you."

She slams the door and locks it behind us.

"You really think she knows Charlie?" Jake asks as soon as we're out of ear shot.

"I played a hunch. But she certainly reacted." I withdraw the photo from under my shirt. "There's something about this pic. I think I've seen these women before."

"Maureen," Jake groans. "For God's sake. You can't just take things. We don't have a warrant. If anything comes of this picture, it will be inadmissible in court."

"This case is never going to court, Jake. And there are lives in danger."

He makes a growling noise in his throat and keeps walking.

"Come back to my suite for a cup of coffee?"

"Depends on what illegal or illicit activities we will be engaging in while there."

"I'm going to run facial-recognition software on this photograph."

"No coffee for me."

"Jake—"

"This case is never going to court. I heard you. But just on the off chance, the farther I am from you and your—methods—the better for all of us. I'm going back to the office to run a deep background check on Ginny and check in with Matt and the medical examiner. For all the good it will do."

I walk him to the door so I can reset the alarm behind him.

"God, I hate this," he says. "Nothing I'm doing will be of any help, but I'm doing it anyway. Please tell me you've got some idea how to rescue that child and kill that thing."

"We've still got time," I tell him, trying to encourage both of us. "If anybody can solve this, we can."

He looks back over his shoulder at me. "Be careful, would you? Don't feed yourself to that spider thing."

And then he's gone, but a warm feeling stays with me. Maybe he's disapproving of my methods. Maybe he hates supernatural adventures. But he still cares what happens to me.

CHAPTER TWENTY-FOUR

"Maybe go in my truck?" Matt suggests. "Get you a hat and a pair of sunglasses and sneak in under the radar?"

If they are going to visit Chuck in the morgue, they have to do it without drawing attention to themselves. But the Shadow Valley hospital is small, and Sophronia is notorious. She often feels called to sit with the dying, to help their souls cross. Some of the nurses are good with this. Others call her the Death Girl and threaten her with trespassing charges.

"You want to put Chuck's body in the back of your truck?" She doesn't even slow down as she calls this over her shoulder, and he takes a few running steps to catch up with her.

"Wait, what? We're not bodysnatching; we're just checking in with Chuck's ghost. Right? Please tell me I'm right."

She opens the door of the van and climbs in behind the wheel. Knowing that she's perfectly capable of driving off without him, Matt mutters a curse and scrambles into the passenger's seat, the raven gripping his shoulder. "Soph. Let's think about this."

"We need access to his body and his *spirit*. Thoth, Matt, don't say *ghost*. It's insulting to the dead."

"Right. Sorry. Spirit. But his body is part of the investigation. It needs to go to the ME."

"It will."

"Do you have any idea how much trouble we can get in for disrupting the chain of evidence?"

She starts the engine and shifts the van into reverse. "Do you know how little I care? Did you see Gee and Val? I was supposed to be protecting them. If you're worried about your precious reputation or whatever, then don't come."

"Soph. Sophronia. You can't blame yourself for—"

"Can't I?" She guns the engine. "It was my job to contain that thing. And what do I do? I let a child get her hands on it. So, if there's anything at all I can get from Chuck that will help us save her, then I need to do that. And I need time to work. The morgue is the worst place in the world for the spirits of the dead. Can you imagine? You're trying to get used to the idea that you're dead, and you haven't crossed yet for whatever reason, and your body is just stuck in a refrigerator like a side of beef?"

She's driving like a madwoman, the rear of the van sliding on the snowpack as they hurtle around the curves. Matt buckles his seatbelt and disciplines himself not to grab on to the handle above his door, or brace himself on the dashboard, or tell her to slow down.

The truth is, he also feels responsible. Once again, he's let an unwanted vision affect his judgment. He's been so fixated on protecting Maureen from Karin that he totally missed what was going on with Gee.

"What's the plan?" he asks as she drives around to the loading dock at the back of the hospital.

"There is actually a scheduled pickup," she says. "But we'll take Chuck instead. Anybody asks, it was an honest mistake. Get my badge out of the glovebox, would you?"

Matt opens the compartment and hands her an ID badge strung onto a black lanyard.

He tells Karin to wait in the van, but Karin as raven is no more biddable than Karin as human. He manages to squeeze out the passenger door without her following, but when Sophie opens the back to remove the gurney, she bursts out in a cloud of feathers.

Matt is torn between relief at the thought of being free of her, and responsibility for the safety of the town in general and Maureen in particular.

"Karin! Come back here!" he shouts.

The raven gives no sign that she's heard him, but the farther she flies, the more her momentum slows. She flaps her wings harder and harder, as if fighting against an invisible wind, but makes no progress. At last, with an angry *kronk*, she turns and flies back to him, thudding down onto the gurney more like a sack of bricks than a creature of the air.

Sophie laughs but not as if anything is really funny. "Looks like the two of you are stuck with each other."

Matt groans.

The raven swears as she eyes Matt balefully. "This is bullshit." It's Karin's voice, clearly emerging from the raven's body.

He knows he shouldn't be surprised. Even normal ravens can learn to talk, but it's still disconcerting.

"Look," he says. "Whatever weird shifter bonding thing happened between us, it wasn't my idea."

The raven makes a gagging sound.

"Well, this is delightful, but the two of you will have to commune later. We don't have time for this," Sophie says. Matt helps her lift the gurney from the back of the van, and they roll it up the ramp to a nondescript gray door. Sophie holds the badge up to the automatic lock, there's a click, and the door swings open, revealing a dimly lit, industrial-looking corridor. Nobody is in sight. Even if some random staff member comes along, nobody will challenge them. They have a right to be here.

The raven, on the other hand, does not. Matt takes the precaution of draping his coat over her.

She struggles and squawks. "Let me out."

"Do you want to guess what will happen to a raven found scavenging in a hospital morgue?"

She subsides and they roll along swiftly. There's no on-site security. Nobody waiting outside the morgue with a clipboard and official questions. Sophie's ID gets them through another unmarked gray door. The room it reveals is occupied. A gowned and masked figure stands over a naked body laid out on the autopsy table, gloved hands deep in the abdominal cavity.

"Hey, Sophronia. Here to pick up Jim Jensen, are you?" The man's eyes glance up, then return to the body on the table.

A whiff of decomposition, faint beneath the sharper smell of disinfectant, reaches Matt's nostrils and he tries not to breathe. He's never been good with the smell of death; it nauseates him. The raven, on the other hand, begins to struggle again and her head emerges from the coat. He restrains her with one hand while draping the coat back over her with the other. The last thing they need is for her to flap over to the body and begin feasting.

Sophie keeps the gurney rolling. "Yep, we're here to pick up Jim," she says. "Anything interesting going on there?"

"Cancer. Abdominal cavity is full of lesions. Want to see?"

"On a schedule." Sophie steers the gurney toward another door on the far side of the room. "Maybe next time."

"It's unlocked," the man says. "Jim's on the left. Got another one in there waiting for transport to the ME."

The morgue uses a walk-in refrigerated room rather than refrigerated drawers, which shields their activities somewhat from the view of the doctor doing the autopsy.

"Give me a hand," Sophie says, and Matt picks up his coat to clear the gurney. The raven flutters up onto Chuck's belly and hops toward his face, her eyes bright with curiosity and probably hunger.

"Don't even think about it," Matt warns, helping Sophie slide Chuck onto the gurney. She rests a hand on the dead man's forehead, her green eyes closed, a look of quiet concentration on her face.

"Karin, come here," Matt whispers, reaching for her.

She evades him, muttering, "You're not the boss of me."

"Suit yourself. When you're seen, we don't know anything about you or how you got in here."

"Come on, already." Sophie's eyes open. She pulls a sheet up over Chuck and fastens straps over him, shooing Karin out of the way. The raven doesn't struggle when Matt drapes the coat over her and tucks her under one arm.

"Take care, Doc," Sophie says as they roll back through the autopsy room. "Will I be coming back for that one? ETA?"

"Yep. She's yours. Somebody should have let you know and saved you a trip. You're welcome to wait, but it will be a bit."

"No worries; I'll come back," she says.

As soon as the door closes behind them, Matt asks, "How long until he notices we've got the wrong guy?"

"A couple of hours, max. Hurry."

Obviously, if they are seen running down the corridor with a dead body, there will be questions, so they keep their pace to a casual walk. Karin squirms and struggles under his arm, and it seems like an eternity before they've got Chuck safely secured in the back of the van. By then, Matt's coat has gone ominously still. He unwraps it with trepidation, half expecting he's inadvertently suffocated Karin.

She's alive but sulking. Her feathers are ruffled and she won't look at him.

"Sorry about that," he says. "We couldn't exactly have you feasting on the eyeballs of the dead."

"Not to mention the talk if the Death Girl is accompanied by a raven on her dark missions," Sophie says. "Get in, would you?"

Matt holds out his arm and Karin hops onto his wrist, digging her claws deliberately into the skin. He hisses with the pain but saves his breath, climbing into the passenger seat. Before he has time to reach for his seatbelt, Sophie slams the van into gear and hits the gas.

Karin hops to his shoulder and he buckles in, grateful for the seatbelt that more or less keeps him in place.

"Hey," he warns. "Getting stopped for speeding isn't in our best interest right now."

"They're all busy at the Manor," she says, and he saves his energy for something practical, like bracing his feet against the floor mat and praying not to crash.

By the time Sophronia pulls up to the back entrance of the funeral parlor, his armpits are sweaty and his jaw hurts from keeping it clamped shut.

While they're lifting Chuck out of the back of the van, Lysander opens the door and stands there, scowling.

"About time you showed up," he growls. "You can't just take off for days at a time. I've been doing all of your work. And taking care of that mangy cur you call a dog."

"You mean Craig has been doing all my work," Sophronia corrects. "And taking care of Morpheus."

Karin ruffles her feathers and lifts her wings, emitting a menacing *kronk*.

Lysander swallows, glancing uneasily from his daughter to the raven to Matt.

"This man is not welcome here."

"Don't be ridiculous," Sophronia says. "What are you going to do about it?"

She takes a step toward him, and he swallows hard and steps back. Karin goes airborne and flies at his head.

Lysander ducks and curses.

Matt has no sympathy for the man and doesn't even try to call the raven off. Lysander is a blustering bully who beat his wife and might have killed her. He's also mistreated his daughter. Last time they met, the older man ended up unconscious on the floor, an act that Matt can't bring himself to regret. Their eyes lock. Lysander's hand goes to his jaw, and he steps back and says nothing as Matt and Sophie wheel in the stretcher.

"I'll tend to this one," Sophie says. "Since I've been gone and all. Go polish the coffins, or whatever you were doing."

"None of your tricks, now," Lysander protests as they move past him. "Just prep the body."

Sophronia ignores him.

Matt goes back to breathing through his mouth. Mostly what he smells is bleach, but he can't help believing there's a tang of death underneath it. He's grateful when, instead of entering the prep area with its embalming equipment and drains, Sophie directs the gurney into a smaller holding room. "Stay here. I'll be right back," she says, leaving him alone with Chuck and Karin. Frankly, Matt isn't sure whether the dead body or the raven makes him more uncomfortable, but before he has time to properly consider the question, he hears footsteps in the hallway and the door opens.

"Craig," Matt says, grateful that he has seen the ruined face before and hasn't reacted with a startled gasp. He knows the man has been badly burned and that working here, and the way people react to his face, is a cruel and twisted joke on the part of fate.

Craig takes in Matt and the raven without even blinking. "Where is she?" he asks, approaching the gurney.

"She went to get something." Matt moves to intercept the other man, who is moving far too purposefully toward Chuck. "She said she's got this one."

"I can help," Craig says. "It will be faster." He begins to undo the straps, and Matt says, "You don't want to see this, man. Trust me."

Craig snorts a laugh. "I've seen everything. Except maybe a raven hanging out in a funeral parlor. That one's new."

Short of a punch to the jaw, there's nothing Matt can do to stop him, and Craig finishes with the straps and begins to draw back the sheet. He stops, staring down at Chuck's swollen face.

"This isn't Jim." Craig's eyes narrow, and he demands, "Wanna tell me what the hell is going on?"

"Not exactly," Sophie's voice says. She's changed out of her usual black into something white and flowing that drapes her curves. She rolls a large, hard-sided case into the room, then walks up to Craig and lays a hand on his arm.

"Pretend you never saw anything."

"There are rules," he protests.

Her face goes soft and pleading. "Please. It's important."

"Sophronia. One of these days—"

"It's a soul matter." She moves her hand to his chest and gazes up into his eyes, a move that is manifestly unfair, given that she knows exactly how Craig feels about her. "You know me. Nothing ghoulish going on here. I don't want you caught up in this."

Craig swallows hard. His hands twitch at his sides.

"Someday," he says, but leaves the word hanging there with no further indication of what *someday* will bring. He clears his throat. "Can I ask what happened to Jim?"

"Still at the morgue. I'll go back for him, I swear."

"Your father. . ."

Sophie's face hardens. "Leave Lysander to me." She spits his name out. "I won't let him blame you. Give me an hour. Then I'll suddenly notice my mistake, and we'll return Chuck and pick up Jim."

Craig hesitates.

"Hurry it up; we haven't got all day," Karin says.

Matt makes a shushing gesture, but of course it's already too late. Craig shakes his head. "You're right. I don't want to know."

He turns and leaves, closing the door softly behind him.

Sophronia lays the case down flat and opens it. "Help me with this," she says, handing up a black candlestick as long as Matt's arm. When he accepts it, she hands him another. "Set them around the gurney. One at the head, one at the feet, two on each side."

When the candlesticks are set in place, Sophronia adds black candles, lighting each one as it is placed, chanting under her breath. Matt can't help feeling a creeping uneasiness when she turns off the overhead and plunges them into a dimness lit only by the candle flames. He imagines the scratch of spiders on his skin and can't restrain a shudder.

Sophronia moves to Chuck's body and touches his forehead lightly. "Don't be frightened," she says soothingly, as if talking to a child. "I swear I'll figure out how to take you across."

Then she returns to the bag and withdraws a bottle of wine and a block of cheese. "No time for a real feast," she says, "but we won't send you off hungry. Open this, will you, Matt?"

He takes the bottle and the corkscrew she offers him while she takes a knife to the wrapping on the cheese and lays it on a small table. "You stay out of this, Karin," she commands, and the raven surprisingly obeys. Next, Sophie pulls out a stone goblet, takes the wine bottle from Matt, and fills it.

Already she has begun to look remote and otherworldly, and when she says, "Guard the door," her voice is cold and impersonal. Matt shifts his position so that his body directly blocks the entrance. Sophie begins to chant again, words he doesn't understand running together in an eerie, monotonous tone. Her eyes glow green. Her hair swirls around her. She lays one hand on Chuck's forehead, the other on his chest, and closes her eyes. The tempo of her chanting increases.

She tilts head back and calls, "Now! Come with me!" The

wind that swirls her hair intensifies. Matt can feel it on his own face now, hot and dry, catches a scent of something pungent and sharp, like pine needles and pitch. The candle flames flare brighter and higher.

The chanting stops. Sophie stands silent, as if listening, then opens her mouth and breathes in, deeply. Bending at the waist, she lowers her lips to the urn and breathes out, then swiftly seals the opening with a perfectly fitted cork. She straightens and her eyes open, glowing green with an unearthly light. She is vivid and wild, fierce and dangerous, and Matt's heart beats with something close to awe.

A memory shakes him. Her lips pressed against his, breathing his soul back into his body after it had been sucked away by a soul stealer. He has belonged to her from that moment, heart, body, and soul. He's tried to keep this from her, but sometimes, the way she looks at him makes it nearly impossible to remember that she is only eighteen, so young, with so much of life to discover. He's told himself over and over that it's only a soul debt that binds them together, not love, but he can't stop wanting her.

Gradually the glow fades and she is a girl again—weary from the power and responsibility she carries on her slim shoulders.

"You have his soul, then?" Matt asks, quietly.

She nods. "I was going to take him across, but then I thought maybe we'd need him. I lied to him, Matt."

To his dismay, her bottom lip begins to tremble and tears well up in her eyes. Matt bites the inside of his cheek, focusing on the pain to keep him from opening his arms to comfort her. If he does that, his resolve will fail. He'll kiss her, opening a door that he won't be able to close. As if she's read his mind, the raven grabs his earlobe and tweaks, sharply.

"Ow!" He lifts his hand to slap at her, but she evades him, fluttering over to Chuck's body, where she sets to preening her feathers.

"Did you learn anything?" he asks.

"His soul isn't like the others."

"His death wasn't like theirs either."

Sophronia slumps against the gurney. "I'm out of ideas. I honestly don't know what to do."

Matt thinks about wings and crawling things, sees that flicker of an image of Maureen lying dead. It's time to engage with the gift and try to see more. "Maybe I can help," he offers.

"How? So, you're a soul guide now?" Sophronia's tears recede, her voice sharpening into her usual sarcasm.

"Not exactly. I don't suppose you've got a crystal ball lying around somewhere."

A comment like this to an ordinary human would result in either disbelief or mockery. But Sophronia isn't ordinary. "You have the sight," she says, in the same tone most people use to discuss the weather.

"Guilty."

"About time you mentioned that," she says. "I've got something that will work."

"Wait, what? You knew? Did Maureen tell you?"

"I've held your soul, remember? I know things."

"But you never said anything."

She picks up the urn containing Chuck's soul and clasps it to her chest. "Why would I? It's private, right? Having access to soul-level secrets? I didn't even know if *you* knew you had the gift, and if you didn't, I wasn't going to be the one to tell you."

"More curse than gift," he retorts.

Sophronia glares at him. "Don't talk to me about curses! At least you're human. At least you don't have responsibility for people's souls!"

Her vehemence hammers at the years of his defenses. She's right. There's no comparison between the weight of who she is and this thing he tries to keep locked up inside him. But then she pushes too far.

"There you are, with this ability to see what's going to happen. To see the future and act to change it and you—"

"Is that what you think?" he shouts, his carefully contained anger erupting under the pressure with the sudden violence of a volcano. "That I see pretty little visions of people's futures? There's a mysterious and handsome dark-haired man who will sweep you off your feet? You're going to travel? Like some fake fortune-teller at a fair? You have no idea what you're talking about!"

"Well maybe if you didn't walk around like a long-suffering martyr with a dark secret in your soul, I'd understand it better," she hurls back.

"I do not walk around like a martyr!"

"Do too." She steps closer, stabbing a finger at his chest. He wants to close his eyes, to shut out the wild intensity of her in this moment, when his defenses are not only down but smashed, when the fire inside him is burning ever brighter in response to her passion. He's swept away by eyes and hair and her lips way too close to his. She smells of winter snow and the first trees of spring, with an overtone of woodsmoke, which makes no sense but doesn't need to.

"Matt, tell me," she says, no longer shouting, her voice low, and he wants to, means to, but there are no words. Instead, he gives way, all in a rush, cupping her upturned face in both of his hands and kissing her. He loses track of any rational thought then, aware only of his hands buried in her hair, their souls meeting, joining, as their lips press against each other in something that is so far beyond a kiss that he has no word to name it.

From what seems like an incredible distance he hears a door open. Lysander's caustic voice says, "Oh, isn't this just delightful? Have you no respect for the dead?"

Matt breaks the kiss. Breathless, he turns his head toward the speaker and reaches for words, but they are too far away.

"You know nothing about the dead," Sophronia hurls back. "Do they talk to you? Can you see their souls?"

"What I see is that this isn't Jim. What are you up to, I wonder?" He takes a step into the room.

Karin dive-bombs his head and he retreats, slamming the door behind him.

"He'll report us," Sophie says. "We have to hurry. Good raven. Come on."

To Matt's shock, the raven alights on her shoulder.

"Are we just leaving Chuck here?" he asks.

Sophronia doesn't hesitate, doesn't even glance back over her shoulder, and he follows her down a hallway and up a flight of stairs to the family living quarters. He moves in a daze, suspended in a shadowy zone somewhere between the sharp-edged reality he prefers and the treacherous territory of the second sight, and has an uneasy feeling that the slim, white draped figure ahead of him with a raven on its shoulder isn't Sophronia but Death.

Her room doesn't help him return to any sense of normal. The walls are covered in framed art posters portraying mythological renderings of the afterlife. Egyptian underworld. Greek Hades. Christian Hell. An array of books spread out on Sophronia's bed are all on the same theme. There's another stack of books on her desk, along with an open notebook and a pen. Matt takes it all in, as if from a distance.

"I've been doing research," Sophronia says. "Looking to see if there's any monstrous creature like this mentioned in the Book of the Dead or any of the other Egyptian papyri. Nothing. I mean, nearly every tradition has some sort of legend built around a spider, but none of them kill like this. Maybe your second sight will help us."

"Full emphasis on *maybe*," he manages. "My sight is erratic and never gives clear information."

"Because you've neglected it," she says, getting on her knees by the bed and drawing out a cardboard box.

He groans as she withdraws a crystal ball as big as her head. "Does it have to be so cliché?" he asks.

"Clichés are always built on truth." She moves a stack of books, sets the abomination on her desk, and gestures at the chair. "Sit."

Matt sits. "I've never used one of these things."

She leans over and lights a candle, shifting it off to the right of the sphere. "Now put your hands on either side, soften your gaze, and invite it to speak to you."

Her hair grazes his cheek and he can't resist reaching up to tuck the silken mane back behind her ear. He catches a whiff of fragrance, as elusive and maddening as she is. Her pale cheek flushes and her breath catches, but she doesn't look at him.

"Do you have the sight?" he asks her.

"Nope. Thought I might. I hoped. I practiced. Nothing. But you do. So, focus already."

He sighs and focuses on the crystal ball. All of his visions have come to him involuntarily and he's never invited them. His practical streak is too strong for that. There's nothing mythical or magical about the paranormals he's run into; they are just lesser-known life forms, with their own DNA, their own rules for existence in this world. Discovering what Sophronia is, the whole bit about soul crossings and stealings, has been unnerving, blowing apart his long-held belief that there is no afterlife.

And now, here he is, looking at a tacky crystal ball fit for a carnival fortune-teller and trying to believe that he can see the future in it. It's ridiculous. But at Sophronia's urging, he places his palms against the glass and lets his gaze drift out of focus. He sees nothing beyond blurred images of objects he knows are in the room. An unpleasant jolt goes through him when he sees the shadow of a black bird, but then he hears the scratch of Karin's claws and knows it's just her reflection.

"Nothing," he says, withdrawing his hands and wiping them on his jeans. The raven flutters onto the desk and pecks at the ball, apparently fascinated by her own reflection.

"Your resistance is so thick, a vision would have to smack you over the head with a frying pan to get your attention," Sophronia says. "Relax a little."

He wants to tell her about the disaster that befell the last time he tried to save somebody from a vision, but he doesn't, can't bring himself to talk about it.

"Try again," she says. "It's for Gee and Val."

He sucks in a breath and once again lays his hands on either side of the crystal. Nothing happens. He hears the rush of wings, and the weight of Karin settles on his shoulder. The next instant, he feels the glass warming beneath his hands. The surface of the ball mists, as if there is condensation inside. The mist swirls, and images begin to move through it.

The mouth of a dark cave, a giant web blocking the opening.

An extraordinarily large raven, feathers shining with an other-worldly light, black eyes and beak gleaming like polished onyx. Maureen, lying motionless and pale, eyes closed. A spider, every bit as big as the raven, crouched on her chest. White bundles hanging from a ceiling, like flies awaiting a spider, only here he can see a foot, there a tip of a finger, and he knows they are human.

"None of this is helpful," he murmurs.

From a great distance he hears Sophronia's voice. "Have you asked it to be helpful?"

Which, of course, he has not, because talking to a ball of glass is stupid. Except that he can't deny the truth that the supposedly inert glass is actually showing him something. Stifling his disbelief, he says, "Show me what I'm missing."

The images shift. *A music concert. A house party. A football game. A group hiking up a mountain.*

"Oh, for God's sake. I'm not suffering from FOMO," he says. "Show me something I need to know about that giant spider."

The scene shifts again. He sees the Manor and then the network of passages beneath it. He sees Gee. He sees Maureen, dead, then he sees what they have all gotten horribly, disastrously wrong.

He removes his hands from the sphere and stumbles up to his feet. "Call Maureen," he says. "Tell her not to go after the Queen Spider by herself, under any circumstances. And we need to go now. Right this minute."

"What the hell did you see?"

"Tell you in the van. Let's go already."

"She's not answering," Sophie says, her phone pressed to her ear as she runs down the stairs behind him.

"Try Jake." Matt slides into the driver's seat of Sophie's van. He's already in gear by the time Sophie climbs in beside him, and he's rolling before she gets the door closed.

CHAPTER TWENTY-FIVE

I make a pot of coffee, not quite equal to Matt's, of course, but it's hot and caffeinated. Ellen settles quietly onto the couch with a cup of tea, the dog curled in her lap. I sit down at the table and go to work on unlocking the secrets of the photograph.

Three women stand together in front of a building—off-white, ordinary, offering no clue as to their location. Ginny looks no older than she is now, so it must be recent. She wears her usual sweater and skirt. A strand of pearls circles her throat. Even though her face looks the same, her hair is longer and there are subtle differences in her makeup palette. The woman to her left is short, thin, and intense. Her black hair is close-cropped, her skin nearly ebony. I am certain that I have never seen her before.

The woman on the right is tall and sturdily built. Fawn-colored hair is pulled back in a high ponytail. The eyes behind wire-framed glasses are focused, staring directly into the camera. She has a familiar face, one I know I've seen before, but the circumstances of our meeting elude me. Have I only seen her in passing? Is she famous, someone I've seen in a picture, or on TV or in a magazine? It's possible, but I'm nearly certain that we've met and talked.

I scan the picture into my computer and pull open my facial-recognition program, then link it to databases that I am not supposed to have access to. Good thing Jake has chosen to go do something else, because I'm breaking laws left and right. While the software does its thing, I do my own search on Ginny. I start with the easy road, one of those sites you can pay to tell you where somebody lives, who their friends are, what's on their legal record. I enter Ginny's information, and it obligingly confirms that she lives here at the Manor. And that is it. According to the report, she has no family. No friends. No social media accounts. No legal record. Not so much as a former residence.

Everything about this feels wrong. Ginny is not an off-the-grid kind of person. I'd expect her to have an extended social network—if not currently, at least in the past. She must have owned a country house and one in the city and maybe a villa in France. I'm not buying this blank-slate business one bit. Deeper digging unearths a birth certificate that states she was born in 1935 in Brooklyn. But I can't find a driver's license. I can't find a credit rating, a bank account, or any history of real estate trans-actions. Is she in witness protection? Or is this something more sinister?

I supply Ellen with a fresh cup of tea and open the encrypted software that stores resident admission records for the Manor. Ginny's file is ridiculously thin. I try calling the emergency contact number listed and get a recorded message that tells me the number is not in service. Her payments to the Manor are automatic transfers from a Swiss bank account. Even running a search on the dark web with her social security number turns up nothing.

I call Jake, who sounds decidedly grumpy when he answers the phone.

"What have you got?" I ask.

"Her background is suspiciously sterile," he says.

"Agreed."

"I don't want to know how you know that," he says. "And I'm afraid to hear your theories as to why."

"Witness protection, maybe," I answer.

"Really, Maureen? I expected something more colorful from you. Vampires or the Unit wiping her record."

"She's not a vampire."

"Of course not." He sighs. "And she's not in witness protection."

"She erased her own past, you think? Pretty effective job of it. She must be hiding from something big. Or the Unit has planted her at the Manor."

"All roads do not lead to the Unit," Jake says. "I very much doubt she's an undercover agent. Maybe she was an abused woman. Faked her own death. Got a name change. Maureen, for God's sake. We have to focus on that spider thing and on rescuing Gee and Val."

"I am. Ginny has got to be part of it."

"Look, just because you hate coincidences, it doesn't mean Ginny has some connection to that abomination of a spider."

"And it doesn't mean she doesn't. You have a better idea? Ellen, what do you want? Hang on a sec, Jake."

I look up at Ellen, who has risen to her feet and is standing directly in front of me, stabbing her index finger at the photo. "Linda," she says. And then, after a pause, "Loeffler. Linda Loeffler."

The name is as familiar as the face, but the circumstances of meeting the woman still don't come clear. Ellen moves to my computer and starts tapping at the keyboard.

"Hey, don't touch that!"

"What's going on?" Jake asks.

"Ellen has just named the woman in the photo and changed the parameters on my facial-recognition search."

Jake groans. "I don't want to know anything about this search. Who is Linda Loeffler?"

"I have no idea. Yet. Wait. . .now, *that's* interesting."

"What's interesting? Damn it, Maureen, talk to me."

"Maybe Ginny *is* a vampire."

Another groan, this one sounding like genuine pain. "Please explain. For the love of God and all things holy."

"We've located records on Linda."

"And this makes Ginny a vampire how?"

"That pic I swiped from her room was taken in 1992."

I wait for him to put the pieces together.

"Ginny hasn't aged in nearly thirty years," he admits grudgingly.

"There's more."

"I was afraid of that."

"I've remembered where I met Linda. I was certain I knew her, but I had the timeline all wrong."

"Let me guess. Linda was a vampire."

"It's worse," I tell him. "Linda worked for the Unit. In DNA research. Are you okay?"

His breathing sounds loud and a little snorty. Like a bull ready to charge. Or maybe a man who was recently shot in the chest, now processing disturbing information.

"What are you telling me? Ginny is a clandestine agent, undercover in the Manor like you and Matt? Hell, maybe everybody in that accursed facility works for the Unit. Why not? Let's play some elaborate practical joke on the local sheriff."

He pauses for more angry breathing and I ask, "Are you done?"

"So very done."

"Good. Because I was thinking that maybe she's a test subject. Not an agent."

"You mean?"

"That the Unit is still conducting experiments and using my

Manor to do it. They never stopped, only now their subjects are elderly. Pregnant teenagers are off-limits because society gets all up in arms if a child is damaged. But who really cares if an eighty-year-old in a retirement home croaks unexpectedly? The chances of an autopsy are minimal. She might have even consented, given her previous ties to the research department."

"Wait," Jake says. "Wait just a minute. Surely, the Unit knows enough about you to know that you're not going to watch people drop off suspiciously without investigating."

"But Ginny was here long before I was. She was here before Phil bought the place."

My blood feels like it's boiling, heating my body from the inside out. I get up and open the doors to the patio, letting in the cold winter chill. How dare Charlie come to me under some pretense of a more humane program. How dare he recruit me back into the ranks and then leave me in the dark, just so that he can use the Manor—my Manor—to run experiments on the residents.

"Maureen?" Jake asks. "You okay over there?"

"I will be. Just as soon as I track down Charlie and kill him. Slowly."

"You can't, now that you said that to me," Jake objects. "Don't make me arrest you, Maureen."

A distracting and completely random image of Jake putting me in handcuffs floats through my mind. Both of us are about half of our current ages and in various states of undress. This does nothing to cool my overheated body.

I get myself under control and answer, "Fine, I won't kill him. We'll have a nice, long, private conversation." Friendly visions of tiny but very sharp knives, needles, waterboard, and electrical equipment replace the thoughts of me and Jake and a pair of handcuffs.

"Maureen," Jake warns. And then, in an entirely different tone: "Speaking of undercover agents, where is Matt?"

I step onto my balcony and look up at the pitch-black sky, the stars so bright and close, I almost feel that I could touch them. Beautiful, cold, and unforgiving. I've had my doubts about Matt. But he's saved my life now, more than once, when he could have let me die, and trust has begun to grow between us. I force myself to consider the cold, harsh possibility that Matt has been deep undercover this whole time, pretending to be a double agent on our side but really loyal to the Unit. What if he's saved my life not out of decency or because he's part of the team but because I'm a necessary asset he's protecting?

"He went with Sophronia to the morgue. Karin is also with them."

There's no need to explain my concern to Jake.

"On my way," he says, and I can hear that he's already moving.

"Take some backup, Jake. And be careful."

"I'm always careful. You, on the other hand, are not. What will you be doing?"

"Having a little conversation with Jill."

"Oh, my God," he says, as the realization dawns. "All that lab equipment. Her insistence on taking over the Manor. And here I thought you were being paranoid."

"Don't worry about me. Check on Sophie."

"Wait for me," Jake says. "Don't go haring off on your own."

I hang up without promising anything. The phone rings immediately. It will be Jake again, angling for my promise that I'll be careful. I don't answer. Living to be old enough to be decrepit or, God help me, senile, is not on my agenda.

"What do I do with you?" I ask Ellen.

She glances up, and for a moment there is clear intelligence behind her eyes. Then it's gone again, and she bends her head to pet the dog. Damn it. It's dangerous to take her and dangerous to leave her. Everything I know about her DNA and her medication came from Jill, and for all I know, it's a bunch of hogwash.

Anubis pokes his nose out from under the couch, still unhappy about the presence of the dog, and slowly emerges, ears back, tail lashing. The dog yaps and the cat growls back.

I call Jill on the radio. "Jill? Come in, Jill."

No answer. Not even static.

"Tea?" Ellen inquires.

"Later. We are going for a little walk."

The decision has made itself, as they often do. I'll have to take her with me. Before we head out, I suit up with all of the weapons I can carry. My new revolver, loaded with three commercial rounds, two silver bullets, and two rounds made of the special amalgam that was Phil's invention, goes into my small-of-the-back holster. The little .22 fits neatly into my waistband. My favorite knife rides in a holster on my right hip. I strap another to my ankle and hook the special flashlight to the carabiner attached to my belt loop. I even hang a silver cross around my neck in case of vampires. I never got my salt sprayer back from Jill, but I don't really think ghosts are involved here.

When I'm as prepared as I can be, I hold out my hand to Ellen. "Let's go."

She comes to me as trustingly as a child, the dog trailing behind her. Anubis hesitates, then decides to follow. We cross the hallway and I knock on Jill's door. "Jill! Open up. We need to talk."

No answer. I use my key. The door opens on an empty room, still in the state of chaos it was in last time I was here. The closet door is open, and so is the door to the secret passageway at the back of the closet. I proceed down the stairs, Ellen behind me. The dim overhead lights, our footsteps echoing in the silence, create a sense of heightened danger. If this was a horror flick, the violins would be playing; viewers would be shouting at the screen, "No, don't go there!"

Unlike the secret stairway that leads out of the closet in my suite, this one leads directly to the Manor basement. Another public-access stairway descends from the hallway by the elevator. Despite the chills running up and down my spine, there is nothing out of the ordinary. Just the water heater and a block of large storage lockers constructed of wood and wire.

Jill hasn't even tried to cover her tracks. The padlock to the locker that contains the entrance to the tunnels is unlocked. The trunk that we placed to conceal the trapdoor has been shifted. I find the ring and tug, and the door lifts, surprisingly easily. I shine my flashlight—just an ordinary, everyday light—into the darkness. The only way down to the tunnels requires descending a long ladder, followed by a trip in an ancient elevator.

"You should go back," I tell Ellen. "It's dangerous. And the ladder is hard."

She shakes her head. "I'm coming."

"It's dark, Ellen. Those spiders could be everywhere."

"Life is short."

"Fine. I'll go first." I clamp the flashlight between my teeth before beginning my descent. Ellen waits until I'm a few rungs down and then follows. The dog yaps and fusses, running back and forth around the mouth of the trapdoor. By the time we reach the bottom of the ladder, my legs are trembling, the bad one aches, and my jaw is cramped from biting down on the light.

"All right?" I ask Ellen as I take the light in my hand and shine it around the small bunker. It looks the same as last time I was here. Bunk beds built into three walls, an ancient elevator cage with manual controls on the fourth.

Above us, the dog is still yapping.

"We have to go down in that." I gesture at the elevator, my own personal brand of hell. "You sure you don't want to go back up?'

In answer, Ellen steps into the mesh cage. I hate all elevators. This is not a phobia but logic. Once you step inside and the doors close, you're trapped with whoever or whatever else is inside. Plenty of time for a vampire to suck the life out of you before the doors open again. This rickety old thing takes that risk to a whole new level. I stop myself from shining my one wavering beam up into the corners to check for spiders. I'm going down, spiders or no. Sometimes, it's better not to see.

I follow Ellen into the flimsy cage, manually close the doors, and push the Down button. There are no floor indicators, but we pass red-lettered signs on the shaft that indicate elevation as we drop from the top of the mountain to a level that puts us below the town of Shadow Valley. By the time the elevator clanks and jolts to a stop, my entire body feels like it's crawling with spiders.

We emerge into a room of the same dimensions as the one above. Instead of bunk beds, it's lined with metal lockers, every one of them still padlocked. If I survive this escapade, the team really needs to see what's in there.

When I shine my light on the floor, I see fresh footprints in the dust. Not just one set but multiple. Which is interesting but not reassuring.

I should drag Ellen back to safety, but I can't face the idea of the elevator again so soon. Besides, how would I contain her? She can walk through walls and go wherever she wants to. I shine my light into the main corridor and we start moving.

At irregular intervals, doors lead into long-disused rooms. Some were for storage, others designed as dormitories, presumably for shelter in case of a nuclear disaster. When we get to the first intersection of passageways, I pause, uncertain which direction to take. But the footprints continue straight ahead and I follow.

We've been walking for close to an hour before I hear the sound of voices ahead and see the flickering of what looks like candle or torchlight.

Slowing my steps, I make a hushing gesture to Ellen, my fingers to my lips, hoping she'll get the message. She nods and lays a finger to her own lips. The closer we grow to the room with the open door, the more slowly and quietly we move. I draw my revolver with my free hand. Gesturing to Ellen to stay put, I rush the last few feet, ready to fire, shouting, "Hands where I can see them now!"

But spiders don't have hands, and the humans in the room are either incapacitated or disinclined to obey.

The floor is moving in a disorienting, ever-shifting kaleido-scope. A wave of spiders breaks over my sneakers, and I shout, "Ellen, run!" But instead, she comes to stand quietly beside me, eyes fixed on the spiders already climbing her legs.

Jill lies on a table in the center of the room, cocooned in spider silk, with nothing visible but her wide and terrified eyes. Gee is seated on a chair next to her, that ghastly blue abomina-tion of an arachnid squatting on top of her head. Ginny stands next to Gee, and for a moment I think she's another victim. But then she says, "Maureen. Welcome to our little party. Close the door and put down your weapons."

"That doesn't seem wise." Never in my long career have I felt such panic, even when the giant slug was feasting on my insides. It takes all of my willpower not to turn and make a run for it. But if I'm about to die in a most unpleasant fashion, I don't intend to do it squealing like Sylvia.

Jill whimpers and begins to struggle.

"I'd suggest you lie still," Ginny tells her, coolly and politely. To me she says, "Please do as I've asked. Come in. Lay down your weapons."

"And if I don't?"

"Your friend dies."

"Go on ahead with that," I bluff. "You'll save me the trouble of eliminating her myself."

Jill's eyes bulge in her head and she redoubles her efforts, rocking her body from side to side.

"I wasn't talking about Jill," Ginny says. "Her fate is already determined."

I glance at Ellen. A spider rests on her right cheekbone, just below her eye. Another is on her forehead, several on her neck. She appears calm, untroubled by either the spiders or Jill's whimpers.

"Yada yada," I say. "I guess we're all going to die. I don't bargain with terrorists."

"Surely, the child matters to you," Ginny says.

Gee sits motionless, her eyes vacant, her mouth drooping slightly open. There's a bit of drool on her chin. The sight of her makes my blood boil, but I shrug and aim Phil's flashlight at the spider on top of her head, drawing on long practice to keep my emotions from my face.

"A little laser burn, and your Queen is spider toast."

"You could try that," Ginny says, "but it's ill advised. I think you'll find there's more to the Queen than either ectoplasm or arachnid. The girl will die."

I can feel spiders crawling up my arms, the scratch of their legs on the nape of my neck. I never expected to live to be old, but of all the ways I expected to die, this never made the list.

Pushing the fear aside, I try to come up with a plan. My job is to get Gee out of here safe and sound. And Jill, too, I suppose, since she's now in the victim camp.

As for Ellen, she gazes at Ginny, head tilted to one side, as if the other woman is a puzzle to be solved. She flicks the spider off of her face, almost nonchalantly, as if it were nothing more than a fly.

"Fountain of Youth," she says, suddenly. "Project 66803. Jennifer Totten. Linda Loeffler. Michael Sweeney."

Ginny's eyes narrow. "How do you know that? It's classified."

Ellen shuffles into the room, sliding her feet forward to clear a path rather than stomping on spiders. "Move if you don't want to be stepped on," she says, making her way over to Gee and bending down to peer at the Queen Spider. "She's grown," she says in an admiring voice, as if speaking about somebody's baby.

"When I saw her, she was a tiny thing. If this is even the original. Has she reproduced?"

"Again, what do you know about 66803?" Ginny demands, in place of an answer.

"I am the only Queen Spider," Gee says, in the voice that isn't really hers. "There is none that compares to me."

"I see that." Ellen still sounds admiring, wonderstruck even. She crouches down and appears to be gazing raptly into the spider's many eyes. "Your Majesty is beautiful in color and form. And of unprecedented size. Might I ask how you reached such magnificence?"

"There was a time of great feasting," the spider says through Gee. "So many souls. A sip here, a swallow there. I fed, I grew. And then they vanished, and I came forth into the light, seeking what is rightfully mine."

"The spirit storm," I say. I can see it all. This creature hidden away in some dark corner of the Manor, sipping at soul energy. And then that inrush of spirits, so many. The spider glutting herself, growing larger and larger and creating a bulk that required ever more sustenance.

"She sensed the influx of souls," Ginny admits, "and was drawn to them. Before that, it was easy to keep her. She required such tiny amounts that she could siphon them from the living and nobody noticed. A little thinning, a little fatigue. But she fed inordinately for a time, and with her increase in size came an increase in need."

"And then Sophie helped all of those souls to cross and left the creature hungry."

"Ravenous," Ginny says. "Demanding. I watched, hoping for a natural death among the residents so that she could feed with nobody knowing. But all were incredibly healthy. She attempted to feed on me, and I knew I had to do something."

"So, you started murdering people to feed your pet."

"I feed only on voluntary sacrifices," the cold voice says.

"Really?" I ask, my voice as caustic as I can make it. "Ida Mae volunteered to sacrifice herself to feed you? And Sylvia? Pardon me if I find that difficult to believe."

"Souls come to me willingly," the horrible voice insists through Gee's lips.

"Jill doesn't look precisely willing."

For the first time, I see a flicker of fear cross Ginny's face. Gee's body begins to shake. A strangled wheezing sound comes out of her. "Gee," I cry, taking an incautious step forward and feeling the crunch of multiple exoskeletons beneath my foot. I freeze, realizing that the sound is a horrible parody of laughter.

"I don't see what's funny." I stomp my other foot deliberately.

The laughter stops. The voice says, coldly, "You will suffer for that."

"How about if you explain what you plan to do with Jill."

"A gift for my subjects."

"And Chuck? He died differently than the women."

"Mmmm. You speak of the male of the species. My subjects were hungry. You, and the one you name Jill, deprived them of their kill before they could feast."

"Spiders don't eat humans," I protest, knowing even as I say it that these are possibly the stupidest words to leave my mouth. Normal, ordinary spiders in the rainforest hunt and consume small mammals, frogs, and birds. And these are not normal spiders. Why would they be? Hell, the whole swarm of them could come from modified DNA. They could be the brood of the Queen Spider, for all I know. That thought turns my blood to ice. I shiver, looking down at my feet and legs, which are being wrapped in webbing. I spread my legs, breaking the still-fragile threads but surprised by the amount of resistance.

"Nobody died in Project 66803," Ellen says in a tone of scientific interest. "The Queen lived on small amounts of energy-siphoning. The subjects all replenished."

"As I've explained, her need has grown," Ginny says. I notice for the first time that her hair is no longer perfect, that she looks tired, the wrinkles in her face carved deeply. "Keeping her fed has become increasingly . . . difficult."

"Are you complaining, handmaiden?" the spider's voice says.

"No. No, of course not." Ginny's lips twitch and she runs a hand over her face, then tries to smooth her hair. "I am grateful for the life you bestow upon me."

"Don't forget your gratitude. Or your place."

Ginny makes a strangled noise, deep in her throat. "Either one of these would serve you well," she says, gesturing toward me and Ellen. "Even the child, if you are through with her."

"The source must be willing. Are you willing, handmaiden?"

Ginny's eyes look almost as wild as Jill's. "Of course. Certainly. But if I offer up myself, then who will care for you? Procure food for you?"

"I have yet to see food. It has been days. In the meantime, my children shall have their feast." Spiders begin to swarm up onto the table where Jill lies. She rolls her head from side to side. Her muffled screams cut through me like a knife through butter. I think about her father, and that maybe I owe it to him to save his daughter from this particular fate.

Hell, I'm going to die anyway. I take another step forward.

"I volunteer for service," I say.

"Willingly?" the Queen Spider asks.

"Conditionally willing. Free the child from your control. Let Jill go. Allow them, and Ellen, to leave this room. And then I will give myself to you."

"But my subjects are hungry."

I shrug. "Them or you."

"You need me," Ginny says, a hint of desperation in her voice. "I have served you well."

Again Gee's body is shaken with horrible laughter, and the cold voice says, "You need *me*. You have needed me since you first brought me into the world. Without me, you will fall into death and decay."

"Release the child, at least," I coax. "Ginny can speak for you, since she already serves you. I will feed you."

Ginny's eyes widen. She shakes her head and takes an incautious step backward, her foot creating arachnid death. "I'm sorry. I apologize. It was unintentional," she flounders, freezing in place.

"Let Gee go," I repeat, beginning to feel like Moses before the pharaoh, pleading for his people. I would gladly face the snakes and frogs he had to contend with over this ungodly swarm of spiders. "And then I am yours."

"Come here," the spider says. Gee's head turns toward Ginny.

Ginny shakes her head.

Gee gets up and crosses the distance between them, spiders clearing a path before her. She stops directly in front of Ginny, so close that her face touches Ginny's chest. The spider's front legs reach out and tap the old woman's chin, then climb over her face and up onto her head.

"Open your mouth," Gee says, still in the spider's voice.

"No," Ginny protests, covering her mouth with both hands. "No. Please. I have served you well."

"You have failed me. You have used me for your own ends."

Gee tilts her head back and opens her own mouth. A silvery mist, vaguely arachnid-shaped, emerges from between her lips. Ginny shakes her head from side to side, pressing her lips more tightly together. The ghostly spider shape moves upward to her nostrils and waits. I can see her holding her breath, her face purpling with the effort. When she finally is forced to breathe, the spider shape is sucked up into her nose.

Her jaw slackens. Her eyes go blank.

Gee steps back. She opens her mouth and screams. The harsh, ear-piercing shriek of terror is one of the most beautiful sounds I've ever heard. She backs away from Ginny and the Queen Spider squatted on her head.

"Get out of here," I tell her.

"I can't leave you," she says, with incredible courage.

"Yes. You can. You will. I need you to go find the sheriff, okay? Tell him what you know. Go now."

She still stands there, indecisive, and I shift my method. "Gee, you have to get Ellen out of here."

"You might want me to stay," Ellen says, quietly.

What is with all of these willing volunteers? I steel my voice. "Go with Gee."

She shrugs. Tears stream down Gee's face, but she crosses to Ellen, takes her hand, and leads her out of the room. As soon as the door closes behind them, I say, "Now free Jill."

"That wasn't part of the bargain," the spider's voice says through Ginny.

"It is now. You want a willing victim, you've got one. But only after everybody else is out of here."

Ginny says nothing. I shuffle my feet across the floor, spiders crunching with every step, and make it to Jill's side. Bending down, I draw the knife from my ankle holster and begin cutting away the cocoon that holds her bound. I begin with her feet and leave her mouth 'til last, on purpose, so I don't have to listen to her scream.

As soon as her feet and hands are free, she's up and running for the door, tearing at the sticky silk on her face as she moves.

I'm very nearly right behind her, but thoughts of all of the people I care about stop me. Jake, Sophie, Matt. Gee, far too brave for her own good. Val. Ellen.

This is what comes of allowing myself to get attached to others. Protective instincts take over.

"You will climb up on the table and lie down," Ginny says in the spider's voice.

I feel a tug at my mind and then an indescribable feeling of my soul flowing out of my body. A deep weariness fills me, as if life has been long and hard and it is time for it to end. Resisting the command feels difficult. For a moment, I stay where I am, but the weariness increases, and all I want to do is lie down and give in.

As I climb up onto the table, an inner part of me tries to panic and resist, but it is a small thing, inconsequential. I lie down on my back and fold my hands on my chest. Even when Ginny dons a pair of gloves and then lays a red-and-green placemat on my belly, followed by a plate, I don't struggle. And when the Queen Spider crawls down off of Ginny's head and settles herself in the middle of the plate, I think only, *So, that's how it was done*, with no real interest.

The room, the spider, my own body begin to fade. Not as if I am being pulled away from them but as though they are thinning, ceasing to exist.

I have a dim consciousness of regret, and then there is nothing.

CHAPTER TWENTY-SIX

Matt calls Jake on speaker phone.

"You're alive," he says when Jake picks up.

"Shouldn't I be?"

"Listen, Jake. This is urgent. Maureen is in danger and not answering her phone. Meet us in the common basement. She'll be in the tunnels."

"Is that what Charlie told you?" Jake asks, his voice thick with suspicion. "How do I know you're not in on it and planning to kill her?"

The mistrust in the older man's voice burns like acid. Matt wants to shout that he should have proved his loyalty by now, that he was willing to spend the rest of his life in prison to make amends, but the words won't change anything.

"You're going to have to trust me," he says. "I'll explain later."

"Kill the spiders," Karin croaks.

"Karin is human again?" Jake asks. "How did you pull that off?"

"She's still a raven, only she seems to have found her voice."

The van careens into the parking lot of the Manor then, and

Matt sees that Jake beat them here. He stands waiting, his service weapon drawn.

"Both of you, stay put," Sophronia orders. "Let me talk sense to him." She gets out first and crosses toward Jake.

"Get back in the vehicle," he orders, but she keeps moving until she can lay her palms on his chest and look up into his face. "You can't really trust any of us, can you? You can't be sure what I might do and whether that other part of me will get out of control. Or whether there's some evil twist to Karin beyond being a shifter. Or whether Matt is lying to us all. But that's what they want, for us to doubt each other. You've got to make a choice."

Matt opens his door and gets out. "Doubt me all you want. Shoot me later. Whatever. I'm telling you there's not time. I had a vision, Jake. She might already be dead."

He sees the indecision in Jake's face and breaks into a run, trusting that the sheriff won't shoot him in the back. He hears footsteps behind him, too light and easy to be Jake's, and he knows Sophie is following. The raven flaps overhead.

His legs are pumping as fast as he can make them move, but he still feels like he's stuck in a nightmare where he's barely moving. He hopes against impossible hope that he's read the vision wrong, that Maureen is safe and has things under control. He flings open the door to the Manor and races down the hall-way, then takes the steps to the basement two at a time, the raven leading the way.

The storage locker and trapdoor are open. A small dog stands at the opening, looking down and whining pitifully. Matt shines his flashlight down into the darkness and sees that the ladder is occupied. Ellen's face turns up to his. One of her wrinkled hands moves upward, grasping a rung. Now Gee's frightened face is visible below her, one hand shoving against the older woman's butt.

"Stop pushing on me, child," Ellen pants. "It's not helpful."

"Hurry, then," the girl says. "As soon as you're safe, I'm going back."

"You are not," Jake gasps. His breathing is labored and harsh, his face creased with pain.

"An experiment out of control," Ellen calls up as Matt grabs her arm and assists her off the ladder and onto the concrete floor.

Gee pops up like a disheveled genie.

Jill comes next, climbing as though pursued by all the bats of hell. Her hair is full of spider webs, her body swathed in them. When she reaches the top, she attempts to swoon into Matt's arms. He sidesteps and she manages to catch herself from falling but bursts into a storm of weeping, slapping her hair and face with her hands. "They are on me. I can feel them. They are crawling, crawling. What if they bite me?"

"Oh, for God's sake, you're fine," Ellen says brusquely. "Not a one of them left that room with you. Go take a shower, if you must."

Jill flees and Ellen turns to Gee. "You, young lady. After her."

"I need to help Maureen."

"Maureen wouldn't need helping if it wasn't for you."

The child's face crumples, tears tracking down her dirty face.

Sophie lays a hand on the child's hair and says, much more gently than Matt has ever heard her speak, "Go on. I know exactly how you feel. Leave it to us from here, okay? Why don't you take Ellen and—"

"Ellen isn't going anywhere," Ellen says. "I'm the only one who understands Project 66803."

"Who all is down there?" Jake barks.

"Maureen. And Ginny," Ellen says.

"Not Val?" Sophie asks. "Is she—"

Gee squeals. "Val! Oh my God, Val! How could I forget? I've got her," Gee yells, already across the basement and running up the stairs. "Get Maureen!"

Before Matt can prevent her, Ellen lowers herself back onto the ladder and begins descending into the darkness.

Jake stands, indecisive, looking down the ladder at the old woman, then up the stairs after the child. "Matt, go after Gee, will you? Make sure Val is okay."

"Sorry, sir. I need to go to Maureen."

Not waiting for the argument, he descends after Ellen, cursing under his breath as they proceed at the pace of a sedated sloth. Jake and Sophie follow. When Matt's feet hit the floor, Ellen is already in the elevator, ready to go. During the interminable descent, she explains about the research project and Matt shares his vision, silently cursing himself. If he'd paid attention to the vision earlier, maybe this wouldn't even be happening. Or maybe it would. The gift of second sight is not a kind one.

"What do we do with Karin?" Sophie asks, as the elevator settles to rest and the door opens.

But the raven is already flying along the passageway.

Jake draws his weapon and aims but hesitates.

"What if she has a job to do?" Sophie asks.

Matt swears and runs after Karin, who seems to know the way. She comes to rest in front of a closed door. Matt tries the handle, but it's locked.

"You sure?" he asks.

Karin *kronk*s and pecks at the door. Sophie runs up and skids to a stop, doubled over with her hands on her thighs, catching her breath.

"Open the door!" Matt bellows, thundering with his fists, but there is only silence within. He aims a well-placed kick just above the knob, but the door is made of steel and the only damage done is to his foot.

"Maureen would pick the lock," Sophie says, with a catch in her voice.

This serves to redouble Matt's desperation and he tries yet

another kick, which leaves him wondering whether he's broken his leg and rendered himself utterly useless.

Ellen and Jake appear and Sophie calls out, as if they haven't figured it out by watching him, "It's locked!"

"Damn it." Jake's breath rattles in his chest in a way that can't be healthy.

Ellen places her hand on the door, takes a breath, and then walks right through it. Matt knows she has this ability, or at least he's been told. But hearing about something and seeing it for yourself are two different things. He'd pictured something complicated or difficult, and she makes it look like the easiest thing in the world—as if the barrier is water or mist rather than a solid steel door that has rendered his entire lower leg numb.

The knob turns from the inside and the door opens, revealing a scene lifted from nightmare.

Spiders and webs obscure the ceiling, the walls, the floor. Maureen lies motionless on a table at the center of the small room. Her eyes are closed, her face peaceful. As with the other murdered women, a festive placemat has been laid across her belly. Unlike the others, a giant, glowing spider crouches in the center of the dinner plate that rests on the placemat, a pool of shimmering silver liquid beneath her.

Karin flaps in and alights on Maureen's chest, which makes the fact that her chest isn't moving abundantly clear. He's too late to save her. All that's left is retribution.

Ginny sits in a chair beside the table, perfectly unscathed.

"Stop right there," Ginny says, a revolver in her hand. She doesn't hold it like an elderly woman who has never held a gun before but in a two-handed grip that means business. She aims at Jake, then Ellen, and finally settles on Sophronia. "Anybody moves, and the girl dies."

Jake growls but stays where he is.

"I'm going to need your weapons, Sheriff," Ginny says.

"You can have them if you'll let me go to her," Jake says. "Please."

"I'm afraid that's just not possible. Drop them. Now."

With his peripheral vision, Matt watches Jake set down his service weapon and his taser, but he can't tear his gaze away from the spider. A silvery drop gathers on the underside of her abdomen, elongates, and falls into the pool of liquid on the plate with a soft *plink*. And then another drop begins to form.

"I've never seen so much elixir," Ellen says, her voice closer to awe than horror.

"What is it?" Matt asks.

"Eternal youth," Ellen answers.

"So it is." Ginny dips a finger into the liquid, then lifts it to her mouth and licks it off.

Sophie gags and chokes. "It's made from souls," she cries. "That's all that's left of Maureen."

"Who wants to be next?" Ginny asks. "I need another volunteer. It's a kinder death than what waits for the rest of you."

"You can't possibly use all of what you have already," Ellen says. "You don't need another victim."

"Never victims. Always volunteers."

"Is that what happened to the others?" Jake edges closer to Maureen as he speaks. "Ida Mae *volunteered?*"

"Stop right there, Sheriff. There's nothing you can do for her now. Don't make me shoot the girl; such a waste. And yes, Ida Mae volunteered."

Matt steps in front of Sophie to shield her with his body, the only action he can take, and one he knows is only symbolic. He can't protect her or anybody. Can't do anything. The grief and horror on Jake's face resonate in his own breast. He's failed not only Maureen but also the others. If he hadn't misjudged the vision, if he'd paid attention, he might have seen this sooner.

Ellen even told them about Ginny while they were in the

elevator, and still he'd underestimated her, because she is old and female. He feels so stupid. So inept. So goddamn helpless.

"You're telling me Ida Mae climbed up on a table in the dining room and volunteered to be soul-drained by an enormous arachnid," Jake snarls.

"Bullshit!" Sophronia steps out from behind Matt and moves toward Ginny. Her eyes are glowing, her hair doing that thing it does when the paranormal side of her is wide awake and ready for action. "You killed her."

"Stay where you are, or I shoot him instead." Ginny aims the revolver at Matt's chest. "Chuck and I helped Ida Mae up on the table. We didn't realize how ravenous the Queen had grown and that the process would kill her."

"Sylvia didn't volunteer," Jake says. "She was terrified when she saw what happened to Ida Mae. That's why she was murdered sitting in her chair. In her room. She refused to get up on a table."

"She did volunteer," Ginny insists. "And then, when she understood death was the result, she became a coward and refused to make good on her commitment."

"Charlie and Ida Mae and Sylvia were all in it for the elixir," Matt says, as understanding dawns. "They thought they were going to live forever."

"I'll admit it was disconcerting when Ida Mae stopped breathing," Ginny acknowledges. "Chuck actually attempted CPR. Which was pointless. Even if he had brought her back, without a soul what would she have been? A zombie?"

"And you—" Sophie takes a step closer. "You're not a volunteer? How come you're not next?"

"Me?" Ginny laughs. "What a preposterous idea. I am her facilitator; with the child released, I am also her voice. Without me, who would find sustenance for the Queen?"

"And who would package it and sell it?" Ellen asks, dryly.

"Each drop is worth a fortune. You created the monster. It was your project in the first place."

"It was. We have been together for twenty years. We need each other."

"What was your part in this project, Ellen?" Jake asks. "Why are you here?"

She shrugs. "I suppose I'm here because the Unit wants me here. But I don't know why. I knew about the project, but I wasn't ever involved."

Ginny's body jerks, as if she's been jolted by electricity. Her eyes go wide and blank. When she speaks, the voice that emerges from her lips is not her own. "I still hunger. This one soul was not enough. Is there another who would volunteer?"

Matt steps forward. "I will."

He would take a bullet for any one of the people in this room. He deserves to die for his many failures. If it buys the rest of them time to get away, to figure out what to do, he's willing to pay the price.

The raven *kronk*s and flaps her wings. Then, with a lightening-swift stab of her beak, she impales the giant spider through the center of her abdomen. A collective gasp goes up from every human in the room.

"No!" Ginny shrieks. She drops the revolver and reaches both arms out toward the spider, as if it is a murdered child. Jake takes two long steps and grabs her from behind. "You are under arrest for the murder of Maureen Keslyn," he begins, snapping handcuffs on her.

The monstrous arachnid squirms and struggles to free herself. Greenish fluid leaks out of her broken belly. Gradually, the creature's spasms grow weaker. At last, all eight legs curl up and motion stops. The raven pins the body to the plate with a claw and withdraws her beak. The other spiders retreat in dizzying waves that make it feel like the room itself is moving, as they clear the floor and climb up the walls.

Matt rushes to Maureen and presses his fingers to her carotid artery, hoping against hope for a pulse. Her skin is still warm; she looks as though she is sleeping. But there is no pulse. No breath. It's too late to begin CPR, but he knows he'll do it anyway.

Evidence be damned. He sweeps his arm across her belly to clear away impediments so he can begin chest compressions. Ellen dives forward with surprising agility and speed and grabs the plate—

dead spider, elixir, and all— and holds it safely out of his way.

"There is one chance to save her," she says. "You must give her the elixir."

"No!" Ginny struggles to free herself. "Do you know what that's worth? I'll cut you in!"

"How would it help her?" Jake demands. "What will it do?" His voice is harsh and ragged, lines of grief scoring his face.

Matt climbs up on the table and straddles Maureen's body, which feels unexpectedly small and fragile. She's always been such a force to be reckoned with, he's expected more muscle, bigger bones. He tilts back her head, pinches her nostrils, breathes a breath into her lungs.

From a distance he hears Ellen saying, "I don't know. Most probably nothing. But the elixir is synthesized from the essence of her soul. It might bring her back."

Matt shifts to chest compressions, counting in his head while the others continue their debate.

"You can't," Sophie's voice protests, half-choked with tears. "Her soul is gone, Jake! Destroyed. If the life force brings her back—she'll be a zombie. She hates zombies."

"We have to take the risk," Jake says.

"You know she wouldn't want this," Sophie cries. "She shot you to keep you from turning into a monster. We can't do this to her."

"I'm not as strong as she is!" Jake's voice breaks on the words. He releases Ginny. Grabs the plate from Ellen's hands.

"Think what you're doing! Millions of dollars!" Ginny wails. "Restored youth for all of us. Wasted. It won't bring her back. It's too late."

"Out of the way, Matt," Jake says.

All Matt has to do to stop this is strike out with a hand. Knock the plate flying from Jake's hands. It will break. The elixir will spill. It's what Maureen would want, given the choice. Gone for good. Not a half-life, called back from the underworld.

He hears a rush of wings and the raven alights on his shoulder. The vision flashes into his head again, only this time he sees Maureen's eyes open, sees her sit up on the table. He can't tell if it's Maureen as zombie or Maureen restored to herself, but it's Maureen. He can't imagine a world without her.

Jake dips his finger in the silvery ooze and rubs it on Maureen's lips. Waits. Nothing happens.

"Open her mouth," he rasps.

Sophie is weeping now, as if she's an ordinary human girl, utterly bereft. Matt lifts Maureen's head with one hand and draws her jaw down with the other. Jake presses the plate against her lips and tilts it. The elixir is thick like syrup, and Jake pushes at it with his finger, gathering it to the center so it will flow into her mouth.

Still, nothing happens.

Jake sets the plate aside and massages her throat with his hand. "Sit her up so it flows down," Jake orders, and Matt lifts the inert body with an arm around the shoulders, supporting Maureen's head so it doesn't flop either forward or back. Silence gathers, broken only by the sounds of their collective breathing.

After a long moment, Jake brushes his hand across his eyes.

"Well. Let her rest, then," he says.

Matt lays Maureen back, gently, tears blurring his vision.

"It's better this way," Sophie sobs.

Ginny huffs. "A life wasted. She was already dead. The elixir should have been—"

"Shut. Up." Sophie's voice is cold and menacing. "One more word, and I will suck the soul out of your body and trap it in a jar. Don't test me."

The old woman's eyes flare with anger, but she presses her lips together and wisely says nothing more.

Jake smooths Maureen's hair. Lays her hands at her sides. "I can't believe this," he says. "God, Maureen. Forgive me."

He bends down and kisses her still lips. The raven *kronk*s and flaps her wings. A sudden breeze surges through the room, smelling of rain-soaked earth and ashes.

"Watch out," Sophie shouts. "Stand back."

Maureen's foot twitches. Her hands fist in the front of Jake's shirt. She gasps and surges up to a sitting position, her eyes wide and staring into his.

Matt holds his breath, ready to intervene if some monstrous thing is looking through those eyes, if some foreign voice speaks through her lips.

"Did you just kiss me?" Maureen demands, her hands twisted tight in Jake's shirt.

"Yes?" he replies, tentative, whether in fear of Maureen or whatever she might have brought with her from the dead, Matt can't tell.

"Well, you might at least do it properly, then," she says.

And to Matt's surprise, Jake does exactly that.

EPILOGUE

I've never been a fan of fairytales, but there are worse ways to come back from the dead than with a kiss. Especially when the kiss is followed by the good news that the monster is dead. But there are loose ends to tie up, and a little bout of kissing, or even the sex that followed as soon as Jake and I could get away alone, has done nothing to mitigate my fury with the Unit.

Another phone message left for Charlie, along with a few well-chosen details and threats, has finally brought him to the Manor.

"Thank you so much for the honor of your presence." I bow deeply at the waist and open the door to my suite wide to invite him in.

"I didn't realize we were having a party," he says, surveying the gathering in the room behind him.

"Did you think I would risk talking to you alone? You've got to stop underestimating me. Besides, all of these people are deeply involved in what the Unit has set in motion." I step behind him and press my revolver to the back of his head. "Please come in. I'll introduce you."

"If I die, there are people who know where I am," he says as Jake closes and locks the door and Matt frisks him for weapons.

"No need for anybody to die," I say as Matt relieves him of a revolver, a Glock, and three knives. "We just need a little information and you're not exactly forthcoming."

"He's clean, at least as far as traditional weapons go," Matt says.

"Do we need to strip-search you, Charlie?" I ask. He shows me his middle finger, and I laugh and gesture him to one of the chairs Matt and Sophie brought up from the dining room to accommodate the crowd.

He sits and surveys the circle of faces arrayed against him. "Really? A child? And you think the Unit is bad."

I hold my hand up to silence Gee, who is ready to launch into her own defense. "That child was possessed by the Queen Spider and very nearly died. She has just as much right to answers as everybody else. You already know Matt, and I'd guess you recognize the sheriff, even if the two of you have never formally met. You know Jill and Ellen. This is Val. And Sophronia."

Charlie stiffens a little as his eyes linger on Sophie. I can't say as I blame him. Her eyes glow with green fire; the ends of her hair are moving in their own atmosphere. If he knows who she is, and he probably does, then he also knows what she can do.

He's a pro, though, and recovers his composure immediately. "All one big happy family, I see. I don't suppose I could have a cup of coffee?"

"What you can have, for starters, is this." I cross to the kitchen counter and pick up a large clear jar. Inside, floating in formalin, is the Queen Spider. I've been keeping the jar where I can see it. When I wake up at night, I find it comforting to turn on a light and see that the creature is still in the jar, still not moving. Sophie confirms that the spirit component also seems to have been destroyed, but she watches me the same way I watch the spider in the jar. Looking deeply into my eyes, sniffing at my breath when she thinks that I won't notice. I've told her to stop being all surreptitious about this and just test me regularly.

When I hold the jar out toward Charlie, he rears back, nearly overturning his chair.

"What the hell? Why would you even have this?"

"Tell me what you know."

He swallows. "You already know. Project 66803."

"What I don't know," I say, holding the jar out toward him, "is why this—*thing*—has been allowed to live and feed on souls in my Manor."

"Could you please move that farther away from me?" he says.

Instead, I shove it against his chest. "We *think* it's dead, Charlie. But we don't know if it's really killable. It would be sad if I broke this jar, wouldn't it? Right over your head?"

"You are risking my life," he grinds out between clenched teeth.

"Tell that to somebody who cares. I have three dead residents. Jill and Val were both wrapped up in spider webs, future dinner for some brand of spider that nobody has seen before. As I already mentioned, Gee was possessed. And the thing sucked the soul out of me. I was dead, Charlie. I came back."

"I see your point," Charlie says. "What do you want to know?"

"Did you know the thing was here in the Manor? That Ginny was tending it?"

Charlie sighs. "I knew. But—" He holds up his hand to stop the tirade I'm ready to unleash. "The spider as I knew her was tiny. Her effect was negligible. Virginia is a scientist. I thought she had things under control."

"Until I called and told you that we had a child here possessed by a giant spider. And you did nothing."

"I couldn't. I had other concerns. Other—projects—I didn't wish to compromise."

"Like framing Ellen for murder?"

He blinks. "Do I want to know how you figured that out?" His eyes narrow, and he focuses in on Ellen, who sits with her little dog in her lap, looking completely calm and competent.

"Yes, that's right," she says. "I've restarted the meds, so don't bank on my confusion to continue with your smear campaign."

"You know it's temporary," he says. "We can't keep you stable much longer."

"You mean you don't want to keep me stable much longer. Too old to be worth the trouble; isn't that it?"

I shake my head at Charlie. "This doesn't look like the kinder, gentler Unit you're trying to sell me on. I've heard Ellen's story. How she worked for the Unit for years as one of your scientists and volunteered to be one of your lab rats. You messed with her DNA and then you not only abandoned her, you wanted her to rot in jail."

"Did I?" Charlie's voice sharpens. "That reasoning is beneath your abilities, Maureen. I'm disappointed."

"What, then? She's a secret weapon set loose in the Manor? I preferred the rot-in-jail theory."

"Quite frankly, jail and the Manor both surprised me. I expect the Unit wanted me euthanized," Ellen says. "That's what is done with 'errors,' isn't it?"

"You knew when you signed up!" Charlie objects. "You signed the agreement. Should your DNA become unstable, should you become dangerous—"

"And am I dangerous?" she asks. "Barring the supposed assault on my husband?"

"It's policy!" Charlie protests.

"Such a fair and equitable policy," I say. "A woman like Ginny, who uses Unit research for personal profit and murders people to make that happen, is beneath your notice. While Ellen, who is guilty of nothing more than an instability in her molecular structure, is supposed to die."

"I tried," Charlie says. "Went out of my way, in fact, to keep her from being euthanized. Jail first, to get her out of her house and somewhere safe. And then here, where I knew you would protect her."

"You also arranged for her to not have her meds, so her brain would go mushy and she couldn't tell anybody about this. You seriously thought it kinder to let her live out her days with nothing left in her mind but empty snatches of song and a penchant for tea, wasting away in a retirement community? Please. When my time comes, somebody shoot me."

Jake shifts uneasily in his chair and avoids my eyes. We've already had a conversation about his willingness to risk me coming back as a zombie rather than letting me die. I've forgiven him, mostly anyway, since he's been making it up to me under cover of night, but we still have a score to settle.

Charlie's gaze shifts to Jill and he shakes his head slowly. "I'll admit I'd assumed that Jill's hatred for Maureen would keep her from collaborating with the rest of you."

"Science always comes first," Jill says primly.

Ever since she helped solve the puzzle of Ellen and I saved her from being the spider's dinner, we've reached a sort of grudging truce. What lies between us is not exactly trust but an agreement that we won't deliberately screw each other over. I'm relatively certain that she won't try to kill me anytime soon, and I'm providing her the same professional courtesy.

"Now that all the secrets are out, what do you want from me?" Charlie asks. "Are you seeking vengeance?"

"That would be interesting, wouldn't it?" Matt muses. "I wonder what sort of torments a soul crosser, a DNA disrupter, a molecular scientist, and a medium might dream up, egged on by Maureen. Oh, and me, of course. The one you were willing to send to death row."

"Oh, I don't know that we'd need to get too creative," I say thoughtfully. "The spider hordes were starving, last I heard. Just because we don't know exactly where they are hiding doesn't mean we can't find them. Or that they wouldn't find Charlie if we shut him away down in the underground passages somewhere."

"It would be rather a shame if he got lost down there, wouldn't it?" Sophronia muses. "Due to his general nosiness. No malice on our part, of course."

Charlie's body goes tight. He glances from one face to another. "What do you want from me?"

"We need the research files from Project 66803 and any others involving spiders."

"I'll check," he says. "But if there is other arachnid research, I don't know of it."

Jake's eyes meet mine. He nods. I lean forward a little in my chair.

"We want a list of all human/paranormal offspring from the HUM era. Parentage, date of conception, date of birth. Date of decease if known. Last known whereabouts if not."

"You know I can't do that."

Karin, still a raven, flaps heavily onto Charlie's shoulder, pokes her beak into his ear, and says, "Brains. Mmmm. Tasty."

Charlie screams and leans away from her, trying to get his hand between his ear and her beak. He overbalances and falls off his chair, crashing onto the floor. The raven follows, leisurely settling on his chest and cocking her head from one side to the other, then darting it toward his face. "Eyeballs. Also tasty."

"How the hell does that thing talk?" Charlie's voice is muffled by his arms, thrown up to protect his face.

"Ravens are great imitators," Sophie says. "But Karin is kind of special."

"You could start by getting us the intel on her," Matt says. "I think you'll find some cross between shifter, raven, and human in the records."

The raven pokes her beak into one of Charlie's nostrils, and when he tries to shove her away, she pecks sharply at his hand. "Softest bits are all inside the skull," she says. "Mmm mmmm mmmm. Karin is hungry."

"Please, somebody get this thing off of me," Charlie moans.

I'm almost beginning to feel sorry for the man but not enough to intervene. Not yet.

"Her name is Karin. She's the Unit's work," Matt says, standing over him. "As for the Unit's other work, do we still have that egg sac, Maureen? Maybe Charlie could serve as an experimental incubator."

"What egg sac?" Charlie whimpers.

"The one the ME found in Chuck's abdomen during autopsy. We're not sure what's in it. I'm guessing maybe the Queen Spider's attempt to procreate. One small incision ought to do it, don't you think, Jill?"

"He could probably swallow it with a little help," Ellen volunteers.

"For God's sake!" Charlie cries out. "Please. I'll do whatever you like, get you whatever you want."

"These are our demands," I say calmly. "Refills on Ellen's meds, and the exact formulation so Jill can replicate it. Those records on the offspring from all human/paranormal experiments. The research we asked for. And anything you can tell us about how to fumigate these spiders."

He screams again as I press a small jar into his hand, before realizing that the spiders inside are all dead and pose no threat.

"Let me go," he moans. "I'll get you the records right away. I know where to find them. And I can do what you ask with the pills. I don't know about these spiders, I swear, but I'll get someone to look into it immediately."

"You'll call in twice a day to report on progress," I say, leaning over him. "No more hiding behind some bogus dry-cleaning firm."

"Yes, yes, of course. I'll call you. I'll give you my personal cell number."

"Give it to me now," I say. He recites a stream of numbers and I plug them into my phone. When I dial, his jacket pocket starts ringing.

"If I call, you answer," I say. "Understood?"

He nods.

"Now. Are there any other experiments going on in my Manor?"

He shakes his head. Sweat drips down off his forehead and into his eyes. I smell the fear on him, rank and hot. All at once, I'm disgusted, both by him and myself for bullying him. I step back. "It's been nice doing business with you. Would you care for a cookie? That cup of coffee?"

His eyes dart around the room. The raven perches on his thigh. Anubis stalks over and bats playfully at his cheek.

"I think I'll just go. If that's all right with you."

"We'd never dream of holding anybody against their will," Jake says, calm and professional. "Everything by the book under my watch."

I can't help thinking that the book Jake is going by is considerably different from the one he went by when we met, and that I like this one better.

As soon as I've watched Charlie down the hall and into the elevator, I close and lock the door and turn to face the eyes that are now all focused on me.

"Are you going to tell us what the plan is?" Sophie asks. "If you don't, we'll all be snooping and digging and getting in each other's way."

It's rather disconcerting, the idea of working with a team this size. It was hard enough getting used to trusting Matt and Sophie and Jake. But we're going to need them all if we're going to track down and reach out to every one of the human/paranormal hybrids that Jake and I have reason to suspect are salted throughout Shadow Valley and the neighboring communities.

Jake comes to stand beside me and reaches for my hand. "I'll tell them," he says, and immediately begins. "When I was a much younger man. . ."

ACKNOWLEDGMENTS

Dead Before Dinner owes so much to so many that I'm hesitant to begin, as I'm bound to overlook somebody important. But here I must thank the following, at least, and if I've left you off the list please blame it on writer brain and a glitchy memory, and know that the book would not exist without your help and support.

To my friend and agent Deidre Knight—thank you so much for retrieving my rights to the Shadow Valley Manor series so I could plunge into this Indie publishing adventure! Words cannot express my appreciation for the way you are always there when I need you.

Susan Spann, my friend and partner in literary shenanigans— you've been on this journey with me almost from the beginning and I can't imagine how things would have been without you. Thank you for being a supporter of this series, and of me, and for all of the advice along the way. Also, thank you for beta reading and for your helpful—and funny—comments in the margins. I love you.

Pam, you have also been with me from the beginning, both as a fearless reader and as a friend and collaborator. Thank you for suggesting the title of this book, and for your many hilarious comments while beta reading, and especially for the socks you ruined while confirming that Maureen could NOT carry a throwing knife in her sock.

Thanks to Richard Shealy for the quick, thorough, and professional copyedit and to the team at ebook launch for helping me rebrand the series with fantastic covers.

As always—my deepest gratitude and appreciation goes out to the readers who have read and reviewed and especially those who have reached out to give me a little nudge about getting this third installment out into the world.

May all good things come to every single one of you.

With love,

Kerry

ABOUT THE AUTHOR

Kerry Schafer writes fantasy and paranormal mysteries featuring fun supernatural chills, dark humor, and quirky characters. In addition to writing, she is enthusiastic about encouraging and supporting other writers as a mindset coach and speaker. When not absorbed in creative pursuits, you'll find Kerry hanging out with her real-life Viking on their little piece of heaven in rural northeastern Washington. She also writes bestselling family dramas as Kerry Anne King.

Visit her website at www.allthingskerry.com.

 facebook.com/kerryschaferbooks

 twitter.com/kerryschafer

 instagram.com/kerryschaferbooks

ALSO BY KERRY SCHAFER

The Between Trilogy

Between

Wakeworld

The Nothing

Shadow Valley Manor Series

Dead Before Dying

World Tree Girl

Dead Before Dinner

The Dream Wars Series

The Dream Runner

The Dream Thief

The Dream Wars

Books by Alter Ego Kerry Anne King

Closer Home

I Wish You Happy

Whisper Me This

Everything You Are

A Borrowed Life

Other People's Things